Take the Cure, If You Dare

Mrs. Elderberry twisted herself around in the chair to nod that she was ready to start—and also to let Neela Zapotnik know that she was forgiven for showing up late. Only when Mrs. Elderberry looked through the plate glass, her hand ready to wave, did she notice that Neela Zapotnik was not in her usual place among the dials and knobs in the control booth.

Mrs. Elderberry blanched. She did not consider herself a biased woman, but felt this was unfair.

She saw a shorter, hairier technician than Neela, one whose competence she felt obliged to question. Residents, interns, even graduate students she had no problem with—but was she really expected to accept her treatment session from the Doctor's famous trained chimpanzee?

Books by Richard Fliegel

The Next to Die
The Art of Death
The Organ Grinder's Monkey
Time to Kill
A Semi-Private Doom
A Minyan for the Dead
The Man Who Murdered Himself

Published by POCKET BOOKS

the man who murdered himself

richard fliegel

POCKET BOOKS

New York   London   Toronto   Sydney   Tokyo   Singapore

This book is a work of fiction. Names, characters, places, and
incidents either are products of the author's imagination or are used
fictitiously. Any resemblance to actual events or locales or persons,
living or dead, is entirely coincidental.

An *Original* Publication of POCKET BOOKS

POCKET BOOKS, a division of Simon & Schuster Inc.
1230 Avenue of the Americas, New York, NY 10020

ISBN: 0-671-74451-8

First Pocket Books printing March 1994

10 9 8 7 6 5 4 3 2 1

POCKET and colophon are registered trademarks of
Simon & Schuster Inc.

Cover art by Tristan Elwell

Printed in the U.S.A.

*For Steve and Bobby, Stanley and Leslie,
who made up the Bronx for me.*

With much gratitude to my editor, Jane Chelius, whose
sense of humor, sensibility, and good common sense
have always been a lesson and a pleasure.

the man who murdered himself

1

**"YOU KNOW WHAT I MISS MOST ABOUT THE POLICE DEPART-
ment?"** whispered Homer Greeley near Shelly Lowenkopf's ear, as the two former police detectives squatted side by side in a dark coat closet on the thirteenth floor of Souchett and Cole Advertising. Fortunately for them, it was early September, and still hot, so that most of the outerwear of the two-man creative team who lived in this office was still buried in closets in their respective homes. There was one long coat, a woman's beige wool trimmed in a starched black fur that ended in long spires like ostrich feathers, which did have to be pushed out of the way; but Shelly was able to make out the chiseled profile of his business partner by the green light of the Xerox machine, glowing through the slight opening of the closet door. The rest of the office snored in darkness, to the rhythm of a never-turned-off computer that served as a printer network controller. The desks were sheets of glass sitting on oblongs of charcoal steel; the rest of the furniture, two chairs and a couch, were made of slung black leather and aluminum piping, cooled by a trace of silver light angling through the huge tinted windows. There was no hoop for a basketball, or putting cup, but a full-size air-hockey board sat in the middle of the zebra rug, its power still on, so that its hiss played counterpoint

to the hum of the computer server and an occasional groan from the Xerox machine.

"You know what I miss?"

"The pay?"

Homer frowned, tiny lines dropping from his cool green eyes. "You want to know, or don't you?"

In the six months since the two former detective sergeants had chipped in together to buy out the Maxim B. Pfeiffer & Sons Private Detective Agency, Shelly had already heard about a dozen things Homer missed most about the force. He missed the rumble of the crowded precinct house when he first stepped through its front door each day. He missed the nods of acknowledgment from the desk sergeant and property-room master, both hard-won and grudgingly afforded; the marks of black heels on the linoleum hallways, and the squeaks that left the marks; the creak of the detective-room door and the smell of old typewriters mixed with cigar smoke that must have permeated the walls for countless years so it could seep back through the peeling green paint whenever anyone risked opening a window. He missed the grimy, slimy daily encounter with the derelict margins of the city, who washed up on the steps of the Allerton Avenue Precinct House like old tires and beer cans on the banks of the Bronx River. He missed the weight of the badge in his wallet, the bracelets at his hip, and the drag of a standard-issue nine millimeter—now replaced by a snugger weapon that did not as comfortably fill the worn leather holster under Homer's armpit. He missed the security of a team behind them, who could be tapped for backup whenever they felt something hinky about to go down. But those were not the things Homer was missing now, Shelly knew, after three nights in the closet. He pushed a curtain of stiff black fur out of the way, the better to see his partner.

"What, Homer? What do you miss most?"

"The significance."

"Of what?"

Homer shook his head as if to take in the entire life they had left behind. "Of everything . . . every case that

2

fell on our desks. Every file had in it some real tragedy—guilty husbands and suffering wives, seniors who had forced themselves to forget whatever they once knew. Children you'd look at and couldn't bear to remember."

Shelly remembered their share of Saturday-night cleanups, too, where one drunk shot another over the bowl of peanuts on a bar. But there were cases where you really got to wonder how one person could treat another so awfully.

"Because we worked homicide."

"Exactly! High-stakes crime, where desperate people did desperate things and then tried to cover them up. Felonies, with consequences, where people invested some planning. Important cases that required real thought to solve."

"This one is important," said Shelly, putting his eye to the crack as something, he thought, crossed between them and the green light on the Xerox machine. He scrutinized a spot of white light that slid across the surfaces of two black plastic file cabinets as he moved his head side to side. Directly in front of him, at the aluminum foot of one desk, a trashbasket overflowed with scraps of paper from the board of white cork that occupied one wall; it was entirely filled with paper and pushpins, some of which also lay in strategic places around the littered carpet. But no one was moving in the room, and he sat back, forgetting the thread of their conversation until he returned to Homer's still-dissatisfied scowl.

"Important? What's important about the two jokers killing time in this office?"

"One of them is a *spy*," Shelly said, leaning on the last word, making the most of what they had. If Homer was bored and wanted drama—

"Not a spy, exactly," Homer said, screwing up one eyebrow. "Spies steal plans for weapons systems and national security codes. These boys are making a few dollars on the side sharing information with their firm's competitors about TV jingles for cleaner teeth."

"Only one of them is doing that."

3

"Maybe. Or maybe they both are. All we were told is the copy seems to be disappearing from this office. On Tuesday nights. So here we are, ready to nab one or the other—or both—with his hands on the toothpaste tube. But do you really think it matters which?"

"It matters to the one who isn't stealing, doesn't it? It matters to their boss. And it presents us with a little puzzle—who's the thief and who isn't? You were always interested in solving little puzzles."

Homer ran his fingers along his temples, pushing back his straight blond hair, to shake out the cobwebs. "Sure —if the big picture matters, so do the details! But this . . . on the trail of a copy thief who spirited off the punchline: 'Because your smile says so much about you'? Not exactly brimming with significance, is it?"

Shelly hauled the beige wool coat to his side of the closet and leaned against it, pinning it to the wall. Then he lit a cigar. It was a new habit, smoking, taken up in the idle time of their private enterprise, that had proved more lucrative than either of them had expected. There was apparently no shortage in the private sector of people with secrets they needed protected or discovered —and so their business was brisk. But there was always time for a break, too, a good cigar, with your feet up on your desk in your own private office. Shelly had sniffed a few brands, listened to the smoke-shop owner extol the virtues of several, and found one that reminded him of something pleasant—Homer had later identified it as the squad-room walls. More than the smoke itself, he enjoyed the whole business of lighting up, which always gave him a few minutes to think before responding to questions that made him uncomfortable.

"It may not be murder," he said finally, "but ad copy means a lot to the agencies that produce it. And what matters to our clients matters to us, now."

Homer listened to this recitation as if he'd heard it too often—as indeed he had. "Do you care which toothpaste you use, Shell?"

"No, but I care that I have toothpaste in the tube, and food in the refrigerator, and a telephone on the desk

4

when I come to work in the morning. I do care about the love and respect of the people I take care of—take better care of now than ever before, thanks to the clients whose insignificant business we look into. Nobody cares about their brand of toothpaste, of course—but as a matter of fact, you do care which brands of shirts and shoes and suits you wear, don't you, Homer?"

Greeley shrugged. "Not all that much . . ."

"How much did that tie cost you?"

Homer touched the knot at his throat and lifted the large dangling end, which sported a swirl of rich colors, blues and purples against cream. "Eighty dollars, I think."

"And the suit?"

It was a soft silk affair, big in the shoulders and loose everywhere else, in a distinctive shade of pale green that brought out the color in Homer's eyes. He shrugged, and the silken sleeves fell flawlessly back into place.

"I don't remember . . . eight hundred?"

"Buy a lot of those when we were on the force?"

Shelly's own suits had come a long way since his policeman's wardrobe of green corduroy and big practical shoes. When he'd first accepted a job with a private firm, his senior partner had led him by the hand from clothier to haberdasher on the Lower East Side, helping Shelly select his first woolen pin-stripes and matching accessories. The change in the weather had left him uncertain, especially after Max had gone to Florida, but Mordred and Isabelle had stepped in to fill the void. Where twenty-five-year-old Mordred was partial to Italian cuts with more flair than made him comfortable, Shelly's sister Isabelle had an eye for substantial fabric and for styles that would last until after the ink on his MasterCard slip was dry. Between them, they helped him spend the money he was earning now—for the first time in his life, more than he needed to make do and get by.

It was always easier for Shelly to spend money on them, and on his son Thom, than on himself. For one thing, after twenty years of dressing himself on a policeman's limited budget, he had never acquired an interest in expensive objects—his two-bedroom apartment in Washington Heights was large enough for his needs, and a car faster than his squareback Volkswagen would only have increased his chances of speeding tickets and accidents. So his first reaction to a larger income had been to buy things for them—watches and earrings and necklaces for Isabelle, leather skirts and suede boots for Mordred, Hebrew lessons for Thom— the last of which elicited less immediate glee, but more thoughtful self-satisfaction than any of the other gifts. But, after the initial pleasure of receiving Shelly's presents, Mordred and Isabelle and Thom wanted to see him spend something on himself. It made them happy. And it made Ruth, his ex-wife, unhappy—perhaps even, he found himself hoping in spiteful moments, made her doubt the wisdom of having walked out on him a decade before. So he went along, trying on for Mordred jackets too high in the shoulders and tight in the waist, and for Isabelle running shoes guaranteed to increase his sprinting speed by seconds at least. Now, as he tipped forward closer to the crack in the closet door, he wore charcoal slacks and a blue sweater that itched his neck but tinted his gray eyes an affluent seaside blue. He had not allowed Mordred's barber near his wiry brown hair, and had resisted his sister's appeal for contact lenses, but a lighter pair of gold-framed glasses now rested on the bridge of his nose, the reduced pressure of which compensated somewhat for the increased pressure he felt to discover the copy thief before the case was taken away from them and passed along to another private firm. The thought of the loss in revenue made him pull at his cigar with a little more urgency, so the cloud of blue-white smoke that emerged was a little thicker, and came with a little more force, than the ones before.

"Do you think you could lose that thing?" Homer said to him, waving a hand between them.

"Sure," said Shelly. It was close in there. The carpeted floor gave him momentary pause, but he shoved aside the black fur trim on the wool coat and crushed the end against the closet's rear wall. When he peered through the crack again, he was aghast to see a film of blue-white smoke floating out from their hiding spot across the airless office. But it made no difference, because at that moment, the lock at the far end of the room jangled in its door, and the line of yellow light became an oblong with a human shape framed at its center.

"Homer—"

"I see it," whispered Greeley, who was down on his belly, his face below Shelly's at the crack. In his hand was the snub-nosed revolver, pressed against the floor.

For a moment the silhouette hesitated: he stood in the doorway, and then entered with care on silent, crepe soles. He did not switch on the light as a security guard or janitor would have done, but glanced back quickly into the hall, and then switched on a flashlight, sweeping its beam around the office like a fisherman trawling with a net. The white cone of light hesitated in front of their closet, illuminating a wisp of cigar smoke that lingered above the wastepaper basket near the desk. Then it swung down low, away from their closet, until it formed a small pool of light at the intruder's feet. A pair of black tennis shoes crept silently across the room, nearly to the closet, but pivoted at the gleaming tube of one desk leg; and a drawer of the desk was soon dragged open. The intruder crouched less than five feet in front of Shelly, searching with desperate carelessness through the documents inside the drawer.

Homer's shoulder moved forward as if to nab the intruder—but Shelly put a restraining hand on him. He could feel the tension in Homer's muscles, the readiness to spring, but he held up a single finger in the unmistakable sign that meant *"Wait."* All they had was "entry," probably illegal—Shelly wanted something more actionable than that. And, as the intruder's guard relaxed, Shelly, in the darkness, hidden from the door by the desk, felt sure they would get it.

After more than fifteen years on the force, he could think like a burglar himself. Shelly knew that the moment of entry is the riskiest, when all antennae are up.

7

Once a burglar has secured himself alone inside, attention shifts to the object of the break-in. A professional maintains a constant watch on the means of entry and exit, but an amateur is often too smitten with his own success to believe he'll be caught in the middle of the theft—after the difficult entry is over. This intruder, Shelly observed, was no professional. He rifled through the desk drawers with abandon, tossing papers over his shoulder, which swirled from the force of his dramatic vehemence and settled on all parts of the rug . . . when suddenly the search came to a stop. The intruder had lifted a sheet from the drawer and then snatched it with both of his hands. He rocked back on his haunches, reading it over by the light of his flashlight, which he held just inches from the page. From the movement of the beam over the trembling page, Shelly counted three readings from beginning to end of the text before the head of the intruder fell backwards in a gesture of awful deliverance, or liberating despair. It was as if he had found what he expected to find, and yet could not stand the shock of his discovery. For a moment he remained immobile like that, with his eyes closed, head flung back, and mouth open toward the ceiling. When in a resonant voice he began to sing.

It seemed to Shelly a grumbling at first, the utterance of a passionate singer who could not stop to find the words. Until, in an incredibly rich baritone, the chorus rang out, vibrant with energy but solemn as the grave—

"Have you ever felt lonely?
Have you ever feared
no one really knew just who you are?
Have you ever wondered
deep down inside
if you'd ever be loved for who you are?"

The singer turned the page over, but whatever he had expected to find wasn't on the other side; he returned to the drawer, emptied it, and then looked around wildly at the papers he had scattered. On his hands and knees, he crawled from one to the next, reading each where it had fallen, without bothering to redirect the beam of the flashlight that sliced across the carpet in front of him, swinging this way and that as he crawled forward on the hand that held it—until he sat up with a start, and boomed out a single line, at once assured and confidential, personal but unlimited in its urgency and universal import:

"New Ultra-Intimate roll-on and spray . . . for just the person you are."

And then, in the profound silence that followed, Shelly would have sworn he heard a sharp intake of breath and a shudder that could only have represented a vain effort at self-control. Because it was followed by more shuddering, and a noise like the mewing of a cat.

The man was weeping. And as he wept, he swept up papers and crumpled them into his pockets—advertising copy for campaigns, to be sold to the firm's competitors. Shelly thought he knew now that the motive was not greed, or even the thrill of industrial espionage, but something more emotional and elemental than those. Passion. Betrayal. Revenge.

The man cried out—a howl. Whether one of triumph or pain was impossible to tell. Homer couldn't take it anymore; he shot out from the closet and grabbed the baritone by the elbows before he could drop the crumpled ball of advertising copy in his hands.

"Don't move. We've got you covered," growled Greeley in his best George Raft imitation.

It was pretty good—but the singer had frozen already, so the only further response he could make was to open his hands convulsively. The copy sheet slipped out and wafted toward the ground, but the flashlight, tumbling faster, crashed to the floor, breaking apart and winking out on impact. The green light of the Xerox machine had been enough to see by earlier, but now, after the blinding brightness of the fallen flashlight, Shelly was unable to make out the paper clips on the desk in front of him. Shelly thought Homer must have fared no better, because a moment after he heard the spring leap from the bulb casing, Shelly heard a baritone "Ay-ya-hah!" and a deep belly grunt from Homer, followed by the rush of a large animal in flight. A rectangle of light glared at him as the office door was yanked open with a gust of air that disturbed all the paper on the rug, and a silhouette disappeared into the hallway.

Shelly did not have to see his partner grunting alongside him to know that Homer would be ready to pummel the man who had winded him, an injury to his professional pride above all else. A private investigator might allow a suspect to elbow him in the solar plexus, but any detective who permitted that sort of move to go unrequited deserved to be retired from the force. Homer was regretting the disuse of his exemplary investigative skills, the exercise of patience in which he methodically put together miniscule details that captured criminals and drove his partner Shelly to distraction—but this karate-chop escape in the dark could not fail to stir Homer's restlessness to the boiling point. With a sigh, Shelly realized the inevitable remedy: They would have to accept Mrs. Davenport's missing-person case. There was no money in it, but it did offer a chance for them to tackle a case with a bit of mystery. Wasn't that what Homer was missing, in the end?

A crash, a grunt, and a whine.

Shelly brushed off his knees in the hall and followed the trail of his partner, who—by the howl from around the corner—must have cornered the baritone at the locked staircase. The howl died suddenly, cut off by a sharp gasp, and was followed by a shudder and snuffling—more tears. Just the way to win Homer's heart. Shelly turned the corner and saw his partner bent over the thief, who knelt on the carpet in front of the elevator, his hands on the floor in front of him. The man was dressed in a black sweater, charcoal-gray slacks, black leather boots, and gloves. He was overweight, with black hair and a pasty face that showed beads of sweat on his upper lip as he twisted around, panted, and rolled heavy thick-lashed lids toward Lowenkopf.

Shelly screwed up one eye. "Don't I know you?"

The man's forehead furrowed hopefully. "Perhaps you saw my Don Giovanni?"

Shelly didn't think so. "Didn't you play an opera singer in a commercial for mouthwash?"

"Breath mints."

"You were the one with your mouth wide open. When the dog at the phonograph keels over."

The kneeling man opened his mouth in a recognizable gesture and sighed, over the disappointments of a career that had not been all high notes. Then he must have remembered where he was, because he looked back toward the copywriting office, and the rims of his eyes reddened.

"They told me I was the only man in the world who could sing it as it needed to be sung," he said softly. "Can you imagine what a fool I must have been to believe such nonsense? But they can make you believe anything." He shook his head in bitterness. "Anything." The tears welled in his eyes and he wiped his cheeks with a glove, then pulled his hand from the rabbit-lined leather and tried again with his thick ruddy fingers. It seemed to Shelly the significance of their evening's work had not been lost on him.

11

2

THE DETAILS ALWAYS CAME LATER, ALTHOUGH BY THE TIME they usually reached him, Shelly hardly remembered the case. He learned about this one the very next day from their client, who was awfully pleased with the results of their detective work, but regretful—although admitting no guilt—about the circumstances leading up to what they were already calling "the incident." The baritone caught with his fingers in the drawer had been employed by the agency to sing the jingle in a test version of the spot for Ultra-Intimate roll-on and spray deodorant, but had been cut from the final production. He was an opera singer who had been cajoled into making the test by the creative team who had dreamed up the ad. They had told him his was the only voice that could deliver the depth of feeling they were after—they had arrived at this decision after having been so deeply moved by his rendering of the soliloquy from *Carousel* ("My boy Bill . . ."). The client's in-house advertising expert, however, wanted to go with a younger voice, with less "boom" than the baritone's. The blow to his pride was tremendous, but the loss of immediate income and then months— perhaps years—of further residuals had unhinged the poor singer. All in all, it made a tragic tale of broken promises, which had for Shelly its most significant

12

consequence in the promise he had made to himself during their vigil in the closet to accept Mrs. Davenport's case.

Roberta Davenport was a self-possessed, childless wife who had accepted her mother's portrait of the world and Roberta's place in it. She looked to be in her early fifties, with stiff blue-white hair and a neat line of tiny pearls around her neck. She wore a print dress with intertwined pink-and-purple blossoms that fell discreetly to her knees. Her white gloves tugged at her hemline and clutched a purple purse with a pearl clasp in her lap. The leather of the purse matched the leather of her shoes, and the pearls in her ears matched the clasp of her purse and the string around her strained neck. She had obviously come out of desperation, but managed to conceal it, in politeness to them—only desperation could have justified the ignominy of her coming to see Shelly and Homer, given what they did for a living. It galled her that she needed their assistance, but need it she did, and that fact humbled her before them.

When Shelly had asked over the telephone what it was she needed from them, Roberta had said in a hoarse but tightly controlled voice, "I'd like to report a missing person." Just as she must have said to the secretary who answered the phone at the Allerton Avenue Precinct. The police do not investigate missing persons cases anymore unless there are children involved or there is reason to suspect a crime has been committed. One meeting with Roberta Davenport would have been enough to make any investigator on the public rolls wonder if her husband hadn't disappeared on his own initiative; but a private investigator's hours were his own, and if Roberta had asked, someone might have given her their number. Shelly was grateful for the referral, as a promise of more lucrative possibilities in the future, and though there was little money to be made in the case, it did have its curiosities. If the details were not too surprising, they were dramatic, in an afternoon-soap-opera way that was rich in promise of complicated human motives. And Homer seemed to need one of those. So, after initially turning down the case when she had first telephoned, Shelly called her back again and invited her down to their office for a chat.

Mrs. Davenport sat on the edge of her Spanish Colonial chair in Shelly's office on Westchester Square in the Bronx, gripping an envelope between her two hands. The chair was one of a set of two, with a tall straight back of dark carved wood and a cane seat that crinkled each time she leaned forward or sat back, which she did often as she spoke. The chairs did not match Shelly's desk in style or color, since the desk was oak, square and solid, with no particular Spanish accents. But he prized the chairs enormously, because they were decorative enough to invite a seat but just uncomfortable enough to persuade the average guest to get to the point of a story. But Mrs. Davenport was not their average guest. She spoke slowly and chose her words with care, either in demonstration of her powerful affection for her missing husband or for the pleasure of maintaining the two detectives' undivided attention.

"You have to understand, Mr. Lowenkopf," she said to Shelly, and then, turning to Homer, "and you, too, Mr. Greeley—Howard had learned to smoke in the old days, when the cigarette companies were the only ones describing the effects of their products. No warnings from the surgeon general—and when those came, they were so watered down against the threat of legal action, you couldn't be certain he had actually made up his mind how hazardous they were! The companies used to advertise on television—are either of you old enough to remember that?"

Was this a stab at flattery, or a lack of judgment on her part? Shelly wondered, knowing he looked every one of his forty-two years. Homer might've looked seven years younger—two years under his actual age, but not a year younger than that. So Shelly nodded for both of them. "Of course—"

"Do you remember those ads? The thundering strains of music while the Marlboro Man lit up on horseback?"

"Dum . . . dum dum-dum . . ."

Roberta nodded vigorously. "Memorable, weren't they? Stirring, even. Well then, how do you suppose they got them off the air? The evidence must have been *so* compelling . . . and still they're allowed to put their ads in magazines, and on billboards, where even children can see camels with noses like—" She trailed off, blushing at the idea of saying that word aloud.

"Mrs. Davenport," said Shelly, "you were starting to tell us about Howard."

She made a face. "Howard grew up on those advertisements. And he believed them—not word for word, of course, but the way we believe all ads: just a jingle playing in the back of your head when you pass a shelf with a certain product on it. So you reach for the thing you recognize—"

"Are you trying to tell us he smoked?" Shelly asked, while Homer resettled himself on the other cane chair.

"Yes," she conceded sadly, raising her index finger, which bore a carefully trimmed pink nail. "He was a terrible smoker! And when I started to read all the stories about cancer . . . and the effects on people around the smoker . . . you can see why I pestered him about it."

Both of them nodded. They could certainly see how she might pester somebody.

She looked cheered by their nods, but her own head dropped. "In a way it was my fault really, because he *couldn't* stop, not by himself. I didn't know that, of course—I don't mean it was *actually* my fault, in any premeditated sort of way, but he was up to two packs a day last summer with no sign of slowing down, so what else could I give him, for his sake as well as my own, but an ultimatum?"

Shelly edged forward, encouraging her to tell them as much of the truth as she could. They were coming to the confidential part, and he didn't want her going discreet on him. "You told him he had to stop? Or else?"

"It wasn't necessary to specify the *else*," she said with a slight tone of reproof. "We don't speak of such things openly, in my set and Howard's. But I felt certain Howard understood the consequences of continuing to smoke."

Shelly was also sure that he did. Homer covered his mouth and coughed.

"He tried to give it up on his own—poor Howard! But he doesn't have the stomach for personal resolve—he's never had a drop. It was my family, you see, who did those sorts of things: circumnavigating the globe in the last century, and braving the West Coast in this one. Howard's line has never been strong on determination, which is probably why they lost all the money they ever had."

This was the Absolute Moral Failing, her tremulous voice implied. It was also the note Shelly had heard the first time, in her phone call, which had led him to put her off. But they were taking this case for the challenge, to keep their skills sharp. So he nodded, to show he had heard she did not have much money to offer. Roberta Davenport saw his nod and relaxed discernibly.

"So he went to a clinic," she said. "Or what he thought was a clinic. I told him he should have it checked out thoroughly before trusting his mind to those people. But there was no other way for him to quit smoking, and Howard was convinced that quit he must."

She blinked her eyes, which were large, pale blue, and lined with red. That made them seem both sad and resolute, which Shelly supposed she was.

"It wasn't a clinic?" he asked.

Mrs. Davenport shook her head, tight-lipped.

"What was it?"

"It was a cult," she said significantly, with a nod of her stiff white head. But she didn't expand on that revelation either, or explain how she knew it, and Shelly was finally forced to prompt her.

"Howard didn't stop smoking?"

"That was the clever part!" Mrs. Davenport cried, placing a hand on Shelly's wrist. "They did cure him of smoking—cured him too well, in fact, because whenever Howard heard even the click of a cigarette lighter, or the

16

grinding when the little wheel is turned, he paled—went pasty white as a midsummer ghost. He was terrified of the sound! Something from that . . . place . . . preyed on his natural disposition. I saw it, gentlemen, crossing his face—again and again I saw it!"

She was clutching his wrist. Shelly eased it out and rubbed it to start the circulation going again. "You mean something from the clinic?"

"Clinic! He hated that place, what they did to him there." It was clear to Shelly from the way she bit her lip that she shared his hatred. Yet there was another side, an admission she felt duty-bound to include. "But he respected it, too, for its power to control his desires. And, you know, people forget when it's convenient for them. Because just six months later, when Mrs. Feldwebel commented how well a little extra weight looked on Howard, what did he do but go sign up for a weight-loss program at the same institution?"

"He went back?" asked Homer. Shelly just looked at him, and Homer sat back on the cane.

"Yes," she said, unable to comprehend it herself but equally unwilling to tell less than her full tale of woe. "He went back to the same place, to those same people who had made him afraid of a metallic click! And the same thing happened all over again! Because when he came back from the weight-loss program—twenty-five pounds lighter, I should say—he had developed another phobia, which could be explained only by his experience at that so-called *clinic.*"

"What sort of phobia?" asked Shelly.

"You can't imagine!" said Mrs. Davenport. But since both of their faces suggested they had no intention of imagining it for themselves, she said, "I'll give you one example. One night I couldn't sleep and went down to the kitchen for a glass of tea. Howard wasn't in his bed, either, and I wondered if the same idea hadn't occurred to him. I found him in the kitchen, all right, sitting at the table in the dark, staring at the closed door of the refrigerator.

"I asked, 'Howard? Is something wrong, dear?' But

poor Howard couldn't say anything at all—he just stared at the door, unable to take his eyes off it, as if some horrible monster were beating at the door from inside the icebox. So I walked right over and opened it. Just as soon as I did—as soon as the light poured out into the dark kitchen—his forehead broke out in a cold sweat and he started shivering violently. I put him to bed, of course, taking him up the stairs one by one, with his weight on my shoulder. But all I could get from him in the morning was, 'The red button, Doctor, please.'"

Shelly made a note. "The red button?"

"There were no buttons on the refrigerator itself— even the little trigger that depresses when the door is shut was green."

"And that's all he said?"

"That's all. And then the incidents subsided. There were no more midnight trips to the kitchen, and no further mention of buttons. In a matter of weeks, my old Howard seemed to return to me—except for the business about the clicking lighters, I mean, and some other odds and ends." She leaned forward again, so that she was hardly sitting on the cane chair at all, and her voice took on a note of anxiety that was almost excitement. "Until one day, about three months after the incident at the refrigerator, Howard announced over breakfast coffee that he had signed up for the most ambitious regimen yet—an eleven-week program of self-esteem and assertiveness training, beginning that very afternoon. You understand, this was breakfast; I had plans for dinner, which included him. He had put off telling me until the last minute, he said, because he knew how I would feel about it, having heard my opinions of *that place*. We had something of a row—it ended with him storming out, without using his napkin, and disappearing for the entire eleven-week period."

She seemed to expect them to share her indignity on that point, but when neither of them made any expression of sympathy, she plowed ahead with confidence in her finale.

"There is of course no law against a man seeking

therapeutic treatment against his wife's better judgment," she conceded, to prevent them from making the same observation. "We can hardly be blamed for the laxness of our legislative bodies! But, before you conclude that my opinions of *that place* were unfairly formed, let me tell you what happened just after the eleven-week course, when Howard returned to me, full of ebullient self-confidence and smug determination."

"That one worked, too?"

"They all work, Mr. Greeley, all of them! Or perhaps I should say they all worked for Howard, or on Howard, who is not, as I mentioned, a man of great integrity or intestinal resolve."

"What does he do for a living?" Shelly asked.

"Howard is a *certified public accountant,*" Mrs. Davenport pronounced, as if it were a title of nobility. "And a good one! At least he was a good one, until they worked him over."

"Who worked him over, exactly?"

"Who? I just told you. The cult—at that place they call a 'clinic.' "

"You mean the people who offered the program of self-esteem training?"

"No. I mean the ones on the next course."

"He went back again?" Greeley broke in. "For a *fourth* visit there?"

"These things are supposed to happen in threes, aren't they? But in Howard's case it was four. He didn't even tell me he was going, then. I found a rambling note taped to the refrigerator door—taped across the opening! Which described at great length the necessity he felt to enroll in a six-month treatment plan that would . . . wait, I think I still have it in here." She fished through her handbag and produced a scrap of yellow paper, which she held up to read. Then she thought better of it, and handed it over to Shelly, who accepted it by one corner, his old habits too deeply ingrained to ignore.

"This is his handwriting?"

She nodded.

Howard's words were written in a cramped, toppling

script that expanded and straightened when he wrote about his intended *"course of treatment."* No details were supplied about the therapy itself, which, in the language of some brochure that must have served as his inspiration, promised to address: *"all the deepest dissatisfactions of contemporary living: loneliness, alienation, a lack of personal purpose in life, and a sinking feeling that our cherished ideals are illusions; that our nation has lost any sense of mission in the world; and that God has abandoned the human race as a failed and hopeless project."*

Shelly handed the note to Homer, who read it over with a sage nod for Roberta Davenport and a roll of his eyes for Shelly, which was meant to dismiss the idea of following up on this case. But Shelly was not so willing to give up on Roberta's plea for help. "Perhaps it will," he told her. "Address these things."

She shook her head. "It didn't."

"The six months are up?"

"Come and gone." She sighed. "And Howard never returned. A week after the day I expected him, I received instead another note." And again she reached into her purse, from which she extracted a brief letter on a single piece of cheap looseleaf paper. It read:

Bertie—

I'm sorry, hon, but I can't give up yet. I'm on to something here. I don't know where it leads, but I've got to stick it out a while longer. One way or another —cleaning dishes in the kitchen here, if I have to.

I'll try to write and explain when I can. Till then—

Howard

"But he didn't wash dishes," she said bitterly. "At least not at first. What he did was go through our joint bank account until there was nothing in it. And then he sold off our rainy-day bonds. Yesterday, I received notification from the insurance company that he had sold off his policy"—she searched through her purse as she spoke—

"his life insurance policy! In case anything happens to him! That's when I knew I had to get help."

"If you don't mind my asking, Mrs. Davenport," said Homer, more gently than Shelly would have expected, "if Howard took absolutely everything, what did you plan to use to hire a private investigator?"

But she was ready for that question, too, and held out her hand for them both to see. For an instant, Shelly thought it was empty, intended as a supplication, perhaps, or a plea for their pity—but she slipped the diamond engagement ring off her finger, and he recognized it as an offer of payment.

"Take this," she said, "as collateral against whatever we'll owe you. If you bring Howard back, we'll be able to redeem it quickly enough. And if you can't . . . I won't need this empty band on my finger anyway."

3

"THERE'S NO NEED TO MAKE YOURSELVES QUITE SO COMFORT-able," said Henry Harrison, Ph.D., with a sneer that elicited a titter of uncertain laughter from the interns and graduate students, patients and guests who had collected for his popular Dependency Group—the only one Harrison himself still conducted on a regular basis. Most of the other programs, including group therapy and individual treatment sessions, had long ago been delegated to the professional staff of clinical psychologists and students in various stages of psychological training. But the weekly plenary meeting of the Dependency Group, when all the smaller treatment modules were brought together for an hour and a half of insight and inspiration, was still conducted by the great man himself, whose reputation as a researcher and therapist had financed and drawn patients to the rustic clinic in the wilds of New Jersey. The Dependency Group meeting was scheduled today as usual in the Council Room of the main building, a ranch-style structure at the geographic center of the clinic's grounds, from whose sofas and armchairs one could see the lake nestled among cabins and trees in the clinic's backyard, and, by craning one's neck, the winding road that led up from the interstate highway to the clinic's front gate. Homer Greeley had

22

driven up that road not forty minutes before, inquired at the check-in desk in the ranch-house lobby, and been told by a formidable woman with blunt-cut black hair that the only way anyone could possibly see Dr. Harrison would be as a visitor to the psychologist's Dependency Group plenary, which was open to all comers as a showcase of the clinic's therapeutic philosophy and not incidentally of Dr. Harrison himself.

Homer could understand why Henry Harrison might want to be glimpsed first among an assembly of adoring and intimidated staff and students, whose credentials and professional advancement he held in his wiry, nervous hands. Harrison stood in the exact center of one of the picture windows, framed by the distant lake, leaning on the backs of two white steel folding chairs on which a pair of graduate students sat, gazing up over their shoulders, unwilling to stir a knee or elbow and thus inadvertently attract the Doctor's attention. It did not take Homer long to see just what it was they so worried would follow his penetrating gaze. Harrison clapped his hands once loudly, and then repeated, "Let's go, go, go! We've only got ninety minutes together. And there's so much I see already deserving of our scrutiny."

Even a middle-aged man in a white lab coat shifted in his seat at the sound of that, as Harrison's muddy eyes held his for an instant and then passed on. The eyes moved with a life of their own, as if they were unconnected from the pale thin mouth, wide nostrils, and thick deep eyebrows that seemed to have dropped across his forehead from the clipped brown hair and settled on the very edge of his overhanging brow. He wore a white lab coat, but different from the others in the room, with more detailing at the pockets and a much better treatment of the collar than had been afforded the rest of the doctors and staff gathered there. Homer had an eye for tailoring, and knew that Harrison's coat had to have been hand-sewn for him. It gave Homer his first impression of the man, a blend of sartorial respect and professional suspicion which made him wonder about the rest of their information about Henry Harrison.

23

The grounds of the clinic were prettier and more expansive than Roberta Davenport's report had led him to expect. The whole place was built on a hill that rose steeply up from the highway, from where only a marble gazebo could be seen at the very peak of the crest. There was a table in the gazebo, covered with a white linen cloth that blew unattended in the wind. The road wound up behind it so that a driver moving in orbit around the gazebo soon found his way around to the far side of the crest, in a parking lot of a ranch house just below it. On this side, the hill sloped down more gently past the ranch house toward two main areas of human habitation farther down the slope: to the south, a cluster of bungalows topped by an impressive glass-and-concrete Research Building; and to the west, some plain residential buildings for guests, made of whitewashed wooden planks, beyond which the tar roofs of quaint, rustic cabins peeked out among the mossy trees surrounding a deep blue lake. The paths were marked with rustic signposts pointing the way to other sites with fanciful names. The Bower. The Glen. The Meadow.

It was enough to make Homer sick. The place had some trees, it was true, many of which were hung with wooden signs with their names burned on them—*London plane tree,* for example, which was just a sycamore with an attitude—but was there really any reason to insist that a stretch of grass running down the side of the hill was not only a meadow but also the "Meadow"?

Somewhere in the back, Homer guessed, hidden away on the north side of the hill, would be the garage, close down by the highway; and somewhere even further in the back would be the septic tank or the cesspool. Would there be a signpost on the far side of the ranch house, he wondered, with woodburnt letters announcing the way to the "Cess Pool"? That rustic spot for a cool evening stroll.

For that matter, with all the Ph.D.'s in the room, was there any reason Harrison's colleagues and subordinates should all be referring to him as the "Doctor"?

"Bring that chair in closer, would you?" the Doctor

called out to no one in particular, gesturing with his palm, a movement which continued as if automatic, even when Harrison pivoted his head like a hungry eagle—because a young woman had dropped an armful of textbooks as she scooted her chair under the front window. She paled when she saw his scowl, but he hardly needed to say anything at all to her, since the students sitting around her picked up the disapproval in his face and reflected it in their own expressions.

"All right," said Harrison when he felt the student had been duly chastened, "we're here today to talk about dependency—what you feel you need, and what you really do. Now—can someone here tell me what people really need?"

There was a silence, as no one wanted to pick up the Doctor's big bat even for that soft pitch of a question. Harrison was both pitcher and batter, asking questions and answering them himself. The students and psychologists in that room knew he always began with an easy one—it was the only way to make people feel, he had written in *Reflexes of the Mind*, that they knew more than they really did. But he'd also written, in *Response to Pain*, that silence itself was a form of hostility which could be confronted and dissolved; and so, to prevent the Doctor from investigating their reluctance to reply to so simple a question, one of the residents on whom Harrison's gaze in any case seemed to have fallen risked replying, "Food? We need food, don't we, Doctor?"

Harrison paused a moment and smiled slightly at the others, as if to imply the resident who spoke had just revealed his own simplicity, articulating what the rest of them took for granted. He said pointedly, "Yes, Mr. Jenkins. Of course, we need food. What else?"

Jenkins adjusted his tortoise-shell glasses. "Water?"

Harrison grinned, sharing his joke with all the rest of the room. "Yes, we need water, too. Anything else?"

And then Jenkins discovered the trap: If he clung to the undeniable in his responses, Harrison would imply he was a fool; but if he ventured to suggest anything more hypothetical, the Doctor would *prove* he was one. Jen-

kins trembled and gripped the wooden arms of his bare
Swedish chair, but opted to appear a fool rather than
eliminate any doubt.

"Oxygen. Rest." Defiantly offered.

"Sleep, you mean?"

Where was the trap, here? The tone implied an over-
sight, but, of course, that could be a trick, too. Jenkins
didn't see it, and he had to say something.

"That's right."

"But, of course, we can do without sleep for forty-eight
hours at least. As many of you will do, I'm sure, when
your licensing examination rolls around."

More titters, and more nervousness—but Jenkins
relaxed back into his chair, apparently believing that
Harrison had taken his pound of sweat and would now
move on. But the Doctor returned to Jenkins, swinging
his beaked nose at the impudent resident in one deadly
motion.

"And besides food, and water, and oxygen, and sleep?
What do we need, as human beings? Come, Jenkins,
we're all waiting, and we've only got an hour and a half
together today. I should say eighty-five minutes now,
after your wonderfully enlightening exposition."

And Jenkins understood no escape would be permitted
him—he resigned himself to humiliation, the faster
enacted the better. But what was it the Doctor wanted to
squeeze out of him? He was ready to be humbled, to have
his limited analysis picked apart for the unexamined
cluster of biases it comprised—but what part of it
exactly did Harrison feel like dissecting?

"Love," he said hoarsely.

And for the first time, Harrison gave him a nod of
respect. The Doctor's sly grin was still visible beneath the
surface of his expression, but he was impressed, too, that
Jenkins had managed to find the wrong thing to say with
no further prodding on his own part.

"Ah," said Harrison grandly, "did we all hear that?
Young Doctor Jenkins here, if it isn't premature to call
him that, believes that human beings need love as well as

those other, more material things to survive. What do the rest of us think—or feel—about that particular idea?"

By his tone, of course, they knew the Doctor had found his heresy of the week, but not even the most sycophantic of them felt much like weighing in with the opinion that people do not need love. There were some in that room whose lovers were also present, and others whose hoped-for lovers were there. And it was shocking in one's own ears to hear the words pronounced that meant, by only a slight implication, "I myself do not need to be loved."

So no one responded.

Harrison cast a dark glance around the room, but then smiled, and they knew he had expected this. He reveled in their silence, accepting it as another performer might have accepted applause. And then he mumbled in a voice just above a whisper, so that they had to listen carefully to make out his words.

"I don't need love," he said. He allowed his sentence to sink in, and then expanded on it, in a louder, more tremulous strain. "Nor do I believe you do, Mr. Jenkins. Or pretty Miss Gunnarson there on your right, either— alas for you, Jenkins! Because"—and here he turned away from the pale-faced Jenkins and beet-red Gunnarson to address the room at large—"because every one of us has experienced a time in our lives when we did not feel loved. Perhaps we were even accurate in those assessments. And this state has gone on for days, and weeks, and years at a stretch. But we did not cease to survive."

If Homer could think of some people who did—who had leaped from apartment windows in their hours of loveless distress—he did not feel any urge to remember aloud, because the assemblage of doctors and staff and patients and guests regarded the Doctor with an awe unequaled since the Sermon on the Mount. Harrison himself contributed to this reception by holding his palms out in front of him and swiveling on his heels, so that his spindly fingers might smooth out any doubts that remained in their duly shaken consciousnesses.

"Let me tell you what you're thinking," he said and accepted their silence for acquiescence. "You're wondering why you feel as if you need love to survive, when in fact it's perfectly clear that you don't."

That was not what Homer had been thinking, and he suspected it might not have been the thought in any number of other minds, either. But it was an interesting question, in a dull sort of way, and since Harrison seemed to have an answer for it, most of them nodded back at him. The nods meant *All right, tell us why*, although from the smug grin on Harrison's face he seemed to think his clairvoyance had been roundly confirmed.

"Because your feelings do not devolve from your needs—they do not! If they did, you would not feel you needed love. Your feelings, like your thoughts, are acquired—learned. And like an old idea rooted out by new science, your feelings can be altered or entirely displaced by other feelings which better serve your actual physical needs."

He had joined his current line of questions to an old line of thought in his books, and once the audience knew where the whole business was heading, they relaxed perceptibly. Most of them could now predict the answers to the Doctor's questions and felt tremendously relieved that they would be spared any moment of humiliation this week. It seemed to Homer that the anxiety over the risk, and the relief that followed once they had located the discussion in Harrison's own chapter and verse, was the part of the game that brought these people back to the plenary session week after week. He wondered if the staff were not required to attend, and noticed that Harrison had avoided threatening any of the paying guests.

There was one perhaps-guest who caught Homer's eye, once the activity shifted from Harrison's opening spiel to a series of psychological exercises designed to demonstrate the veracity of his observations, and to plant them deep into the minds of his listeners. This guest, if that was indeed his status, had not been in the room when Harrison began, but must have slipped in during the interrogation of Mr. Jenkins. His appearance made slipping in unnoticed a simple accomplishment—a thin, frail man with a creased brow and a look of imposed peace on his forehead. His eyes closed repeatedly under heavy lids, which nonetheless fluttered unsteadily until the lashes linked. He wore a stained cloth apron over a sleeveless undershirt and a pair of dirty white pants, but, except for the humbleness of his attire, Homer would have been sure the man matched the description of Roberta Davenport's husband.

Howard?

Homer tried to cross over to the man in the apron, but his hand was seized by a chunky intern with blunt-cut black hair and too much mascara. She wore a dark blue sweater, red plaid skirt, and sea-blue pantyhose. Her large brown eyes were filled with water and fixed on Henry Harrison, although the hand that reached for Homer's right held it fast when the Doctor announced, "I'd like you all to link hands now, with the people on either side of you. That's right. Just for a moment."

Jenkins looked at Harrison suspiciously, but how could they refuse? He glanced at Gunnarson, a pretty young woman with a blond ponytail, who blushed and turned away, slipping her hands into the pockets of her lab coat.

The chunky intern held Homer in a grip of steel. He made one attempt to wriggle free, eliciting a glare of disapproval so stern he desisted at once—less a professional than a maternal rebuke, the sort of expression his mother might have given him had he publicly disobeyed Daddy. Hadn't Homer heard the Doctor's instructions, to join their hands together? What on earth could he be thinking, then, preferring not to do so?

"Introduce yourself to the person on either side," Harrison intoned magisterially.

The chunky intern turned to Homer brightly, with genuine interest in him now. "I'm Neela Zapotnik," she said, turning to the woman on Homer's left. When the woman said nothing, Neela made a face and went on as if making introductions at a charity ball. "The woman

29

holding your other hand is Dr. Helen Kaufman, my supervisor and best friend in this place."

Dr. Kaufman smiled at Neela and then gave Homer a cooler, more reserved smile. She was a slender woman with poised auburn hair and an air of competence about her. She wore a Chanel suit in white and red, and matching red pumps. Her strong, delicate fingers were linked to Homer's by only the slightest pressure. Yet there was no question she might drop his hand accidentally; her touch was like a surgeon's, he thought, just firm enough to do the job required, but not an ounce of pressure beyond what was necessary—avoiding any suggestion of a more personal connection.

Her detachment put him at ease far more than the anxious cordiality of the intern.

"Homer Greeley," he said to both of them, and then, more quietly to Kaufman, "Are we about to do something here that's supposed to make us feel better?"

Her eyes hooded for a moment but she allowed the trace of an ironic smile to linger on her mouth.

"Not with Henry."

Neela gave them an impatient blink and refocused her gaze on the Doctor.

"Now," said Harrison, "there are things I could say which might make us all feel very comfortable about our *closeness*," and from the way he minced the last word, Homer could tell that was not about to happen. "But there are other things I could say, too—which might change how we felt about so much proximity. Just feel for a moment the palms linked to your own. And think—who is this person? Would I allow him—or her—to hold my hand in public under any other circumstances? After all, hand-holding is a token of intimacy in American culture, is it not? And how much intimacy do you actually feel for these people—who happened to stand on either side of you this morning?"

Homer looked over at Neela Zapotnik, who was staring at him uneasily. Her palm started to sweat, and slipped from his own. On his left, Helen Kaufman's hand remained dry and her grip true; but when he glanced at her face, she was smiling at him ruefully. "Feel good?" she asked.

"Creepy."

"Really knows how to get under your skin, doesn't he?"

Homer released her hand, as most of the people in the circle did the same to their partners. There was a moment of awkward shifting, which Harrison encouraged for as long as possible before he said, "So what can we learn from this?" He looked around but couldn't restrain his impatience enough to solicit a reluctant volunteer. Instead, he nodded, as if in prior agreement with the conclusion he himself was about to supply. "What feels good when one set of words are presented, makes us feel quite uneasy when another set of words define the context. Same act, same linking of hands—but very different feelings as a result."

He gave them a moment to acknowledge the brilliance of his observation before closing in and pounding home his thesis. "Every one of our feelings is like this—we experience some inchoate sensation and then interpret it as an emotion in light of the cues we pick up from the world around us. Do we feel a peculiar queasiness in our stomach today? Why, what could it be? After lunch, we conclude it must be indigestion. Face to face with a barking Doberman, what could it be but fear? And when we watch the object of our heart's desire walk off with a rival? Unrequited love."

You could tell by the way he finished, he expected to hear a silence with no pins dropping to disturb it. Helen Kaufman snorted and Liza Gunnarson sneered but the rest of the room seemed to raise no objection, and Homer was tempted to say something himself, just to have it said aloud by somebody, when he noticed that the man in the white apron was no longer watching from his spot on the far side of the room.

Howard had gone.

Homer saw him through the picture window, crossing the lawn in bounces as the ties of his apron danced behind him. He was headed toward the wooden bungalows in the shadow of the Research Building—toward one particular whitewashed shack with a roof of pink and black shingles. Slipping out of the Council Room was no easy feat in itself, and Homer exhausted his store of apologetic smiles and eyebrow-lifts in making his way through the assembly. But the threat of Harrison's intimidation was a powerful ally—no one else was willing to join with Homer in disrupting the class, so they let him pass with a few scowls but no real resistance. Homer tried two glass doors that separated the Council Room from the world outside, but both were locked— Homer drew the Doctor's gaze when he rattled them. Helen Kaufman stepped discreetly to his rescue, leading him by the elbow. The others turned their heads back to Harrison when they saw Kaufman had the disrupter in her grasp, and that was apparently enough to appease the Doctor. She directed Homer through an unmarked door at one end of the room that led into a vestibule of exposed cedar with an emergency exit emptying onto the lawn. When he looked back to thank her, she was gone.

Homer did not notice Neela Zapotnik watching him through the window as he bounded across the lawn, following the man he took to be Howard Davenport. And he did not see the expression on her face when Harrison observed she was paying no attention to him, and called her name in rebuke. Neela turned, saw the Doctor's frown, and stepped on her own toes—for which she also blamed the blond disrupter.

Homer was fleet of foot and happy to be out of the Council Room; he flew across the lawn on winged feet. For that reason, he reached the whitewashed shack only minutes after his quarry did—soon enough to hear the squeak of air forced from the pipes as a sink tap was opened and too much water splashed into a basin. He followed the noise and found the aproned man whistling as he scrubbed a glass beaker in an ancient porcelain sink under a window. Sunlight poured in through the crooked, broken blinds as the man worked a sponge on a long plastic handle, moving it in and out of the beaker in time to his whistling. A large pile of dirty test tubes and ceramic bowls sat piled in a plastic laundry basket at the man's feet, and he worked methodically, plunging each one under the stream of clear water, and scooping out its insides with a swipe of the long-handled sponge. Facedown went a beaker on the plastic mat to his right, and he dropped into a squat, reaching behind his back for the next vessel, the glass bowl of an alcohol burner, which he flipped over his shoulder and caught with his free hand in the sink.

"Mr. Davenport?" said Homer, once the test tube had fallen into the man's waiting palm. He had evidently not heard Homer over the noises from the sink, and he glanced over that shoulder before returning to his cleaning.

"It's Howard, here."

"According to your wife, you're Howard everywhere," Homer said evenly, leaning against the counter to Davenport's left, out of range of the splashing sink water.

Howard grinned at him. "Roberta sent you?"

"She's worried about you." The line sounded flat in Homer's own ears, and he wished Shelly were there to handle this part of the job. Shelly usually handled the interviewing for them, which freed Homer for what he enjoyed far more—poking around for what he thought of as *the facts*, the details that showed you more than people would ever tell you about what was really going on. What would Shelly have said to this man? Something more provocative than *She's worried about you . . .*

"I'm worried about her, too," said Davenport after a while, twisting off the tap.

Homer hated to leave things vague. "She's not in actual danger, is she?"

Davenport thought about it. "Not *danger*," he was forced to admit, "if you mean immediate risk to her life or limb, or even to her pocketbook—which to Roberta may be worse. Just the slow, inexorable wearing away of a life without meaning."

Now what was Homer supposed to say to that? He knew Shelly would've thought of something. He should have come. But their landlord had insisted on a meeting to discuss the installation of a centralized air-conditioning system for their entire office building, and one of them had to attend; and Shelly, having taken over the role of office manager when Max had handed him the keys, was the only reasonable choice. For one thing, Shelly understood their lease, while Homer had fallen asleep reading it after the fifteenth clause. For another, Shelly had felt that the ride out through Jersey would do Homer some good. "And this clinic," he had said, "is just the sort of place we'll need your nose for snooping around." That was intended as a compliment, Homer knew, and a gift, too—but here he was, face to face with a man talking about the meaning of life, and where was Shelly when he really needed him?

"You're talking about your own life, aren't you?" Homer ventured.

Howard smiled broadly. "Indeed I am. A life I have now left behind. Which Roberta, alas, has not. I'd offer her my hand, as a way out of it. But each of us has to find our individual way."

Homer was struggling to find his own way, all right, out of this conversation with Davenport. "Then you're not in fact a prisoner here?" is what he said finally, although that wasn't what he'd intended to ask at all.

"You mean of a *cult?*" said Davenport, raising his eyebrows, pronouncing the word as Roberta herself had said it. Homer didn't see any point in quibbling.

"Of anything."

Davenport grinned. It might have been the bright sunlight reflecting off his white apron, but he seemed to beam as he mastered his smile, and the contentment that lay behind it, long enough to reply:

"I've never been happier in my life."

34

4

THE BOTTOM LINE ON THE GREAT AIR-CONDITIONER OFFER,
Shelly concluded, was that their landlord wanted to
centralize the air conditioning in the building as part of
his larger plan to renovate the hallways, modernize the
elevator, and raise the rents on all their offices according-
ly. In four or five of the rental agreements—including
their own, bless Max Pfeiffer—a clause had been inserted which prohibited the landlord from doing so
without their consent. The landlord was willing to buy
their consent, in principle, but his greed kept getting in
his way when it came down to negotiating the dollars and
cents of a waiver. Shelly was glad he had gone to the
meeting himself, since Homer would have been bored
out of his mind during the first hour; but he also sighed at
the fact that he himself hadn't been equally petrified. He
thought of Homer driving out to the clinic over the
George Washington Bridge and felt a twinge of something else, too—not jealousy, exactly, since he had
wanted to send Homer, but regret that he actually
considered his time better spent this way.

Still, it was worth it, Shelly told himself later, when he
picked up Thom at Ruth's place in Pelham and they
drove down together into Manhattan to see Isabelle,
whose birthday was just the sort of occasion he had never

really been able to celebrate properly before. This time he was going to make it up to her—he and Thom stopped off at a jewelry shop on 47th Street, where Shelly allowed his eleven-year-old son to choose any of the half-carat diamond pins the boy liked best. They stopped for flowers, too, and candy, and again in a stationery store, where Shelly found a card in the birthday section that began *Dear Sister,* and Thom found a card in the Far Side section which seemed to compare his favorite aunt to a dyslexic giraffe. They reached Isabelle's apartment half an hour late but loaded with gifts. When she said she was just beginning to worry about them, Shelly waved his hand in the air as if to suggest there was nothing to worry about, ever, anymore.

Shelly would have liked to take Isabelle out to one of the chic places she would know about, as the manager of a restaurant herself; but Isabelle reminded him that she managed a diner, nights, and never really felt comfortable in places where the staff were better dressed than the customers. Instead, she said she would like him to take her out to a restaurant she had shown him many years before, when she had first moved out of their parents' house into student housing at NYU. It was an Italian place in the West Village, which had wandered from Greenwich Avenue onto the side streets when the rents had gone up. It took them a little while to find it, now, driving up Bank Street and down Twelfth, and then a little longer to find a parking spot. But Shelly still had a cardboard sign in his window which misidentified him as a working member of the New York City Police Department. He parked the car in a red zone half a block from the restaurant, made sure the rectangle of cardboard was visible, and left the squareback Volkswagen. Isabelle frowned at the car, and Shelly knew she meant—again —it was time he bought another vehicle more consistent with his financial situation. But though he had no objection to better suits and better ties and even better shoes for himself, he wasn't quite ready to divest himself of his past entirely.

Inside, though the location had changed, the food was

better than ever. The veal was tender and delicious—he had to hand it to Isabelle for insisting on the place, despite all his temptations of other, more stylish alternatives. They had Neapolitan ice cream after, a brick of one part chocolate, one part vanilla, and one part strawberry. It tasted cool and sweet, and as it slid from his spoon down his throat it reminded Shelly of something old and special which had to be earned. He finished his first, and as Thomas and Isabelle spooned through their own portions more slowly, he sat back in his chair and took out a cigar from the inside pocket of his jacket. They were sitting in a little garden with cobblestones underfoot and tiny white lights in the branches of the trees around them. He checked the wall to see if there was any prohibition, and, seeing no sign to that effect, lit his cigar in three satisfying puffs.

He drew in a cheekful of the white smoke, and while the taste was not his favorite part of a cigar, there was something gratifying about the way it issued from the side of his mouth when he expelled it a moment later. There was no ashtray on the table, but he enjoyed watching the ashes lengthen on the tip of the cigar until, when the ashes started to slip, he knocked them off with a single smart rap of his index finger on top. The round column of ash instantly broke apart and flew off in every direction—and as he looked up, watching them go, he noticed that both Isabelle and Thom were staring at him.

The same scowl, a family resemblance—it was eerie, like a disapproving house of mirrors.

"What?"

"Must you do that?" asked Isabelle.

It was her birthday, and she still had the last curve of strawberry ice cream on the end of her spoon. No, he decided, he didn't have to smoke. He knocked out the lit end on the sole of his shoe. But it was an expensive cigar, and he'd only smoked the very end of it. He tucked the rest of it back into his jacket pocket, and drew another scowl from Isabelle, although a kinder, gentler one.

"It's not that I mind the smell of a man's cigar, myself," she said, shaking the soft curls at the end of her hairdo. "My nose developed before we had all this information about second-hand smoke! But it's not good for"—and here she gestured toward Thom—"as a model of behavior. And, of course, it's not good for you, either."

Thom looked at them and shook his head. "Don't worry about me—I think it stinks."

Shelly knew it wasn't good for him—he understood that plainly enough. Cancer, heart disease, shortness of breath—he had read the warnings the Surgeon General had placed on every cigarette and cigar pack, and believed them all. And yet, somehow what he knew and believed didn't have much influence over what he desired and did. He played little games with himself—just one cigar today, just after a meal—but despite all inductive and deductive reasoning to the contrary, there was something deeply satisfying about the image of himself in his own mind when he lit up a cigar that led him to do it again and again. Those first three puffs, with the match or lighter under the end, and then leaning back in a comfortable chair . . .

"It's Edie Adams," snapped Ruth, later that night, when Shelly stopped inside his old house in Pelham to see that Thom was safely home. His ex-wife Ruth was still a good-looking woman, which meant she still exuded a certain animal musk that was half dabbed and half her own, a smell he remembered from snuggling up behind her on weekday mornings when he opened his eyes a few minutes before the alarm. When she dressed, she still tried to show off her shapely legs, but even now, in a quilted pink robe and furry brown slippers, there was still enough zing to her to cause him a momentary pang of envy for Clem, upstairs. And she still knew him—as soon as the door had opened and Shelly stepped through behind Thom, she had wrinkled up her pert, aging nose and said, "Smells like your Bug is burning oil again."

It wasn't the Volkswagen she smelled, of course, and Shelly didn't drive a Bug, of course, which she knew as well as he did; but rather than going into all of that for the thousandth time he just said, "It's fine."

"He's taken up cigars," said Thom.

"Cigars?" Ruth looked at him with her head atilt, thinking perhaps about his new affluence, and the difference it might have made to their marriage. Then she shook her head sadly and said to him, "It's Edie Adams, isn't it?"

Thom gave her a sidelong glance, kissed his dad good night, and started the long climb to his room on the second floor. Ruth held the door for Shelly, but placed herself in the doorway too, so he had to pass quite close to her to make it through.

"G'night, Ruth."

"Does *she* like it?"

She was, of course, Mordred now, whom Ruth envied but not for her relationship with Shelly. Whatever he said was likely to strike Ruth like a match. He opted for a neutral shrug. "She doesn't complain."

Which Ruth interpreted as a personal insult. "If they're young enough, they don't—is that it?"

"I didn't mean to imply anything about you—"

"I know just what you mean, and what you don't, and just how mean you can be, sometimes."

"I apologize."

"If you'd taken up that habit when we were together, I would have left you even earlier."

She meant cigars, not apologies. He tried another. "I'm sorry."

"How do you *know* she doesn't mind? Even though she doesn't complain? According to you, she never complains about anything. Have you asked her?"

The truth was, it hadn't occurred to him. But when Shelly returned to his apartment in Washington Heights that night and found Mordred waiting for him, lovely as ever, in a purple satin nightshirt through which the tips of her nipples stood erect like soldiers awaiting review, he kissed her; and when he kissed her, and smelled cigar tobacco on his own breath, he remembered what Ruth had put into his head, and asked Mordred seriously, "Do you mind the cigars?"

"No," she said quickly.

Too quickly.

"But you don't like them?"

Mordred was ideologically opposed to prohibiting personal vices in one another. She did not herself smoke cigarettes, and was sexually loyal to an endearing degree, avoiding even the appearance of a wandering eye—especially sensitized, he thought, by the fifteen year difference in their ages. But she did have a taste for tequila, an occasional joint, and had even dragged on Shelly's cigar once or twice—and the idea that personal vices should not be her own personal decisions to make seemed to her a particularly suffocating sort of closeness to impose on each other. There were occasions when she would pick up and disappear for weeks at a time, on photo assignment, and Shelly's lack of any resistance was a continuing joy to her. So she was not inclined to deny him his cigars, which did seem to make him happy, in some symbolic way. But did she actually have to *like them?*

"I've smelled worse."

"Worse cigars? Or worse things?"

"Both."

"Like what?"

"Bus exhausts. Burning tires. There's a factory along the New Jersey Turnpike . . ."

Shelly knew the place—an industrial plant at the bottom of a curve in the Turnpike, which so fouled the air throughout its valley he habitually rolled up his car windows the exit before. And these were the things his cigar smoke evoked?

"Would you rather I stopped?"

"If you want."

"Would you rather I wanted to stop?"

"I'd rather you wanted to do whatever you feel like," she said, but there was a slight strain to her voice, and Shelly surmised the truth—that she preferred not to tell him what she actually preferred, which was for him to prefer to give up the wretched habit on his own for himself.

"I think I'll give them up."

"If you want."

But he didn't want, not really. The first few hours of the night were easy enough—Mordred was there with talk of her day, to distract his attention and chase away any fleeting impulse, any doubt, which the cigar might otherwise have assuaged. So he didn't want one then.

But later, as he was taking off his clothing before climbing into bed, he took the two cigars out of his inside jacket pocket and placed them on top of his bureau— and it required an act of deliberate will for him not to slide one over to the night table at his side of the bed. Mordred noticed his glance, and leaned over the bed, kissing him, occupying his mouth with her own, her tongue and soft full lips pulling him down on top of her, right on top of the quilt. She barely gave him a chance to catch his breath, and occupied the rest of his mind and body for the better part of the next hour, during which there was no place in his imagination for the thought of a cigar.

Afterward, she lay curled up in his arms, her beautiful soft features smiling in sleep, the crimson hue in her black hair doused in moonlight from the open window. Shelly held her gently, his hands on her smooth arms, her head cradled into his shoulder. He looked around their room, at her clothes dumped unceremoniously at the foot of their bed, at the new television set with built-in videocassette player he had bought to please her, at the Captain's bed and matching bedroom set of two night tables and two dressers, including his own bureau, on top of which the cigars in their plastic wrappers gleamed back at him, blue with moonlight.

Winking at him.

But the weight of Mordred's head on his shoulder was enough to fortify him—it would mean disturbing her, if he reached for one of them, and Shelly's reluctance to disturb her sweet dreams was more than enough reinforcement for his flagging will. He closed his eyes in determination if not in contentment, and ran his hand over her head, brushing the hair away from her temple and ear, until he was sleeping as peacefully as she was.

For an hour, at least.

And then Shelly dreamed: He was in the middle of a dark forest, with thick trunks rising like sequoias straight up, tall and leafless in the lower quarters except where the roots tangled in the dense brush of the forest floor. There was no order to them, no pattern, and, as he turned left and right trying to pick a way through them, he felt a curious tingling, and sensed another presence slipping among the trunks around and behind him . . . though each time he snapped his head around to see who or what it was, it disappeared again between them. It must have been some sort of forest sprite, a tree nymph or sylvan spirit, because he heard a sound each time the presence seemed to loom at the edge of his periphery. It was a serenade, a siren song, inviting him to dally in the forest, drawing him deeper among the straight trees until he would lose himself completely among their tall, bare, undifferentiated trunks. He knew enough to resist, to move away from the beckoning sound, but it attracted him, and he followed it just a little farther into the shadows of the trees.

And then darkness.

He woke in a cold sweat, the moonlight blinding compared to the dimness of the forest in his dream. Mordred was beside him, her breath rising and falling, curled away from him now, engaged in a struggle with the top sheet. He looked around the room again as he recovered his breath, allowing his heart to slow and his palms and forehead to dry. The closeness of the smooth trunks, and the song of the woodland sprite returned to him, not quite as waking music but as a rhythm beaten out against the back of his skull—DA-DA-DA-DA-DUM! DUM-DEE-DUM . . .

A trombone—and the words fell right into their places among the beats.

. . . "I could see you were a man of distinction, a real big spender. Hey, big spender . . . spe-e-e-e-e-end . . ."

Shelly sat up against the headboard, and the tree nymph looked up at him out of the thicket of his dream—he recognized the big eyes of Ernie Kovacs's wife, Edie Adams, batting sultry as a siren's from under her sweeping red hair, slinking around just as she used to in the old Tiparillo cigar television ads.

". . . A little time . . . with me!"

That was enough—so what if Ruth knew him? Mordred lay asleep, head on her arm, her mouth open, snoring.

Shelly reached for the cigar on his bureau top, and fished a match from the night-stand drawer. He tore the plastic wrapping off the big cigar, struck the match, and sat back against his pillow, lighting up in three deep puffs.

5

HOWARD DAVENPORT FINISHED WIPING THE LAST OF HIS TEST tubes and dried his hands on a white cotton towel imprinted with the insignia of the Care Clinic.

"Please tell Roberta I'm fine," he said as a farewell to Homer. "I don't want her to worry. But just between you and me, she could probably stand six good months at this funny farm herself."

"Would you be willing to write her? Or call?"

"Can't now," said Davenport. "On my way to a treatment session. But why don't you write something about the place yourself? That should reassure her."

And he headed off toward the concrete building next door, leaving Homer alone in the equipment shack. Homer was ready to write his report, which might reassure another woman, but wouldn't do much to reconcile Roberta Davenport to her husband's newfound obsession. Still, there wasn't much else he could do. Homer walked out of the shed, and began climbing back up the sloping lawn to the ranch house and guest parking lot behind it. He sighed, wishing again that Shelly had been able to come along. If all they could do was console Mrs. Davenport for her husband's determination to have his brain reshuffled, it would prove a lot easier to do if

44

they had learned something that might be presented as consoling.

As he passed the back porch of the ranch house, however, Homer saw a strange sight: a blonde in her middle twenties, slender as a princess pining away for her prince, sat with her elbows propped upon a small cafe table covered with a pink cloth, sharing a box of Belgian chocolates with a dapper chimpanzee. She wore a pink dress, gathered at the waist and then flaring to her ankles, where her feet were cupped in tiny pink slippers. The chimp wore a stiff collar with rounded corners, held in place by a string tie clasped by an oval of acrylic resin in which a scorpion lay embedded, its stinger curled. It gave him a vaguely Western air of accomplishment, as if the treacherous creature were a personal trophy. The chimp held a saucer under his teacup while the blonde filled it halfway to the brim from a finely wrought silver pot lifted above its matching tray. About a third of the chocolates had been removed from the box, their wrappers crumpled on the table and the floor beneath the couple's feet, but the rest of them were still visible in the open box, within easy reach of the chimpanzee's long arms but politely undisturbed by him.

"There, Joseph," the blonde urged after pouring their tea. "Taste another chocolate, won't you?"

The chimp tilted his head at her, as if to make sure she had meant it; and when she nodded in confirmation, he reached over, hesitated in making his selection, and chose a chocolate-covered nougat nut cluster, which he nibbled, offering her a taste. She refused, nodding again for him to enjoy the entire thing himself. Then she turned around and removed a thick black platter from a hand-cranked Victrola phonograph behind her, replacing it with another from a stack of 78's beside the record player. Its faded label had once been colorful, in the heyday of its speed, Homer imagined. The blonde set down the needle by hand, and not at the beginning of the record; she looked up at Homer, whose eye level cleared the porch railing just as the lush strains of violins and other strings gave way to the lyric, "I know you, I've danced with you once upon a dream . . ."

It was the *"Sleeping Beauty Waltz"* as performed for the Disney animated feature.

Was this romantic setting . . . for the chimp?! Some kind of experiment, perhaps? Or was there actually some liaison between them? Homer tried to keep his anthropocentric biases in check, but as the blonde held his gaze with her large violet eyes, Homer couldn't shake the impression that the whole scene had somehow been arranged for his own sake. He was not usually given to gawking at even spectacularly beautiful women, but the proud set of the blonde's head on her long slender neck; her impossibly skinny limbs; the delicacy of her grip on the teacup as she held it level with the chimp's matching cup—these things touched Homer in a place he didn't know could be touched. Her brow wrinkled; her gaze became an inquiry; he felt a pressure in his chest to answer a question that hadn't been asked.

The chimp was a sophisticate who did not seem troubled at all by Homer's intrusion into their privacy; he slipped out of his seat across the table from her to make room, it seemed to Homer, for another biped to assume his place.

"Joseph?" she said, and then turned to Homer. "Do I know you?" she asked, when it seemed that he and the chimp had worked out an arrangement between them.

Homer said, "Not yet."

"It isn't polite to stare," she scolded. "It isn't polite in the very best places, but in a lunatic asylum, it's positively bad manners."

"This isn't a lunatic asylum."

"You see?" she said. "I thought it was. I must be crazy." It was a joke—when he didn't smile, she had to herself, and her smile was wonderful.

"I didn't mean to chase off your lunch partner."

"Joseph? He comes and goes. And we weren't having lunch. It was an early tea."

Homer surveyed the table top. Linen napkins, silver

teapot, china cups and saucers, and expensive swirls of white and brown chocolates. "No scones?"

"I prefer chocolates," she said, taking a square for herself and offering the box to him. He shook his head and she bit into her square, squeezing creamy pink liquid out the side closer to Homer, which she recovered with a quick lick of her small pointed tongue. "They have something in them—some chemicals—which're supposed to be the same ones released into your bloodstream when you make love."

"Endorphins," Homer said.

She shrugged—the wonders of modern chemistry did not interest her. "Are you sure I can't tempt you with one?"

Why the hell not? Homer took a step closer to accept one, leaning on the porch railing. As he did, he caught a splinter of painted wood in the elbow of his jacket. He tried to brush it off, but it stuck, until she lifted his forearm delicately by the wrist and extracted the splinter in one surgical tug.

"Thank you."

"They really ought to repaint this railing," she said, sadly accepting responsibility for the injury he had sustained on her behalf. "I think they painted it like this in the first place to give it that lived-in rustic look, you know? Flaking Off-White." She smiled and he matched her, tooth for tooth.

"Are you a client here?"

"A *client?*"

Homer wasn't sure of the psychologically acceptable term. "A patient—someone receiving treatment from the Doctor and his minions."

"A nut case."

"I can't believe that."

"Believe it," she said, tossing back her head to jangle her blond curls, but catching herself in the act of flirting, and stopping herself. "With the rates they charge for residence at this place, nobody spends eleven weeks here who doesn't really need to."

47

"Are you spending eleven weeks here?"

"Going on twelve."

"Why?"

"It was the only camp my daddy thought was right for me."

"Your . . . father put you here?"

She nodded. "Not my sugar-daddy."

His stomach uncramped inside. "What makes it right?"

"The diet."

"You eat only special foods?"

"I eat all foods," she said expansively. "And eat and eat and eat them."

"I don't believe it," Homer replied, eyeing her waist—part compliment, part genuine incredulity.

"You don't believe a lot, do you? What are you, a cop or something?"

That took him by surprise, though he tried not to show it. "Not anymore."

"Oh," she said, her tone dropping while her eyes went dull, about a thousand miles further removed. "My dad sent you out here, didn't he?"

Homer shook his head, aghast. "I'm not here to investigate anything to do with you."

Her eyes refocused. "Who's it got to do with, then?"

"Can't say."

"I like secrets," she told him. "And I can keep them, too. Everyone knows that."

"How do they know?"

She laughed. "I tell them." It was a sweet laugh, and the logic was endearing. Homer wasn't sure whether he admired her, or was annoyed with her, or just couldn't figure her out. But he offered his hand, anyway.

"My name is Homer Greeley."

"Homer," she said, "that's a nice name—like the father of Western literature. You have a poet's name."

He didn't know what to say to that. Most people thought of Bart Simpson's father.

"It was my mother's idea."

"She was a classics major, huh? They get the best training. *Mens sibi conscia recti,* you know."

A mind knowing what is right? That was Virgil, from the *Aeneid,* which his mother used to recite to him! Homer couldn't *believe* this girl—his scalp tingled with an eerie sense that she knew all about him, and his family, without ever having met him. They seemed to have what could only be called a natural affinity. "And your name is?"

She let his question hang a moment, as if she didn't know what was expected of her. Then she grinned, broadly, showing big white teeth, imperfectly aligned. The unevenness only added to her charm, Homer decided. It was the flaw that proved she was an actual, living woman. She declared herself, "Adrienne Paglia."

"You have a wonderful smile."

"That's my dad's."

"Your smile belongs to your father?"

"No, it came from him. He's an orthodontist. Fixed all of them—I mean *all* of them."

"Even the ones that didn't need fixing?"

"Who am I to say which of my teeth needed work? He was the professional, after all. So if he said I needed to have my jaw broken, professionally, so that it could be straightened and made shorter, who was I to quarrel with his assessment?"

"He broke your jaw?"

"Not him. His classmate. To correct my bite. And gave us a bargain price."

"And now?"

"Now I'm beautiful, don't you think?"

Homer certainly did. "Yes."

"Tell him."

Then a thought crossed Homer's mind, in the voice of his absent partner, which he expressed before he had time to consider fully what it meant, or how she might react to its presumptions. "Is that why you have lunch with chimpanzees?"

For an instant she looked as if she might be angry, but

49

the lines that leaped across her brow receded, and she turned away from Homer, calmly surveying the slope of the hill tumbling down to the lake. She turned back to him with a smile that did not seem composed. "Early tea."

He nodded, tempted to bow, accepting the correction. But she didn't give him a chance to apologize for anything. "Don't you want your chocolate?"

It sat on the edge of the railing, where she must have set it down when she lifted his wrist to remove the splinter of wood from his sleeve. It was a rectangle of semisweet chocolate, almost black, with a flat bottom and rounded upper corners. Homer picked it up with his thumb and index finger, and bit into it, tasting cool syrup and a fresh whole cherry. He had to engulf the second half, pushing it into his mouth, or it would have dripped down over his fingers. Adrienne seemed to enjoy his trouble in keeping himself clean, and held on to her linen napkin an extra moment to give him time to struggle on his own before offering him aid.

"Good, huh?"

He swallowed, open-mouthed. "What's in that?"

"Cherry brandy." She searched through the rectangles still in the box, found another like his first, and offered it to him. When he declined it, she popped the whole thing into her mouth, chewing vigorously. "Ummm." When she swallowed, she closed her eyes in rapture and then raised her eyebrows at him, as if they had shared a sensual experience. Homer wiped his syrupy fingers on her napkin.

"This what you do all day long?"

"This is what I'm doing today," she said. "For fun. It is not part of what the doctors call my treatment modality. For that I have to go, like everyone else, into the concrete bunker down at the bottom of the hill, built by the favored architect of the Soviet KGB."

Where Davenport went. Homer squinted as the sun reflected off its grim walls. "No windows?"

"So no one can hear you scream," she said.

Homer started to smile, acknowledging the joke, but

Adrienne wasn't smiling; and when a question started to form in his mind, she stood and brushed invisible crumbs off her dress, retreating behind her chair before turning back to him.

"See you around."

"Wait! Did you mean what you just said?"

For a second he thought she might answer him directly, but a grimace of anxiety wrinkled the corners of her eyes, which she smoothed again with her fingers. She passed her hands over her eyebrows, and took a deep breath before replying, "Of course not. This is a hospital. Goodbye."

"Wait—"

"I can't. I have to go now."

"Where?"

Her mouth curled and she looked at him as if she had thought him too polite to ask such a question; but since he had asked, she had no choice but to answer honestly.

"To throw up."

Was it his question? Something else he had said? Homer was horrified that he had revolted this young woman, without knowing how. He wanted to ask her to forgive him, when he heard a moan float up from behind him, rising across the lawn that separated the ranch house from the concrete bunker.

"Unh-hnhh . . ."

There were no words to the utterance, but Homer realized you don't need words to recognize a voice—at least not the nasal whine he had heard only forty minutes before, straining over the pounding of tap water into a sink.

Homer turned, and saw two orderlies in white coats rushing out of the concrete bunker called the Research Building, pushing a body on a wheeled gurney between them. On top, reclining on his back under a tight-wrapped white sheet, was Howard Davenport, his head flung back on a pillow, mouth open to the sky. Homer glanced up at Adrienne, who watched, horrified, and withdrew through the doorway of the ranch house behind her. He looked down the lawn again and saw the two orderlies steering the gurney along a path that led to a cluster of cabins near the lake.

Homer went after them, bounding down the lawn again, which already seemed to him the only mode of transit across it. He caught up with them as they neared a cabin, one of the smallest in the cluster, which were not as spiffy, he noticed, as the newer guest quarters closer to the ranch house. The two men in white lab coats were hoisting Howard on his gurney up the three steps into his cabin, where Homer stepped in to hold open the screen door. Inside was a sparse but clean room with a cot and a dresser of badly stained dark wood, with a frame for a mirror on top but no mirror in it. There was a metal desk with an office chair—a swivel model in gray steel and cracked green plastic. The floor was bare boards, and the windows were unadorned except for dysfunctional blinds. The orderlies unwrapped Davenport from the gurney and lifted him into his bed, dumping him on top of the woolen blanket. As he hit the springs under the thin mattress, Davenport opened his eyes with a start, and eased back again. He noticed Homer at the door and the two orderlies nearer his bed, and mumbled, "Thanks, fellahs."

The big one sighed. "Too much juice again, Howard."

Howard managed a weak smile. "Gotta watch that damn dial better."

"You said it, man," the smaller orderly muttered, waved, and followed his larger colleague out the door.

Which left Homer alone with him again. Davenport avoided the detective's green eyes for a moment, and then asked in a wavering voice, "You're not gonna put this into your report now, are you?"

"Can't leave it out, Mr. Davenport."

"Look," said Howard, "my wife's paying you, isn't she? All of her money comes from me. So you could say I'm paying you, couldn't you?"

"No," said Homer.

"All right," said Davenport. "So put it in. But it's just going to upset Roberta for no reason."

"No reason?"

"A little too much enthusiasm for personal improvement is all that happened. I feel fine."

"You didn't look so fine when those two gorillas in the lab coats brought you in here."

"You can't always feel wonderful," Davenport said. "Not if you want to make yourself a better person. There are efforts involved, and risks."

"This a risk you're prepared to take?"

Davenport sighed, his frail body trembling despite his best efforts as the air escaped from his chest like a punctured tire. "Yes," he said resolutely. "It's like Dr. Harrison says—'What are you prepared to risk to save your life? Your vanity? Your smug sense of individuality? Your money?' I'm prepared to risk this sort of thing every day of the week." He tried to raise himself to an upright position, but his elbows trembled as he put his weight on them, until he sunk back into the pillow, closing his eyes from the exertion of his declaration.

And Homer had nothing further to say to the man, recognizing the unmistakable strain of courage in Davenport's twisted resolve.

6

THERE WERE TWO DINING SPOTS AT THE CARE CLINIC. ONE OF them was the Eating Room, an airy, barnlike cafeteria where patients and staff gathered at long tables to pass around plates of runny eggs in the mornings and turkey sandwiches with potato chips in the afternoons and beef stroganoff over wet noodles in the evenings. This was where "family-style" meals were available, as the brochure referred to them, which meant each guest was expected to bus his or her own plate and silverware at the end of the meal. There were waiters, college-age kids from the local area, who brought the large plates and bowls of food to the various tables, but the ethos of the room implied that their services were not to be taken for granted but appreciated as favors from one human being to another. This alone was evidence to the discerning eye that Dr. Harrison had not had a hand in the dining arrangements, at least in the Eating Room, where he never ate his own meals anyway. Anyone who wished to eat with the Doctor, who had earned that distinction with service or financial generosity, needed to troop over to a marble gazebo at the very highest point of the grounds, where Harrison would have his daily meals brought to him so that he could contemplate the higher reaches of psychology, and the cars passing below on the highway. On the day of Homer's visit to the Care Clinic, Harrison received two luncheon guests at his gazebo, who came together to lunch with him as a package deal: Dr. Helen Kaufman, director of internships at the clinic, who had seldom before lunched with Harrison in his special eating place; and Neela Zapotnik, a graduate student, who by that fact alone should never have been invited to join them. But according to the waiter, Harrison was in one of his moods, his customary irritability aggravated by something on his mind, which perhaps explained the lapse in his usual strict hierarchy of who might be invited to lunch with whom, and where.

For her part, Neela Zapotnik was conscious of the honor the invitation implied, and had even nearly bragged about it to her next-door neighbor, Adrienne; but as the two of them crossed the grass together, Helen was not so excited, and she thought there might even have been a wrinkle of worry in the center of her forehead, had Neela been capable of noticing it.

"Is that for us?" asked Neela, blinking as the vista came into view through the white pillars of Harrison's gazebo—a white wrought-iron table covered with a white linen cloth, which blew and fluttered in the breeze. The Doctor himself sat at one of three chairs, entirely in shadow, a silhouette with his chin on his fist and his elbow on the table, gazing out abstractedly in the opposite direction. Below him, and completely unnoticed by him, the table was set with fine bone china, heavy silver implements, sparkling crystal, and a bottle of red wine, which had already been opened. A deep purple liquid lolled at the bottom of the goblet balanced in the fingers of his free hand.

Kaufman nodded at the girl. Should she have allowed this encounter? It was difficult to know for certain. Although every synapse in her trained clinician's mind was firing its separate warning blast, there was no way she could have turned down the Doctor's invitation without discussing it first with Neela—and once she told Neela about it, of course, there was no way of discouraging the girl from accepting. She tried to suggest her suspicions about the lunch, that it felt to her like the kind of trap Harrison set for unsuspecting colleagues and professional rivals; but what could she tell the girl, really? Neela was not the shrewdest of this year's brood, although she certainly was intelligent enough—but there are things from which intelligence will not protect you. Helen had sighed inside, and had managed only to get herself invited along, to offer Neela what protection her presence would afford. She owed that much to the girl's mother, she felt. But the sight of the brooding Dr. Harrison, waiting for them in his windswept gazebo, confirmed Helen's worst fears.

"Don't let him start asking you personal questions" was all she could say to prepare Neela, who gave her a quizzical glance in return. Helen had no chance to explain before Harrison marched down the three sweeping steps and offered his hand to the frightened child.

"Miss Zapotnik, isn't it? Or do you prefer Neela at lunch?"

"Neela is okay," she replied in a tiny voice, with a quick glance at Kaufman.

"Then it's Helen and Harry all around," said the Doctor.

"Harry?" asked Helen.

"I'm usually Henry," Harrison explained to Neela, as if her understanding were the crucial point to him, "as Dr. Kaufman is well aware. But I feel like Harry, right now—do you know what I mean by that?"

Neela nodded uncertainly.

"Redefinition of the self," said Harrison, just to make sure she did. By her expression, that was not what the poor girl had taken him to mean, but she nodded again; and so did the Doctor, each of them confirming the other's insight.

Helen Kaufman did not feel at all comfortable about so much empathy, but what was there to object to, on the face of it? She checked her watch and saw she had forty-five minutes before her supervision group was scheduled to begin. Could she usher Neela in and out of this lunch by then? Not unless she could hurry things along.

"Neela has been very interested in your research, Doctor," she prompted.

"Oh, yes!" agreed Neela. "It's wonderful, watching Joseph! I've never seen anything like him before."

Harrison nodded self-effacingly but made no comment. He was not planning to discuss psychology, it seemed, since he reached across the table to locate a plate of tuna *carpaccio,* sliced very thin and garnished with capers, which he offered to Neela without comment. Neela flushed, uncertain what it was, and Kaufman had to lend a hand by putting some of the cold fish on her own plate, providing an example. Neela Zapotnik declined to do the same. Harrison offered her another appetizer, a smoked salmon *caprese,* rolled with eggplant and cheese, which she also refused. But when the Doctor made his final offer, a *bruscietta,* she felt she could not turn it down without insulting the man and moved the smallest piece of toasted bread onto her plate, from which finely chopped tomatoes and onions fell off into the napkin on her lap. When she tried to lift the pieces discreetly from her napkin, they rolled onto the pleated skirt over her thighs. Neela looked up at Helen, who gave her a little expression of encouragement, and at Harrison, who never watched while she did these things but seemed to take them all in anyway. Each time she dropped a bit of onion, smothered in oil, on herself, his eyes seemed to be elsewhere; but every time she wiped herself off, and tried to sit up correctly again, she caught a glimmer from the corner of his eye that showed he had witnessed her secret embarrassment but was altogether too polite to acknowledge it. This only made poor Neela even more self-conscious, of course, and she proceeded to drop *fettucini Alfredo,* and a spinach dish in a cream sauce, and even a thick glob of *gelato* on herself in sequence. The Doctor and Helen kept up a running conversation about the plays they had seen and the books they had read; now and then Harrison would cast his eyes in Neela's direction as if to include her in their conversation, but she had nothing, she felt, to contribute, and splattered herself with dish after dish, listening in intense fear of being directly addressed.

"Have you read Horney's analysis of anxiety and clumsiness?" Harrison surprised her by asking.

"No," said Neela, shaking her head, coughing, and spitting up onions; she reached for her napkin to cover her mouth, and dropped the white linen on the ground.

"Pity," he said, observing the whole performance.

Neela knocked her wine over with her elbow.

Helen tried to change the topic once or twice to subjects that might allow Neela to participate; but topics seemed hard to come by, were quickly exhausted, and always caught the girl unexpectedly. In the middle of a discussion about learning disabilities, Kaufman said, "Neela, weren't you telling me about your mother's speech impediment?"

"My, uh, mother's?"

"Stutter? When she's upset."

"Right," said Neela, grateful for a topic she knew something about—or she thought she did, before she had to speak about it. "She, uh, stutters. But only when she gets upset." Did she have anything more to say about it, really?

"Why do you think she stutters?" asked Helen helpfully.

"Because she's . . . upset," Neela responded. "Of course, when she stutters, that makes her upset. So she stutters."

"That's an interesting cycle," said Helen.

Dr. Harrison watched her with interest, without comment or reproach.

But he must have seen something in her, despite her efforts, because when Helen Kaufman stood and said, "Well, thank you, Doctor, it's been lovely. But I do have to lead a supervision group in ten minutes in the Council Room," Harrison nodded, accepted Kaufman's withdrawal, but turned an inquiring eye toward Neela.

"And you, Miss Zapotnik? Do you have to be running off from me as well?"

It must have been the sly *"from me"* that he slipped in so smoothly, Helen thought, but Neela's eyes widened and she did not seem to be able to manage a discreet *"'Fraid so."* Instead, she looked at the Doctor, and then at Kaufman, and at Harrison again, who sat waiting like a spider for her.

"I don't have to be going right away," she said quietly. "Do I?"

"Of course not!" roared Harrison, showing his good nature. Dr. Kaufman shot her a look of alarm in response to the Doctor's good humor, but it was too late for Neela to do anything about it. Because Harrison smiled broadly at her, and sat back in his chair, wiping his mouth with his linen napkin, and said, "Very good, Miss Zapotnik! Then you and I will have a little time alone to discuss your future."

The sound of it was almost enough to make Helen Kaufman call the ranch house and cancel her supervision group. But there was no real excuse she could use to do so, especially for Harrison, who must have waited until she committed herself before springing his wire on Neela. Helen gave Neela a last glance of warning, and then smiled at them both maternally, as if her face could set the tone of their conversation by example.

"Good luck, dear," she said to Neela. And then, sweetly, as if making a joke, she added, "Don't let him pin you down."

Then she was gone, crossing the wide lawn in giant strides, already late for her group. Harrison waited until she had gone inside the ranch house before leaning back in his chair, tilting his head to one side, facing Neela.

"Now, let's talk about your research. I understand you've had some trouble lately. Perhaps I can help you straighten it out. One researcher to another."

Mrs. Wanda Elderberry knew she had time for just one more dessert before her afternoon treatment session, a thought which made her selection at the dessert table more anxiety-provoking than it would have been anyway. At one-hundred-and-ninety-three pounds, she had come to the Care Clinic for help and was indeed receiving it: she was pleased to discover that she had, in fact, developed an aversion to the chocolate éclairs that under other circumstances would have been enough to make her mouth water. Now she gazed at them unmoved and marveled at the efficacy of modern psychological science. Her induced revulsion to chocolate éclairs pleased her so much, she decided to reward herself with an extra scoop of vanilla ice cream on her nice thick slice of hot apple pie, and topped it off with a strawberry and a healthy dollop of that sweet syrup in which the waiting strawberries swam in their bowl.

She had just enough time to cram it in and wash it down with a cup of decaffeinated coffee and saccharin, when she heard the soft chimes of the one o'clock bells, discreetly intoning over the Eating Room's speaker system. Several of the patients and staff in the room looked up at the big clock on the fireplace mantel. They gathered up their papers and books, collected their plates on their trays, and carried them over to the trash and recycling bins. Mrs. Elderberry watched them go, and acknowledged with a sinking feeling inside that there would be no time for a slice of the tempting peach cobbler as well.

And yet, as she followed the last of them out of the Eating Room, the crowd dispersing across the wide lawn, she thought she saw her therapist heading diagonally across from the gazebo at the front edge of the grounds—that young Miss Zapotnik. Or was it Dr. Zapotnik? Mrs. Elderberry couldn't tell who was a doctor and who wasn't at the Care Clinic, who was a staff person, and who was a student. All she knew was that the young woman with the staff badge that read "Zapotnik" was the one who adjusted the controls on the conditioning machine when she was strapped into it; and since Mrs. Elderberry was herself on her way to that machine, shouldn't Zapotnik have been heading there also?

But she wasn't. She was headed toward the residential

cabins around the lake at the back of the grounds. True, she had felt the girl was a little chunky herself to be administering weight-control treatments, but Neela was always nice and patient with her, and it made Mrs. Elderberry uncomfortable to think she might have to get used to a new therapist instead. Mrs. Elderberry called out to her, "Dr. Zapotnik!" and on receiving no answer followed up with "Neela?" But she received no response to either name, and decided to head straight for the lab building as she was expected to do, where Zapotnik would surely show up shortly. A moment before, Mrs. Elderberry had been a bit worried that she might be running late. This feeling was now replaced by a gratifying sense of indignation that she might be held up by an even later therapist.

And so she was—because when Mrs. Elderberry arrived at Room 226 in the concrete Research Building, her conditioning room was open, but Zapotnik was nowhere in sight. Mrs. Elderberry put her face to the plate glass that separated the treatment room from the control booth where Zapotnik usually sat, monitoring the flow of electrons or whatever it was they were zapping into her chair. But no one was in there, and Mrs. Elderberry stood uneasily in the treatment room for a moment, before deciding what-the-hell, she might as well sit down in the chair as stand on her aching feet until Zapotnik, or whoever they sent to replace her, finally arrived.

So she eased herself into the treatment chair as Zapotnik usually eased her, settling her head on the new paper over the padded headrest, centering it beneath the video monitor overhead, which was now just a hissing screen full of random noise; and, since her hands felt uncomfortable in her lap, she slipped them through the rings on the armrests of the chair, gripping the posts at the end of each arm as Zapotnik usually showed her she should do. It felt the way it always did, and Mrs. Elderberry snuggled into the padded seat until she had pretty much installed herself into the chair for a treatment.

"This should save us some time, at least," she an-

nounced to herself, "once we finally get started, here."
She wondered if this waiting time would be counted
toward her therapy hours, and if she would be charged
full price for it. "After all," she said aloud in case anyone
was listening, "I don't expect Dr. Harrison to treat me
himself, personally, but there's no reason I should have
to treat myself."

It seemed as if somebody agreed with her, because the
chair began to hum as it always did when the power was
turned on in the control booth next door, and the video
monitor in front of her suddenly came alive with wrig-
gling lines as if a tape were being cued up on a cassette
player that fed it. Reflected on the thick glass surface of
the monitor, she saw somebody enter the other room,
slip into a white lab coat, and take up a position at the
control panel. The speakers alongside Mrs. Elderberry's
ears began to buzz with a familiar staticky silence, and
then that nice voice began to whisper into her ears,
murmuring at a level that was just audible to her.
"Welcome back, Mrs. Elderberry," it said in a man's
deep voice, which she imagined was the voice of the
Doctor. "Our staff have had a chance to review your
charts with Dr. Harrison, who feels you are making
excellent progress. The following video has been prepared especially for you, to help you achieve the goals
you have come to this place for and have been working so
hard to achieve."

There was a pause, in which Mrs. Elderberry heard
herself think, "Indeed I have!" It was so satisfying to hear
her efforts recognized and acknowledged. And then the
familiar litany of instructions as her individually designed treatment plan kicked in with a jolt to her
forearm.

"Settle back now . . . relax into the chair. We'll start as
usual with some music to soothe you. I think you'll find
today's selection includes some of your favorites. After
that, we'll begin with some pictures. Please close your
eyes now, and keep your hands on the contact plates on
the armrests. Now, shall we begin?"

Mrs. Elderberry twisted herself around in the chair to

nod to Zapotnik that she was ready to start, and also to let the poor girl know that she was forgiven for showing up late. Only when Mrs. Elderberry looked through the plate glass, her hand ready to wave, did she notice that Neela Zapotnik was not in her usual place among the dials and knobs in the control booth.

Mrs. Elderberry blanched. She did not consider herself a biased woman, but felt this was unfair.

She saw a shorter, hairier technician, whose competence she felt obliged to question. Residents, interns, even graduate students she had no problem with—but was she really expected to accept her treatment session from the Doctor's famous trained chimpanzee?

7

RALPH WALDO KOTLOWICZ BELIEVED HE HAD FOUND HIMSELF his own little piece of heaven, although he had to keep it to himself. As maintenance director of the Care Clinic, all sorts of tricky business fell his way which would not normally fall within the purview of a maintenance supervisor—mostly technical problems in the labs, where machines that should never have been plugged in were overloading circuits that had never been designed to support them. When Harrison had hired him for the job, it was with specific instructions that the Doctor never again be informed of technical problems on the grounds—he was handing over total responsibility for the physical plant to Kotlowicz, who ought to know better than Harrison himself what needed to be maintained, and how. There was a grounds crew to maintain the horticulture and a cleaning crew for the buildings. Ralph's responsibilities were limited to machines that blinked and beeped and turned wheels and gears and went *perclunk* when no one was watching in the night. Unfortunately, the Doctor did not hand over at the same time the authority to do what was necessary, so when Ralph had had a chance to study the electrical system, and recommended that the entire lab area be rewired, Harrison had vetoed the necessity for it. As a result, the circuits would overload around two in the afternoon, when the late starters had begun to use their labs' therapeutic equipment, and the early birds hadn't knocked off yet. Then Ralph would be a familiar figure around the Research Building, turning off machines that did not need to stay on continuously, trying to help people manage their temperamental computers. That was how he had met Helen Kaufman, working together to recover a computer file which represented her entire morning's data analysis. She had sat in the swivel chair at her computer while he squatted, then knelt beside her, both of them staring at the blinking screen, his shoulder brushing her arm as he reached across to tap her keyboard, struggling to bring up the failed system and recover her files from the void into which they had disappeared when the A/C power on the fifth floor was shorted out by a coffee maker with a bad *on/off* switch two floors above her.

God bless Mr. Coffee.

Ralph had never considered himself much of a catch, or much of a looker, either, in his blue work shirt unbuttoned at the collar so that the loop of his T-shirt showed above the topmost button. He was forty-seven, in fairly good health but spreading above the belt, with thinning hair and clean-shaven cheeks with a stubble that was turning increasingly silver. His mustache, once an unruly walrus-style, was now trimmed neatly, and his long, graying hair was bound in a ponytail that hung to the center of his shoulder blades. When not in overalls, which he wore without a shirt, he wore a big silver buckle, worked with turquoise by the Navajo, and his watch was set in a similarly worked wristband. In the evenings, in his fringed buckskin jacket, he looked like an aging Buffalo Bill after a successful hunt. And yet this impeccably tailored professional woman had sat silently staring at her screen while his shoulder touched her arm, electric through her sweater, and then as the rough edge of his hand met hers side by side on the keyboard. By the time they succeeded in recovering all but the last ten minutes of her data, Ralph knew she would agree to a cup of coffee to celebrate their success; and by the time he had finished his third cup of coffee, he knew she would meet him for dinner. He knew she liked him because she laughed at his jokes, and whether she did it to make him feel good or because she thought he was really that funny didn't matter at all—either way, she liked him, and he liked her better than any woman he had ever bought a coffee for. She was a great listener, of course, given her job, but the thing was, she didn't make you feel she was listening to be polite—she was listening to what you said because she cared about what you said, about the subject itself. He had the strong sense she would have changed the topic to something she cared about if she didn't. And this *honesty* made Ralph feel respected by Helen for what he was and what he said and what she felt about what he had said. Besides, from the first moment he saw her, striding across the lawn in her smart Chanel suit, he had wanted to lie down on a pillow beside hers, stroking those curls away from her face, murmuring promises to her. Promises he would keep.

There was just no figuring women—Ralph had spent a year and a half with the office manager of a plumbing and heating supply firm, and she had done her best to make him feel like an unwashed ignoramus; and here was this truly well-educated woman, skilled at her demanding profession, who gave credence to his opinions and judgments and sometimes changed her mind in light of what he had observed. The truth was that he was undoubtedly better read than either Helen or Audrey when it came to the Transcendentalists, and American literature in general, which had been his passion as an undergraduate at Buffalo; he had taken Thoreau's model literally and had dropped out in the early sixties to head south, where he learned his craft rewiring churches bombed in voter-registration drives at the start of the civil rights movement. The Zen of maintenance work had exerted a powerful influence over him, and his skill with machines that did not work when the *on* button was pressed made him a welcome visitor at hog farms and other communities throughout the sixties and seventies. When he decided it was time to find a place to make his stand, as Gary Snyder had phrased it, he looked for geography above all other considerations—and the grounds of the Care Clinic were just what he had in mind. He was able to pick his own spot on a patch of level ground above the lake, and to build his own cabin with his own hands, an ax, and the trees that grew there. It was Emerson who wrote in his essay *Self-Reliance*, "Whoso would be a man must be a nonconformist." Although Ralph's lifestyle resembled Thoreau's more closely than Emerson's (since Thoreau had been the bachelor, earning his living by carpentry, surveying, and other forms of measuring, while Emerson was a celebrated public figure and family man), Ralph had always preferred Emerson's sociability and desire to reach concord with other men to Thoreau's personal competitiveness and isolationism; and there was no doubt that Emerson's aphorisms stuck in his mind better than anything from *Walden*—the one book of Thoreau's Ralph thought held any literary merit. He had raised these considerations with Harrison during his interview, but the Doctor didn't give a damn why he wanted the job, so long as he kept their machines up and running without hiring additional staffers. Ralph couldn't help agreeing with Helen whenever she pointed out that Harrison was an asshole; but he also recognized that his needs and the Doctor's complemented one another. Ralph wanted a job in which he could be responsible for something and left alone to take care of it, and Harrison wanted exactly the same thing.

So Ralph was able to live a life in which his familiarity with the objects of the modern world bought him time and space to live without them. He put in a spigot outside his cabin but kept himself warm with his quilt and extra blankets and a fireplace. The kitchen in the ranch house was well enough supplied for him to dispense with a refrigerator, and the lack of a telephone he considered a personal boon. He had no television, but a boom box to play his CD's and cassettes with plenty of spare batteries on hand. He read in bed each night by electric torch, or kerosene lamp when the mood came over him. A two-burner propane range was sufficient to boil water, and his paper screens made excellent coffee, if he wanted a cup before the ranch-house kitchen perked theirs. He had found his place: the sound of the lake lapping at the nighttime shore, an occasional visit from a hunting owl—these pleasures more than compensated for the lack of TV game shows and telephone solicitors. His evening conversations were with crickets and bullfrogs, and when it came time to retire, he slept the untroubled sleep of a woodland denizen at peace with his neighbors. "If a man would be alone, let him look at the stars," Emerson had written in *Nature.* "Most persons do not see the sun." Ralph was certain he wanted to see the sun as children are able to, with an appreciation of the eternal that sustains it; but as he sat in front of his cabin under the sky each night, he was not sure he wanted to be so alone.

And then, into his pastoral if lonely existence came Helen. That first night at dinner, after coffee, they had sat at the far end of a table together, across from each other, hardly talking but looking up at one another from time to time with glances that seemed too revealing for them to allow anyone else to see. When she had asked for the salt and he passed it to her, and the edges of their hands brushed against each other—what could've been more obvious than that? She blushed deeply, this restrained professional woman, and he studied his plate, unwilling to allow anyone else in the room to intrude upon their thrilling foreplay. Afterward, by common if unstated consent, they retreated to Helen's room upstairs in the ranch house, where they made noisy and responsive love well into the early hours of the morning; after which they lay in a daze, skipping breakfast, Helen missing her morning rounds with the interns and Ralph unavailable when the sprinkler system around the gazebo failed to shut itself off, drenching the grass through which Harrison had to walk for his butter croissants and coffee. That afternoon, Helen had expressed a desire to see Ralph's cabin, and when she did, a preference to spend their nights together there, and their lunches as well, whenever they could both free themselves for a secret rendezvous. It was not that fraternizing among the staff was forbidden by clinic policy, or even that Helen felt embarrassed by the liaison she had struck for herself, but Ralph did not think their love affair was anybody's business but their own—and there may also have been an unexpressed concern that Helen not reduce her status among the complex pecking order of residents, interns, and other doctors by her association with a maintenance man. Helen guessed this motivation, and confronted Ralph with it; Ralph denied it, and she allowed him to do so; and the outcome was they kept their secret, which they called their privacy, and met one another at Ralph's cabin by the lake every evening and every afternoon their schedules allowed.

Ralph, it turned out, was the one who most often could not free himself at the appointed lunch hour, so he usually found Helen waiting for him when he could. But on this afternoon, when he finished relining the brakes on the delivery truck and made his way to his cabin, Ralph did not see the straightened doormat outside his cabin door which usually signified that Helen had passed over it; and when he stuck his head inside, calling her name in two lilting syllables, he discovered that she had not in fact managed to join him. She had suspected as much that morning, when she kissed him goodbye, and yet the speed with which he finished the brakes on the delivery truck, and his own unexpected availability, had stirred an optimism in his heart that sank slowly into the wooden floorbeams.

He had rebuilt the place for her, it seemed to him, piece by piece. She had not asked for anything to be changed, insisting that she didn't want to change him; but it didn't take Ralph very long to feel he needed to make things better there for her. She took certain medications, he noticed, which she usually stored in a refrigerator in her own room. When she spent the night in his cabin, she left them in a bag outside the door—to keep them cool overnight, he guessed. So he realized he needed a freezer or a refrigerator to accommodate her, which meant, of course, he needed a source of current. He installed a generator outside the cabin, in back, and bought himself a small fridge that ran off it. He installed a sink beside the fridge, and ran a hose from the spigot outside to the taps whenever she stayed over. Ralph went so far as to buy an old space heater at a local garage sale, but she never let him plug it into the line from his new generator, preferring, she said, to keep the cold as an incentive to snuggle closer.

What wouldn't he have done for Helen? He loved the feel of her slender waist when he wrapped his big hands around her, and the *zip* of the zipper on her hip before she wriggled and stepped out of her skirt. He had never known a woman with so much lacy underwear, fancy stuff, which made her look round where she might have been lean, and soft where she might have been bony— not that any of it mattered to him, really. When he took her around, all of the differences between them vanished. He called her "Baby" one night into the hair by her ear, and she rubbed up against him with so much contentment he used it, sparingly, as a secret name between them. After all day responding to the emotional needs of all sorts of critical people, Helen found nothing so renewing as to feel Ralph throw his big arms around her, and take care of her like a baby.

He usually took care of their arrangements—planning where and when they might see one another, and what they should do when they could. He tried to spare her any concern, which meant not only any pain but also any trouble. It was important to him that she felt no need to seize control of the world whenever they were together. Today was no exception.

Ralph had brought along with him foodstuffs from the kitchen, which would serve as their lunch, when they were ready to fix one: fresh rye bread, newly sliced by himself on the kitchen's slicing machine, and, wrapped in white paper, a turkey breast, newly removed by himself from the refrigerated turkey, along with toma- toes and lettuce and a dressing he had blended from ketchup and mayonnaise and relish. He gave Helen another few minutes to show up late, anxious with explanations and even more anxious for him to take her to their bed. But she didn't show, and Ralph consoled himself by fixing a double-thick sandwich, popping the cap of one of the two bottles of beer in his bag, and retreating thus fortified to the edge of the lake to face the humiliation of the loons.

The birds, he meant, who flocked along the far side of the lake this time of year. The other sort, who waded into the water from the grassy edge near the cabins, or plopped into the lake from badly handled rowboats, he kept as far away from as he could manage. This was a clinic, Harrison had explained to him, but there was a psychological benefit to be gained by associating the work done in their laboratories with the images of summer camps and vacation spots normally associated with fishing and swimming and so on; and while Ralph had put his foot down against water skiing, Harrison had persuaded him that a little innocent boating might not be the worst photograph to appear on brochures for the Care Clinic.

So Ralph had built a boating dock, and cleared an area for swimming, marking it off with floats and lines. He placed it as close to the guest cabins, and as far from his own cabin, as was geometrically possible to arrange. Now, as he walked down his favorite path to the far side of the lake, he turned his back on the guests splashing around in the swimming area, knocking oars into the dock or losing them in the lake, and headed for the spot he knew would interest none of them, blocked by tall rushes from even the most ambitious Sunday sailors. He expected to see no one there, and no one on his way there. But he was wrong, on both counts.

First, he saw Ray Singh, the clinic's research statistician, striding briskly down the beaten path that ran around the lake. Singh wore a short-sleeve shirt in white cotton with epaulets, and khaki shorts, almost knee-high white socks and penny loafers; on a strap around his neck hung high-powered binoculars, thumping against his slim chest with each step. Singh was a bird watcher,

Ralph knew, who liked to do his observing in the quiet time before breakfast; it was unusual to see him near the lake during the lunch hour, when so many other people were disturbing the wildlife. And there was something else unusual about Singh, he thought—whereas the statistician was normally formally polite but rather sad, Ray seemed to be in rare high spirits, whistling, in fact. Singh gave Ralph his usual greeting, a two-fingered salute, and stomped off down the path.

The second surprise was even more disturbing: Ralph came upon it at the far end of the lake, where he abandoned the path and raised his arms, easing his way through the waist-high grass to a rock at the edge of the waterline. It made a lovely seat, covered with moss and flat on top, where one could sit and enjoy the tiny wildlife that clung to the rim of the lake. Ralph was resigned to his daily discovery of candy wrappers and cigarette butts along the boating dock and shoreline bordering the swimming area; he even managed to remain stoical about having to fish floating aluminum cans out of the lake center now and then. But he had come to expect that this spot, among the thin blue flowers that sprouted at the crest of the river weeds, would be spared the detritus of human beings who could not bring back from their encounters with the lake all the things they had brought to it. Today, right there, floating beside a submerged log that was home to a goggly-eyed orange frog, Ralph saw an article of clothing some woman had left behind—a pleated skirt, it seemed to him, of dark blue, judging by the hem, which was all he could see of it through the weeds.

Now how could a woman manage to leave a skirt behind? She must have worn her bathing suit underneath it, and slipped out of the skirt to swim; and then gone back to her cabin wearing only the suit. Her outfit must have passed from her consciousness as she turned her thoughts to her next therapy session, or to lunch, or whatever other activity came up next on her schedule. And how did the damned skirt find its way across the lake from the swimming area, and through the weeds, to moor itself here on the far side?

Ralph couldn't imagine, until he reached down to pull it out and found it resisted him stubbornly. *It must've caught itself on the bottom of the log,* he figured, but when he scrambled down to the water's edge, and tugged at the hem with both hands, it did not seem to have snagged in any particular spot. And, by the color of the water beneath the log, there seemed to be a lot of it down there.

Ralph had to climb into the lake, which was deeper than it appeared, the water level high as his solar plexus; and when he reached for the skirt from this angle, something kicked him in the belly. It floated to the surface, breaking through first as a heel, then a sole—a woman's shoe. His stomach fell, and he felt an even more awful sensation, as if someone were watching him from behind. He turned and saw through the weeds the face of a girl tilted skyward, her nostrils just clearing the water-line. Then the rest of her swam out from under the log to meet him: a knee filling out the hem, with a calf and foot attached to it. And he realized he was holding on to the clothes of a girl who was still wearing them. The shock flushed through him, overcoming the chill of the lake water on his chattering bones. But Ralph reacted quickly, hauling her out from under the submerged log, shoving her up onto the grassy bank beside his moss-covered rock, while the water streamed from every opening in her. Her skin was cold but her limbs were not yet stiff, her eyes glazed over but not yet vacant. He would have thought her dead but for one fact: He thought he recognized her as one of Helen's, and he wasn't about to tell Helen that one of her interns was dead. So there was nothing for him to do but try and save her.

Ralph had taken Red Cross lifesaving nearly twenty years before, and all that remained in his memory banks was the general idea of forcing water out of her lungs, and oxygen in. For the rest he had to depend on movements of his arms and shoulders, and the rhythm of his own breath, which seemed to him most likely to accomplish those two objectives. But what else could he do? She was Helen's student, the one she had been talking about the day before, worrying about her—with a funny name, Kneeling Zapata or something like that.

Neela.

As the name entered his head, the girl opened her eyes for a moment, blinking at him—and closed them again. But she lurched on the ground convulsively and vomited water, and he rolled her over onto her side, where she vomited again with more conviction. Ralph hadn't a clue what he might say to her, so he just patted her damp arm, encouraging her to expel the lake from her insides. When she finally stopped heaving and began to shiver, he picked her up in his arms and carried her like a lover along the path to the boating dock and the ranch house behind it. She did not say anything to him either, but her arm hung around his neck, and her head fell upon his shoulder. He felt her shudder, the length of her frame, a spasm that shook them both. When it subsided and the warmth of his body began to thaw hers, the stiffness ran out of her and she melted against him, shaking in a different way. Ralph looked down and pushed the matted brown hair off her face, gently, as he knew Helen would have done. He saw that she was a young girl, really, younger than her years and education might have made her; and he saw also that she had curled herself up as tight as she could, and was weeping into her fists uncontrollably.

8

"HE LIKES IT THERE," HOMER SAID TO SHELLY AFTER THE drive back through Jersey to their offices in the Bronx. "They zap him with electricity now and then, but it doesn't seem to do him any permanent damage, and he doesn't mind it." Homer dropped heavily into his green leather chair and put his hundred-dollar loafers up on Shelly's desk. "It's a creepy little place, all right, but the doctors there seem to know what the law allows them to do to consenting adults."

Which meant, no crime for them to investigate and no case to pursue. Shelly reached across his desk for the ashtray into which he had dropped Roberta Davenport's diamond engagement ring. It was a gesture on her part, leaving the thing with them—but it was a good one. "What do we tell her?"

"We tell her we're sorry, but there's nothing we can do to help her. We send her back her ring and with it a bill for my time today. If you like, we can even suggest she drive out there and talk to Howard herself."

"What would he tell her if she did?"

"To stay and get zapped right along with him, I suspect. Or go home without him."

"Which do you think she'd choose?"

75

"Having seen the place? I'd say she'd high-tail it out of there as fast as her heels could carry her."

Shelly grunted. Not only had this case failed to gratify Homer's need for significant inquiry, but they had run into a dead end after a day's work. Shelly did not like turning away a call for help, but he positively hated responding to one and then being unable to offer any. It was more than the failure itself, which irked him, it was true, but not as much as the crestfallen hopes of the people who had put their trust in him only to have it disappointed. Shelly did not know Roberta Davenport before she called his office, did not particularly like her once she did make herself known, and had certainly not promised her anything he had been unable to deliver—and yet, he felt he owed her more than they had delivered on this case.

Homer watched the cogitations going on behind his partner's grunt, and said, "There's no point in taking any more of her money, Shell, if we can't help her."

That was true, too, and Shelly nodded, indicating that he understood the professional thing would be to surrender the case and move on to the next one, which might be more amenable to their investigative talents. But Shelly kept nodding, and Homer knew that meant he wasn't ready to do that yet—at least, not without one more personal stab at it. *So what was the point of my going out there alone?* Homer wondered, *if you're just gonna go back without me?* He pushed back his chair and stood up, brushing invisible crumbs from his trouser legs, still cramped from the long ride through Jersey.

"Well, sorry, Shell. I did what I could. See you tomorrow. I need a shower."

Shelly picked up his partner's irritation and couldn't blame him for it. He said, "I'm sure you found whatever there was to see, Homer. As a matter of fact, it's what you saw that I'm most interested in seeing for myself."

"The treatments."

"If that's what they really are."

"That's what Davenport called them. And Adrienne Paglia . . . and everyone else I talked to."

"Then maybe I should try some."

"You? For what?"

Shelly took a cigar out of his desk drawer and planted it squarely between his teeth.

"I'll think of something."

The woman at the registration counter at the Care Clinic gave the cigar the same sort of look she might have given a live serpent wrapped around Shelly's neck. Smoking was one of their big draws, he knew, along with weight loss and what the brochure described as *"the healthy development of self-esteem."*

"Does this stuff really work?" he asked, as he was handed a release form to sign.

"Stuff?"

"You know, the treatments."

"Absolutely." The receptionist was a woman in her late forties, with square-cut black hair, a short-sleeved print dress, and thirty pounds more than she needed on her. She checked his signature against a credit card and said, "I used to stutter all the time myself. Now I've got it practically b-beat."

"Really?" said Shelly, replacing the cigar in his mouth and puffing thoughtfully.

"Almost." She took the cigar and crushed it in an ashtray before handing him a wooden rectangle with the key to Cabin 15. "It's the first cabin on your right as you face the lake. Enjoy your s-stay!"

"I thought nobody *enjoyed* these things."

She shrugged, impervious to nettling. "People enjoy all sorts of things, I guess. And you're here, aren't you? So you must expect to enjoy something."

Shelly turned to pick up his overnight bag, but it wasn't on the ground at his side where he had left it. Instead, he found it in the grip of a five-foot chimpanzee, who stood quietly next to him, waiting for him to follow.

"Hey!" said Shelly.

But the receptionist only yawned. "That's Joseph. Haven't you ever heard about him? He's Dr. Harrison's most f-famous accomplishment—the highest functioning chimp in the world, they say, entirely trained by our methods here at the clinic! He's a wonderful help around this place, especially in the nursery, taking care of the guest children, and all. Don't worry so much! He's our best luggage handler." She leaned over the counter, making eye contact with the chimp, pinning something on Shelly's shirt. It was a card from his registration packet, with his name in red letters on a field of gold plastic. "He's in Cabin 15, Joseph—and don't forget to show him where we k-keep the towels, please."

Joseph curled his lip at the receptionist and led the way, rocking side to side with Shelly's bag in one hand and the knuckles of his other on the floor. He paused at the screen door until Shelly had gone through first, and then regained the lead in the loose stone driveway, glancing back from time to time and showing his yellow teeth to make sure his guest was following. When Shelly flagged, taking care not to slip on the loose gravel, Joseph chattered at him in a high-pitched chimp rebuke that could only be translated, *Step on it, mac.*

"I'm coming, I'm coming," said Shelly, determining silently to reflect the chimp's impatience in his tip. But they never made it to Cabin 15, the first on their right as they faced the lake, because at that moment a voice floated across the driveway at them, full of delight and surprise, expressed with British Indian intonations.

"Joseph! How nice to see you!"

The chimp stopped in his tracks, looked over, and lit up with joy himself. A man in a white shirt with epaulets and baggy shorts was standing there, arms open, waiting for him. Joseph looked as if he might like to run across and leap into those open arms—but he remembered his business, and lifted Shelly's bag into the air, shaking it back and forth for the man to see while he chattered some noises of explanation.

"I see," said the man, glancing at Shelly. "You have a guest to locate comfortably in his quarters. Well, business is business, and it must come first." He shook his head sadly at the chimp and then offered his hand to

Shelly. "Excuse me, sir. My name is Ray Singh. A member of the staff of the Care Clinic, like Joseph here."

"Shelly Lowenkopf. A smoker."

"We'll cure you of the desire for that."

"Can you really do that?"

"Indeed."

"Are you a doctor?"

"Not an M.D., no," explained Singh, evidently a Ph.D. "Just a number cruncher, I'm afraid. A statistician. I was speaking on behalf of the clinic as a whole."

Joseph thumped Singh on the back, shrieking his importance at Shelly.

"I get it," Shelly replied. "He's a pal." Then he said to Singh, "He certainly seems taken with you, doesn't he?"

"Joseph and I are old friends," said Singh with nostalgia in his voice—which dropped out when he squatted and addressed the chimpanzee at his own eye level. "I'm worried about you, Joseph—you don't look at all well. Are you all right?"

The chimp shrugged, rattling Lowenkopf's suitcase.

Singh frowned, shaking his head. "He doesn't like to worry me. And we each have our jobs to do, don't we, my friend? So you'll go your way and I'll go mine."

He gave Joseph's hand a squeeze, nodded at Lowenkopf, and started across the gravel, whistling. Joseph imitated his shrug and started off in the opposite direction, down the drive to the lake, with a short burst of chatter over his shoulder intended for Shelly. But before they had made any progress, yet another voice reached them from across the driveway.

"Joseph! What are you doing?"

It was Harrison, the Great Man, standing on the front steps of the ranch house. Shelly recognized him at once from Homer's description, by his glistening forehead where the hairline was bent on receding into a thicket of tight brown curls, and the air of self-importance he wore like a cheap magician's cape. Behind him, a delivery truck idled without a driver, grunting in the morning sun. The chimp at Shelly's side winced as if he'd been caught with his hand in the banana pile; he looked at Harrison and showed all his teeth in an unconvincing imitation of a smile. Harrison crossed to them, shaking his head sadly and extending his hand. At first, Shelly thought the hand was for him, until it lowered to the chimp's height, and, when Joseph refused to take it, grabbed him by the wrist.

"Come along. I've told you about this sort of thing! I'm sorry, Mr.—"

"Lowenkopf."

"Mr. Lowenkopf, but this is a highly trained animal that should not be passing himself off as a bellboy. To think of the hours that have gone into him! For him to be carrying bags to the lake . . ."

Shelly felt less sympathy for Harrison than Harrison felt for himself. Perhaps it was because the Doctor's hours were already invested in the chimp, while Shelly would have to carry his suitcase now. And he had already developed enough of a relationship with Joseph that he regretted losing his company so unexpectedly. There was also something in Joseph's response to Harrison's voice that made Shelly want to keep him a little while longer. He said, "Your name is?"

"Dr. Henry R. Harrison," Harrison said coldly, as if the name should frighten Lowenkopf from asking further questions.

"And your friend?"

"Friend?"

"The chimpanzee."

"Joseph is not my friend. He is a subject of my research methodology."

"He seems to feel as warmly about you."

"His feelings are not an issue."

"Still, he's a crowd pleaser, isn't he? Must be wonderful for business—reputation, I guess you'd say. A singular feature of your camp."

"Camp? This is not a camp."

"Your establishment, then. An impressive job of training, even to a layman."

Harrison stuck his pinkie into his ear, wringing it out,

and scowled at the chimp, who was doing the same, imitating even the rhythm of Harrison's brisk ear cleaning. "Sometimes he seems too well-trained, doesn't he?"

"That would have been your error, wouldn't it?"

"My error?"

"Since you trained him?"

"Of course. My error. Can't very well blame the chimp for being trained, can we?"

Harrison said the last with a grin, as if it were a joke, although Shelly didn't see the humor in it. But Harrison wasn't a man who noticed whether other people enjoyed his humor. He walked off grinning to himself, dragging the chimp by the wrist toward the porch. Joseph gave Shelly a backward glance, baring his teeth and screeching, just before they disappeared behind the idling truck—and Shelly couldn't shake the feeling he knew what that screech was intended to communicate.

He sighed, picked up his bag from where Joseph had put it down, and turned toward the cabins at the lake. *First cabin on the right,* he thought, and then from somewhere in his consciousness added, *and straight on till morning*—but when he turned to face the downhill slope, he saw Ray Singh, still standing where Shelly and Joseph had left him, a troubled expression on his face. At first, Shelly thought the statistician was concerned about him, by the lines of concentration at the edges of his eyes—but he realized Singh was in fact staring past him at the front porch of the ranch house, where Harrison had hauled Joseph up the steps and slammed the screen door behind them. Singh did not stop staring, and Shelly realized he must have been thinking about something else—when the delivery truck parked in front started to roll forward, its heavy tires crunching over the gray and white gravel of the driveway.

There was something missing from its sound as it began to lurch over the stones—no sudden change in the grumbling idle that had become all but subliminal, a change that marked a vehicle's transition from *park* to *drive.* Shelly hadn't heard the rev of its engine or shift of its gearbox when the truck began to move. So he peered through the windshield and saw no head behind the steering wheel, either.

Shelly paused for a moment as the truck picked up momentum, rolling past him down the driveway. From his vantage point on the hill, Shelly had a clear view of the driver's seat inside the closed cab—and there was definitely no driver behind the wheel. The truck threw back a spray of gravel, and Shelly leaped for the door on the passenger side, his fingers clamping on to the handle, which was locked from inside. He rattled it, to no effect, but hung on anyway, as the truck rolled forward, headed straight for Ray Singh, who stood fixed to his spot, gazing at the grille while immobilized in horror.

Shelly yelled, "Jump!" and waved his free hand.

But Singh just stared at him, unable to react to the danger, as the truck roared for him as if guided by personal animosity. Shelly dangled there, clinging to the door with his left hand, waving his right wildly at the immobile statistician until he was forced to let go or be trapped himself in the crash. The last thing Shelly saw before he went flying was Ray Singh's thoughtful expression, blinking at the oncoming bumper, grille, and fenders. Shelly felt the metal tear away from his grasp, and covered his face to protect himself against the gravel, which leaped up from the road like jumping beans as the truck ploughed straight into Singh.

There was no one inside the cab to step on the brake, even after the sickening crunch of impact; and the mass of Ray Singh was not enough to stop the truck's forward momentum. It tore through him, dragging him under, until it cracked into a big oak tree eight feet from the edge of the driveway. The branches of the oak shook from the contact, and the truck rose up on one wheel and then went over on its side, tires turning uselessly in the air. Where Ray Singh had been standing only a mess of bloody stones remained; his body lay ruined beneath the truck, which was crushed on contact with the tree.

Shelly was the first to reach him, but for an awful moment there was absolutely nothing he could do. And then they were overtaken, first by a slender woman with black hair streaked with gray, wearing the standard white lab coat over a tasteful silk skirt. From her first reactions to the emergency, it was clear that she had kept her head when all about were losing theirs—and in the case of Ray Singh, that seemed an imminent possibility. She raced from the ranch house and knelt by the body, tearing off Singh's shirt to expose his chest. She listened for an instant, and then placed her hands two-finger-widths above the center of his rib cage, where she began pumping with fierce precision. Her blue eyes narrowed; her delicate jaw clamped and her lipsticked mouth whitened, and she leaned into Singh, letting the weight of her upper body do the work instead of her arms. She evidently knew what she was doing, and Shelly stepped back, out of her way, when he became aware for the first time that someone on the porch was screaming—squealing like last-minute brakes.

There were several people on the ranch-house porch, in fact. The woman from the registration desk was there, and a new guest, the sign-in pen still clutched in her hand. Howard Davenport was there, and an elderly man Shelly had seen dozing in a wing chair in the lobby. There was a muscular maintenance man in overalls but no shirt with a ponytail behind him, talking to a skinny kid in a sleeveless undershirt, who stared at the truck in horror—the driver, Shelly guessed, by the implication of guilt and fear in the kid's huge brown eyes. But it was the receptionist who was screaming, her imperturbable countenance evidently perturbed by the grisly scene in the driveway. She shrieked twice more for emphasis, and then threw up her breakfast into the hedges beyond the porch railing. The elderly man from the wing chair clucked and patted her back gently in sympathy as the maintenance man dashed for the delivery truck, its wheels still churning upended against the tree. The driver seemed immobilized; the new guest stared at the pen in her hand as if it had inserted itself there on its own steam; Howard Davenport took it from her, went into the house and came back again without it, banging the screen door each time he crossed over the threshold. He

was followed a few seconds later by a redheaded intern
who did not seem confident of her ability to steer a
padded steel gurney down the porch steps, and, behind
her, a group of sweaty people who had been having a
weight-loss session in the Council Room when the crash
took place outside their picture window. They rushed to
the railing, watching the scene like tourists at Marine-
land who finally had something they could write about in
their letters home.

The woman with gray-streaked hair asked Shelly's
assistance in loading Ray Singh on the gurney, which was
rattling in the hands of the unsteady intern. Singh was a
mess; there was hardly any place to grab onto. The
woman with gray-streaked hair folded Singh's arms
against his sides, and had mercifully left his feet for
Shelly. It took him a moment to find a grasp at the back
of the arches. But his care was wasted; the doctor looked
away as she settled him onto the gurney, and Shelly
understood that Singh was beyond any further risk.

9

RALPH WALDO KOTLOWICZ WAS SURE OF ONE THING: THE brakes on the delivery truck had not slipped on their own. He had just repaired those brakes himself, three days before, replacing the pads and grinding the shoes until the damned things were so tight they squeaked when you stepped on the pedal. He had done them Wednesday, the day he found Neela Zapotnik floating in the lake—but not until now, while his fingers worked automatically on the familiar pads and cylinders, did he have a chance to recollect in tranquillity what he'd experienced, and what he thought about it. As he turned the incident over and over in his mind, the crucial moment seemed to arrive as he stood in front of the infirmary with the unconscious girl in his arms, still soggy with algae and lake water, but also still alive.

They had taken her from him, he remembered that— the feel of the burden lifted, replaced by a muscular panic as his stiff, cramped forearms remembered the life cradled between them. Agnes Fleming had checked him for shock when the others took Neela inside. She had sat him down on the steps, and covered him with a blanket, and taken his wrist in her hand for his pulse, and wiped the cool sweat from his forehead. When she felt certain he was not in danger, she tried to elicit whatever information she thought might be useful to the doctors working on Neela inside. She was comforting but efficient, propping a pad on her white knees as she asked him what had happened. It had taken him two false starts before he found the relevant train of events, but once he began talking about the body in the lake, she started to scribble violently, nodding her head in encouragement until the whole story spilled out of him like lake water. She held his arm with her hand every now and then, as a sign he should pause so she could write down every word he told her. Helen had come running from the direction of the ranch house, an expression of fear hollowing her cheeks. When Nurse Fleming told her that Neela was still alive, on the respirator, about to be transferred to Jersey General, Helen let out the most horrified sigh Ralph had ever heard from her. And when Agnes explained how Neela had been brought in to the infirmary (beefing up Ralph's role, it seemed to him), Helen threw her arms around his grizzled neck and nearly kissed him right then and there.

So finally, unexpectedly, a public display of emotion. What hadn't he tried to convince her to acknowledge him before? And then, unanticipated, the girl bobbed up in the lake, and Helen had clung to his neck.

What was it Emerson wrote in *Fate?* "The secret of the world is, the tie between person and event. Person makes event, and event person." And this event, his happening to be there at the lake to pull the poor girl out, had nearly made Ralph a socially acceptable person in the eyes of the local circle of medical professionals.

Nearly. Well, even the socially unacceptable Thoreau had a Harvard education, hadn't he? Education still had its status, Ralph conceded. Still, he had seen it in her eyes, an impulse to smother him in kisses, to hell with who saw it—and he saw also how sad her eyes were when she restrained herself. Was that restraint supposed to be for his sake, now? She might have done it anyway, had it been just Agnes Fleming there to see; but at that moment Henry Harrison had shown up, looking deeply concerned about the nearly drowned girl, and what her

accident might mean to the reputation of the clinic—
well, Ralph thought, somebody's got to think about those
things, and if it weren't Harrison himself, who would it
be? They had all listened together to Fleming's report on
Neela's prognosis, but Ralph had noticed that Helen
edged just a bit closer to Harrison, and farther away from
himself, as the nurse tried to put the best face on what
seemed likely to prove a suicide attempt.

Though they would do their best, he knew, to conceal
that. It was *Experience* that occurred to him this time,
from the always consoling Emerson: "Dream delivers us
to dream, and there is no end to illusion." Ralph sighed,
unable really to blame her in the end. "We live amid
surfaces, and the true art of life is to skate well on them."

There were surfaces and surfaces, Ralph thought, the
mirror of the lake beneath the ice in winter. Helen had
devoted her life to seeing beyond them, while he was just
an amateur.

But this business about the brakes giving out on the
delivery truck—that was another matter. Ralph didn't
believe it for a second and was not reticent about
expressing this view. His professional reputation was on
the line, he said, to anyone who would listen: the police
who came to verify that it had indeed been an accident;
Dr. Harrison, when he listened to the police confirm they
believed it was; even that strange guest, Lowenkopf, who
had tried recklessly to stop the truck and been swept up
in the investigation. There was perhaps another reason
for Ralph's insistence. It had less to do with his reputation as an auto mechanic than with the inner voice of his
conscience, which kept denying the suspicion that he had
rushed the brake job in order to make time to see Helen.
She hadn't even been at the cabin that day when he found
Neela Zapotnik in the lake—but he had no way of
knowing Helen wouldn't be able to get free for lunch, so
mightn't he have rushed the brakes, just to see?

He hadn't, he told himself, he had given the brakes his
full attention until the moment they were done, had
tested them and remembered a nice, snug squeak. But if
he hadn't neglected them, if he had done his usual good

work, why had they given out on Eduardo that morning? He had told the kid more than once never to leave the truck idling—there was always time to crank up the engine after you made the delivery. Eduardo had assured him that he perfectly understood—he'd turn off the engine, make his drop, and goose it up again. But of course, this morning he was just stopping off in the lobby, dropping off packages from their post-office box in town. He had not expected to run into Ralph in the lobby, or that Ralph would keep him talking so long about the sink in the ladies room on the third floor of the research annex. He did not want to *tell* Ralph he had left the engine idling in front of the ranch house, and Ralph had no other way of knowing; but it gave him one more bit of culpability, one more reason to wonder if Ray Singh might not still be alive, if not for Ralph's absorption with Helen Kaufman?

Nobody else blamed him, exactly, though they didn't seem to believe him either. Harrison had said, "Well, Ralph, an accident is an accident, either way," which, of course, left unanswered the question of whether the accident had been his responsibility; and when the cop from the local precinct had nodded at the Doctor, drawn into the same conclusion by Harrison's fateful eyebrows, which lifted so gently as if to suggest an equivalence between the workings of fate and those of the unconscious—a marvel to see in action, *either way,* weren't they? The cop had nodded, as any sophisticated observer of human nature was bound to do, wrapping up the case without any need for further elaboration. And yet those words, *either way,* stuck in Ralph's memory like the aftertaste of a spoiled piece of fruit. *One way* was his fault, and the other way wasn't.

Ralph couldn't say why the patient, Lowenkopf, was the only one who seemed to appreciate the difference it meant to him. The man had been thrown against the gravel driveway with some force as the truck had ploughed into Singh. The fatal damage done to Ray had all but eclipsed the bruises suffered by the other man in the driveway. Lowenkopf had stood, brushed himself off, and on wobbly knees assisted the paramedics in getting Singh the hell out of there. His trousers had been torn at the knee, and he was bleeding at one elbow and the opposite palm. But he had taken a bandage from the first-aid kit, wrapped up his wounds, and gone down to check himself into one of the cabins near the lake. It was the sort of self-reliance Ralph found particularly affecting, and when Lowenkopf came nosing around after the accident, anxious to find out about the man he had tried to save, Ralph showed him more than he might have shown the average patient: the linings of the brakes, the shoes and pads, even the drums—all in perfect working condition. Lowenkopf glanced at each piece, but seemed more interested in Ralph's opinion of their condition than in the evidence before his own two eyes.

"You're saying they're working fine?"

"Look! Try them yourself."

Lowenkopf watched one piece of padded metal contracting against another, and then turned to Ralph to interpret its significance, as if they were disemboweling a sacrificial calf and looking for omens in its entrails. But Ralph wanted Lowenkopf to find the truth for himself.

"Isn't that the way they're supposed to move?"

"It is."

"So you don't see anything that might suggest they gave out on their own?"

Ralph shook his head, struggling with impatience. "And then fixed themselves again?"

"You haven't repaired them since then? Haven't replaced any pads or anything?"

"Nothing! This brake was just the way you see it now, when I first took the drums off."

"So earlier—"

"They *couldn't* have slipped. No way."

Lowenkopf nodded, convinced that Ralph, at least, believed what he was insisting. But something had caused this truck to run down Ray Singh—Shelly had seen it happen. So if the brakes hadn't slipped, someone had released them. He poked his head into the cab of the truck.

"Could the control have released itself? If it was less than fully engaged?"

Ralph opened the door. "Try it."

Lowenkopf would have been satisfied with a *yes* or a *no*—this learning by experience was more in Homer's line. But he humored the man, reaching across the driver's seat to the emergency-brake lever, which lifted with an impressive series of clicks.

"Sounds like it works."

"It does!" concurred Ralph, pleased that Lowenkopf had at last decided something empirically for himself. "With all those clicks, you can't engage it halfway— either the brake is off, in which case the truck never would have held on the slope at all; or else the brake is on, in which case there's no way it could've disengaged itself."

Lowenkopf nodded, accepting the point with evident respect for the handyman's intelligence. Ralph saw it in his eyes, a moment before they flicked to the floor of the cab and narrowed on something shiny he spotted there. Lowenkopf reached under the driver's seat and picked up something—a crushed piece of aluminum that had rolled back under there. Unfolded, it made a small cup of foil, half an inch deep.

"What's this?"

Ralph took the bit of foil from him and examined it closely. "Where'd you find this?"

"In the front. Ever see anything like it before?"

Ralph studied the thing, opening and closing the end before replying. It was a matter of professional discretion, Shelly understood—how much to tell one guest about the ways of another. Lowenkopf did his best not to act like a guest, and his old policeman's manner must have made the difference, because finally Ralph handed the thing back to him and said in an offhand tone, "Illuminati's group wears them."

"Who?"

"The Initiates of the Church of the Unflagging Eye— in the last two cabins on this side of the lake. They wear these little foil cups on their fingertips sometimes. When they do their initiation rites."

"Here? On the clinic grounds?"

"The Reverend sends them all up here for a two-week course of training."

"In what?"

"In whatever the Reverend wants them trained," said Ralph with a shrug. "They're a contract group—every couple of weeks, another busload arrives for whatever sessions Harrison has worked out for them."

"What does Henry Harrison know about training religious Initiates?"

"He knows plenty about training, period. Illuminati planned the curriculum, including whatever mumbo jumbo he thought should be common knowledge among his followers. And the Doctor arranged for them to learn it as quickly and painlessly as possible. As quickly, anyway."

"You mean there's pain involved?"

"I don't know what's involved," Ralph said. "But there's always pain of one sort or another in finding your true calling, isn't there?"

That wasn't the sort of pain Shelly thought Ralph had meant a moment before, but he didn't want to press him further on so deliberate an evasion, which might end his willingness to talk at all. "Is this your calling?"

Ralph looked surprised but not displeased at the question, having given a lot of thought to the issue of his true calling. "Auto mechanics? No, that's just something I picked up along the way, between electricity and electronics, you might say." Then he seemed to realize one possible implication of that confession and followed up with, "Not that I don't know brakes well enough to do a creditable job. It's just that my interests range wider than a chassis."

"This is an interesting place, isn't it?"

"I'll say," Ralph agreed, easing in to a topic he felt more comfortable discussing. "Lots of interesting people passing through, between the staff and patients and all—and plenty of interesting machines, too, in the Research Building and in the other treatment sites."

"Machines?"

"Psychological tools—you must know, from your own treatment sessions."

"Haven't had any yet."

"Well, you will."

"You wouldn't want to give me a preview, would you?"

Ralph shook his head. "One thing I don't mess with is the treatment plans. Those things are carefully planned, mostly by Harrison himself. Your doctors will tell you what you need to know, when you need to know it. If I go ahead and describe this or that, maybe I'm upsetting the timetable."

"Maybe you're just informing me about what to expect as well as they should have. I'm a cigar-smoker, not a sniper dragged down from a water tower. Don't you think I have a right to know what I'm getting into?"

"You signed up for this on your own, didn't you?"

"Uh-huh."

"Then you had a chance to ask whatever you wanted, before deciding to come."

"Not really."

"No? When you registered, you signed one of those forms, didn't you?"

"You mean the ones that say the clinic isn't responsible if I jump out of the window during a therapy session?"

"Or anything."

"Like what?"

"Like anything. The point is, now that you're here—you've kind of signed away your rights to ask those kinds of questions, I guess."

"I don't remember anybody explaining that."

"Someone's supposed to."

Ralph was starting to feel just the least bit uncomfortable talking about this, but Lowenkopf seemed satisfied with what he had heard and moved in closer to inspect the brake pads—when his available time was suddenly cut short by a young man in a white coat. He was led into the garage by a skinny kid with a twisted lip, in a stained, sleeveless undershirt—the kid Shelly had seen Ralph talking to on the porch of the ranch house, just after the delivery truck had struck Ray Singh. He was the truck's driver, doing penance in the garage, perhaps, barred from driving until Ralph had sorted out the true details of the accident to his own satisfaction.

"Eduardo?" Shelly guessed.

Eduardo thumbed the other young man, who was about the same age but doing his level best to resemble the driver in no other respect. He hugged his white coat, the unmistakable sign of the professional stratum to which he belonged or aspired—some sort of doctor-in-training or laboratory technician—then adjusted the fit of his tortoise-shell eyeglasses and cleared his throat against the fumes of the garage before asking, "Mr. Lowenkopf?" as if he weren't quite sure which one of them might respond to his call.

Politeness, Ralph thought. He recognized the kid as someone he'd seen around Liza Gunnarson, but couldn't remember his name. His memory was spared the trouble, because Lowenkopf looked up and the resident said, "My name is Arthur Jenkins. I'm supposed to take you to your treatment session."

Shelly said, "What for?"

"For smoking," Arthur explained. "That's what we call it here. Some of the first-timers don't think of it as a treatment, but it really is."

"Oh, I'm sure you'll give me the treatment," Shelly said.

Eduardo grinned at that, but Jenkins frowned, unsure whether he was supposed to reinforce that sort of comment. He settled on ignoring it, opting for the neutral-sounding but collaborative, "Are we ready?"

"I am," said Lowenkopf.

Eduardo glanced at Ralph to check if it was all right and smiled again. Jenkins knew he didn't want to respond this time; he took a step toward the garage door and waited for Shelly to follow him.

Lowenkopf slipped the bit of aluminum foil into his coat pocket and gave Ralph a shrug that might have meant *When you've gotta go, you've gotta go*. Or maybe, *If you don't hear from me in an hour, send in the marines*—which, given the limitations of his staff, could only mean Eduardo. Ralph grinned in spite of clinic policy, and returned to the delivery truck, where he saw nothing else to do but replace the wheel over the same damned brakes—as Eduardo stepped up behind him to watch over his shoulder. As Jenkins marched Lowenkopf across the lawn toward the research building, Ralph's clear whistle sailed after them, in a lively rendition of "Whistle While You Work."

10

SHELLY HAD NOT LIKED THE LOOK OF THE CONCRETE BUNKER from the first moment his Volkswagen pulled up at the clinic. He had hoped that it might be one of those structures of limited access, where staff were forced to spend their hours in air-conditioned discomfort while patients were seen in the homier ranch house and rustic cabins by the lake. The Research Building, Shelly hoped, might be a showpiece, a forbidding scientific structure that lent credence to the more personal clinical work that went on between patient and therapist in friendlier settings. But as Arthur Jenkins led Lowenkopf around the edge of the hill from the garage area off the main entrance road, and the topmost floors of the concrete bunker came into view, Shelly knew he was in for a taste of scientism in its least secure and most insistent incarnation.

"First time at the clinic?"

"Uh-huh."

"We're not half as bad as they say," Jenkins promised, and then, with a grin, added, "of course, that would still leave a half that is, wouldn't it?"

Is this chit-chat intended to reassure or distract me? Shelly thought. It only succeeded in making him wonder what they felt he needed to be distracted from? Shelly had received a telephone-message slip at his cabin informing him that his first appointment had been scheduled for eleven o'clock A.M. in HRB 542, which he now understood to be a lab in the Research Building—*the Harrison Research Building, perhaps?* He had not thought much about it either way at the time, but now he began to ask himself, *What sort of therapy requires a fetch-it man to make sure I show up?*

The doors to the Research Building opened automatically when they approached, and not by a hidden trigger underneath a rubber mat; there was nothing on the ground but tiles, while an orb like an irisless eye above the door attended and responded to their approach. Inside, the small lobby was carpeted in neutral grays, with a bank of three elevators made of mirror glass. Two other guests were waiting, and when the door opened silently and no one stepped out, Shelly and Arthur followed the two others into the car. They were a thoughtful pair, wearing white robes tied about the waist with a length of TV antenna wire, and leather sandals with a hole for their big toes. After pushing the button for the fifth floor, they did not look up at Shelly and Arthur but kept their attention focused on the ground, although they half-chanted and half-hummed a tune that Lowenkopf recognized as the theme to "The Beverly Hillbillies." They were both in their early twenties, with close-shaved heads and rings beneath their eyes. One of them removed a hand from inside the folds of his robe, and Shelly caught his breath: three fingers on his left hand were covered to their knuckles in newly wrapped aluminum foil.

When the elevator car reached the fifth floor, the two men in robes were mildly surprised to see Arthur hold the door so they and Shelly could step out together. But it was a shock that wore off quickly, or else they were too tired to think about it, because they quickly turned their attention to the narrow hall leading off to the right of the elevator, while Arthur held out a hand for Lowenkopf to walk to the left. As he turned his back, Shelly heard the chanting resume, then rise toward a crescendo at the line

"said California's the place you ought to be . . ." But
when he turned to face them, they were gone, disappearing into one of the row of erratically numbered doors.
Shelly saw that the doors on his own end of the hall made
just as little sense: Room 529 was adjacent to 516, which
was immediately after 533, which was right next door to
542—his own treatment room. Jenkins held the door for
him, and Lowenkopf went in.

It was a small room, without a window, painted in
some neutral color. It looked pink under the ceiling light
that illuminated the few pieces of furniture arranged on a
piece of carpet continuous with the gray hallway. In the
center was a big chair, like an old barber's chair down to
the white paper on its headrest, already craned backwards. The arms were porcelain, but into each armrest
was inset bright rectangles of shiny aluminum. There was
a footrest which swiveled out from the lower portion of
the chair itself, onto which Arthur Jenkins now encouraged Shelly to step, on his way into the chair. There was
no alternative: He would have to assume his seat here, or
abandon the clinic's antismoking program. Shelly stepped up tentatively on the stiff footrest, which kept him off
balance until he settled into the padded vinyl seat
cushion of the chair. There were vinyl straps to either
side of his calves, but Arthur did not fasten these,
concentrating instead on swinging into position directly
in front of Shelly a video monitor with a cluster of thick
black cables running from its back to a machine on a
small table in the corner of the room. There was a swivel
chair at the table, and Jenkins sat in this, rolling back and
forth between a small control panel there and the connectors on the back of the video monitor. The screen in
front of Shelly was dark but alive, hissing and popping as
Jenkins twisted his dials. There was a chart in an
aluminum folder hanging on a nail over the table.
Jenkins took this down and read through it, glancing
occasionally at Lowenkopf in his chair; then he propped
up the chart behind the control panel on the table and
made another series of adjustments to a second hidden
machine that did not seem to register on the video

monitor at all. Shelly felt a sudden heat below his wrist, and yanked his hand off the armrest. Jenkins noticed and shook his head as a sort of apology, readjusting one of the dials on the hidden control panel.

"Need some help with your shoes?"

"Help?"

"Taking them off."

"No," said Lowenkopf. "I think I can manage myself." He slipped off his loafers, set his stockinged feet on the footrest, and felt a metal grille through the weave. There was no way to place his arms on the armrests without leaving the undersides of his forearms on those aluminum squares, so he arched them until he was leaning on his wrists with his elbows in the air and his lower back aching. Jenkins came over and placed his feet flatter and more squarely on the footrest grille.

"Comfy?"

Shelly thought the man insane. How could he be comfortable in this torture device? "Not very."

"Then we'd better see what we can do for you," Arthur said, rather like a nurse adjusting a hospital bed, "before we strap you in for good."

Lowenkopf sat forward, upsetting Jenkins's careful placement of his forearms on top of the metal squares.

"Pardon?"

Arthur hesitated—what did they tell these people ahead of time? Only to settle their bills in advance, it seemed. "You knew we had to strap you in, didn't you?"

"No—"

"For your own protection, Mr. Lowenkopf! So the current doesn't vary."

"What current?"

"Not much, really. A few hundred volts, at most—"

Lowenkopf was out of the chair in a single bound, heading for the door. Jenkins tried to interpose his body between Shelly and the hallway, but one glance from Lowenkopf made him think better of it. Shelly could read the entire thought process on Arthur's worried face. His charge from Harrison was evidently to keep the clients happy if he could, but to keep them at all cost. And *cost* was the operative word in those instructions. But how was Arthur to accomplish this? Lowenkopf's was an elective procedure—quite different from Arthur's last placement, on the chronic back ward of a mental hospital, where no one but the staff knew the patients, or cared what was done to or with them. Arthur remembered that patients in a clinic such as Harrison's were, in actuality, *clients,* who might walk away and abandon therapy forever, or—even worse—find another treatment modality they preferred. It made dealing with them a lot more troublesome, but it was also the only way to make any money in their field—something Arthur was determined to do. That was the reason he had sought out this residency at Harrison's celebrated clinic—to learn from the master how to make psychology a vocation not only gratifying but *rewarding,* which for Arthur meant it had to include a profound financial reward. Now Lowenkopf was walking out, and Jenkins would have to report at the weekly staff meeting how and why it had happened. He began to panic. He couldn't command an orderly to come and recapture Lowenkopf, as he could have done on the chronic back ward, so if he was not to lose the client entirely, failing them both so miserably, not to mention Dr. Harrison, who had placed so much trust in him, Jenkins had to convince Lowenkopf of the benefits of returning with him to his treatment chair.

"Mr. Lowenkopf!" he said, following Shelly into the hallway. "You haven't even given yourself a chance! It was important to you to give up cigarettes, wasn't it?"

"Cigars," said Shelly, pressing his thumb to the elevator button and leaving it there.

"Cigars, then!" shouted Arthur, pleased to have won even this much acquiescence. "You're not going to give them up this way, are you?"

"I don't know," said Shelly. "I might. I'm not going to give them up *that* way, for certain."

"Are you afraid it hurts? It doesn't, you know. All of the patients say so."

"Really? Then why don't you sit in the chair, and I'll turn up the dials?"

"Because I'm not the one with the problem."

Shelly released the button and hit it again, but still the car wouldn't come. He began to wonder if the call button worked at all in this direction—it would be just like this operation to allow you into the Research Building, but not to allow you out. Jenkins did not seem concerned about the likelihood of their talk being interrupted.

"Aren't you?" Shelly said.

"I work here."

"My point exactly. Doesn't it ever trouble you?"

Jenkins understood the implication, but he shook his head proudly. "We do good work here, Mr. Lowenkopf . . . important work, even. Henry Harrison is a leader in his field, with a proven track record in the most promising area of psychological research today. I'm sorry that our methods frighten you, but breaking new scientific ground always frightens somebody." From his tone, anyone would think they had just invented the telephone. Arthur cast down his eyes and murmured regretfully, "The saddest part is that we might've been able to help you beat your awful habit—which you did want to beat, remember? And now you won't be here long enough for us to prove it to you."

The last words stuck with Shelly—if he wasn't there at the clinic to work on his cigar smoking, what excuse could he offer to investigate the place? Homer had already tried poking around as a visitor, and if Shelly's partner hadn't been able to find anything that way, Shelly would do no better. And yet, from what he had seen in his first few hours, he *knew* there was something to find. He wasn't about to go back to that chair, but how could he keep himself around?

And then the answer suggested itself, as a chorus of voices rang out from behind an opening door: *"A poor mountaineer, barely kept his family fed!"* One of the two robed men who had come up the elevator with Shelly and Arthur appeared; he settled a paper bag full of clinking beer bottles into a trashcan in the hall and was about to retreat back into the noisy room, when Lowenkopf strode down the hall behind him, peering into the dark laboratory from which a dim blue light flickered.

Inside were three other men and two women, sitting on the floor in a semicircle around a television set. Two men sat in a full lotus position, while the others sat looser, cross-legged but without the strain on the ankles the full lotus demanded. In the center of their semicircle was a large bowl of popcorn that had evidently been heated in the microwave oven on a table in the corner, just where Arthur's controls over Shelly's chair and monitor had been located. But here, instead of the wired barber chair, was only a videocassette player and a television set on the carpet. One, then another of the gathered group would lean to touch its glowing screen reverently with the tips of their foil-covered fingers.

Arthur Jenkins came after Lowenkopf, anxious to pull him out of there, but to evade him Shelly circled around until he saw what they were playing on the big television screen: an episode of "The Beverly Hillbillies" in which Jethro was decked out as a rock star, with the banker's assistant Jane Hathaway as his drummer. The sight of prim Miss Hathaway swinging her drumsticks at a swaying cymbal elicited from Shelly a grudging grin——and with the *crash* came an idea.

"Mr. Lowenkopf," said Jenkins, "this is a private session! We can't interrupt this . . . treatment." Arthur didn't look so sure himself about using that word for this activity, but he brushed any doubts aside. "As a psychological resident, my advice to you would be to return immediately to your own laboratory; but, if you absolutely refuse to do that, I'm afraid I'll have no choice but to ask you to pack up and leave our clinic."

"I don't think so," said Shelly.

"You don't think so? Why on earth not? If you're not going to use our facilities, you'll have to make room for someone else to take advantage of——"

"I will be using your facility, after all," Shelly told him, drawing up a patch of floor at one edge of the group semicircle. "Forget about my cigars! I've just discovered a real interest in the practice of these people here."

"What?" said Jenkins. "Just now?"

"Faith is an unexpected thing," said Shelly. "It takes hold when you least expect it."

One of the women smiled at him, then glared at Arthur in support. Lowenkopf tore a piece of aluminum foil off a crumpled sheet under the popcorn in the bowl, and began wrapping it around his index finger. The woman took hold of his hand, and drew it forward gently until the foil-covered tip of his finger rested on the surface of the screen. Shelly closed his eyes as the others had done, and sighed contentedly.

"What are you talking about?" snapped Arthur, his professional patience already exhausted.

Shelly gave him an expression of glowing inner peace, which all of the others reflected.

"I've decided to become an Initiate of the Church of the Unflagging Eye."

11

"NOW TELL ME AGAIN," SAID HOMER OVER THE PHONE, WHEN he got Shelly's call on Saturday. "You want me to drive all the way out to the mall in Paramus and check out . . . an appliance store?"

"A church," said Shelly patiently, matching his tone to his partner's. "In back of the appliance store."

"Behind it?"

"I don't think so. They tell me it's in the back," and here he hesitated, looking through the glass of the telephone booth behind what was called The Commissary, a whitewashed shack opened from three to five, where toothbrushes and sanitary napkins were sold for four times their supermarket prices. From his booth, Shelly could see along the perimeter of the lake to the cabins at the far end, where the other Initiates were killing a free hour in their schedule, playing smashball on the fifteen-foot patch of stony sand the brochure called "the beach." Since joining the group in the Research Building, Shelly had not been allowed a moment of solitude by the Initiates until he admitted he had not brought along the requisite box of aluminum foil. The failure on his part to observe the precepts as written caused consternation among the Initiates, until Roger the Group Leader decided that Shelly's infraction could be forgiven because he had not elected to join the select until after arriving at the clinic. He was allowed a fifteen-minute period of private penance and reflection during which he was expected to run up to The Commissary and buy the foil he would need to participate in the remainder of their initiation ceremonies. This decision was arrived at only after a consultation with the group's absent spiritual leader, the Very Reverend Eleazer Illuminati, who was keeping vigil at their home church, located "in the back of an appliance store in Paramus, New Jersey." This he had been told by Roger the Group Leader as they waited for the call to be answered; Shelly suspected Roger might not have been so forthcoming if his question ("Where is it?") had not come at the moment the Reverend answered their call. Shelly was using his time of penance to place the call to Homer. He had his roll of aluminum foil tucked under his arm, and was expected to return momentarily to the Initiation Camp. So he had little time to explain to Homer all that he might want to know.

"Could you spell that name again?"

"I-l-l-u-m-i-n-a-t-i. Reverend Eleazer Illuminati, pastor and financial leader of the Church of the Unflagging Eye. The name of the appliance store I haven't picked up yet, but how many could there be in the mall, Homer?"

"How do you know he's the financial leader?"

"Most of our conversation concerned what they should charge me for joining at this stage of the game. Roger here asked the questions, and the Reverend answered them."

"How much are they charging us?"

"Don't ask."

A pause from Homer's end. "Who did you say was our client on this one?"

Now it was Shelly's turn to pause. "Let's call it follow-up on the Davenport case. A man was killed today, Homer. Murdered, I think."

"Is that what the police think?"

"They're still calling it an accident, officially."

"And unofficially?"

"An accident, too. But it wasn't."

"You're sure?"

"You would be."

That was Shelly's shorthand, Homer knew, for something like *My doubts are based on material evidence, things you can touch that don't fit together, and not on any analysis of human motives and personalities alone.* Homer sighed audibly into the phone. "What am I looking for, exactly?"

"Your impression of the operation, and the man who runs it."

"Isn't that usually your department?"

"Give it a shot, will you? These people won't let me out of their sight. I've got a piece of molded aluminum foil in my pocket and a perfectly new set of brake pads that usually fall into your domain."

That touched Homer—he had been to the clinic three days before, and hadn't noticed a thing that made him suspect a murder was about to take place. If Shelly was right, Homer had missed his usually keen rapport with *things* of all shapes and sizes—and if Shelly had in fact spotted something as innocuous as aluminum foil, the only way Homer could right the balance was by sizing up a human being. It was Saturday, and the last place he would've thought to spend it was New Jersey. On the other hand, Homer had no plans for the day, and the only woman his mind turned to when he let it wander was Adrienne Paglia anyway. He would have to go to the clinic to report to Shelly after visiting the mall, Homer thought—and if by chance he ran into Adrienne again while he was out there, he wouldn't be working this time.

"All right. I'll let you know what I find there." And he hung up before Shelly had a chance to suggest any other reporting arrangement.

Homer did not himself own a car. He lived on Bank Street in the West Village, and when he had worked at the Allerton Avenue Precinct House in the Bronx, the fastest route up was the subway. There was no garage in his building, and alternate-side-of-the-street parking was in effect on Bank Street, so owning a car required renting a space in a garage or gas station. Since the only use for a car in the city was to escape to the country on the weekends, Homer did without one, preferring to rent when he felt like a trip to the Hamptons. Shelly had arranged for the rental on Homer's last trip out, an economical Reliant which he supposed was intended to remind him of their unmarked police car. This time, Homer was doing the renting himself, and so the first place he called was not Rent A Wreck but a number he had written down from a poster of a two-seater T-bird. The Thunderbird was out, of course, but the rental agency did have a spiffy red Mazda Miata—which was not from his childhood but still conjured up images of sleepy summer days in little American towns, with a cheerleader in the passenger seat and two pom-pom girls hanging on for dear life, propped on the rump of the trunk as the car streaked down Main Street, their blond hair and short skirts and pom-pom confetti flying in the wind . . .

Or was that just the ad he had seen for the car?

In the end Homer opted for a '65 Mustang convertible, baby blue with white interior, that showed over 36,000 miles on the odometer. He did not ask about the first hundred thousand as he revved the engine, which sounded fine, loud but untroubled, and signed for all the extra insurance the rental agency offered. If he had to drive out to Paramus on a Saturday, he was going to do it in style; let Shelly figure out how to write off the expense in their accounting of the case—if they had a case, which by all that he had seen, Homer figured they didn't. At least not one for which they'd be paid. And if he had learned anything in the short time since leaving the police force, it was the private investigator's very different definition of a case, as *something you got paid for*.

The drive out in the Mustang was a whole 'nother experience: even the George Washington Bridge looked different, fantastic really, this beautiful span of gleaming steel over the expanse of the Hudson River, separating New York from New Jersey. On one side, in Washington Heights, stood the forested fastness of Inwood Hill Park and Fort Tryon Park, where a transplanted castle called the Cloisters Museum watches over the river, holding John D. Rockefeller's Unicorn tapestries within its stone walls. On the Jersey side, the gray granite cliffs of the Palisades rose to meet the bridge, leading, on the left, to the glass towers of Fort Lee apartment buildings, and on the right, to the lushly landscaped Palisades Parkway, which traveled up the shoreline, another gift from the estate of the shrewd old skinflint robber baron.

So the evidence of greed was all around him, which Homer enjoyed to its fullest. The salty air ripped through his blond hair as he sat in traffic in the right-hand lane in the middle of the bridge. *Construction on the Parkway,* an orange sign informed him; *please use alternative route.* The wind snapped through the cables suspending the span, making them sing. Homer glanced at himself in the rear-view mirror and considered raising the top— but what was the point of a convertible with its ragtop over it? So he suffered the bitter wind in his face, doing his best to resettle his hair, until the line crawled forward and released him from the bridge. There was no toll on the shore for cars headed into Jersey, only a double toll into the city, which the Bridge and Tunnel Authority had hoped might reduce traffic in New York City; as a result, once his tires crunched onto Jersey macadam, Homer was able to pick up a little speed for the short drive to the Paramus mall—which proved to be a two-story structure with outside parking, housing Macy's and Sears but no movie theaters. Its central lobby was distinguished by an artificial waterfall splashing into a turquoise tile pool. Customers pitched pennies at bright coppery circles painted on the bottom, although these seemed to Homer unlikely to grant any wishes, as he watched from above, riding the escalators up and down in search of a store directory.

There were, in fact, three stores in the mall that advertised major appliances, but Greeley was spared checking out each of them, because the directory also had a listing for the "Church of the Unflagging Eye," which turned out to be located not in fact in an appliance store at all but in a TV and VCR outlet that went by the name *Illuminations*. The name of the church was stenciled on the frosty front door. Its display window was entirely filled with television monitors, all of which displayed the same images, evidently fed by a tape loop. First came a trio of Neanderthals squatting under huge black leaves in the primordial jungle night, thumping a hollow tree stump. The sound surprised them, and they jumped back, listening to it echo off the mountainsides. One of them—the bravest—returned to the stump and banged it twice, and then sat and wrapped his legs around it, beating out the pulse of an uncertain but regular rhythm. He grinned, and then in a fast pastiche of intercut images, a network of drummers picked up his beat, spreading the news. The darkness was soon illuminated by a series of signal flares on hilltops, igniting in sequence, one to the next, while below, in the bay water off the coast, a sailing ship, then a fleet of ships, followed a course marked out by the flares. From the deck of one ship flashed the dots and dashes of a message, answered a moment later on the deck of another, where a sailor tilted his light directly into the camera—when in the sudden glare of light the scene dissolved night into day: Homer saw telegraph operators clicking away and telephone operators plugging connections, replaced by computer banks making the same hookups thousands of times faster; telephone wires gave way to fiber optics, splintered brilliantly into laser beams, and struck communication satellites orbiting the Earth, which swung around, revealing the planet linked in a single network of lines and relays, stretching around the turning globe in a dizzying whirl that resolved suddenly into a corporate office, where a trio of three executives, two Caucasian men and a woman, stood before an enormous video projector on which a Japanese woman spoke; one of the men typed something into a computer keyboard, and a moment later the woman crossed the room to retrieve something coming in over the fax machine. It was a picture; she held it up for the two men to see, and as the camera closed in on the graphic, Homer saw three

Neanderthals squatting under huge black leaves in the primordial jungle night . . .

"Can I help you?"

The voice was deep and resonant, insinuating itself over Homer's shoulder as if it were addressed not to his face but to the back of his skull through his ear. Homer turned and saw a stocky man in a pin-striped gray suit with a diamond tack in his red tie. Most striking was his hair, bleached snow-white and brushed straight back from his face so that a ragged crown stuck out stiffly behind his ears, climbing along the nape of his neck. Light blue irises showed beneath heavy eyelids, and his thin nose flared at the nostrils as his lips trembled, barely holding back the many things he was bursting to share with Homer, whom he obviously held in that place of awful respect and honor—a customer.

"I was just admiring your tape," said Homer.

"Thought provoking, isn't it? One of the Initiates— junior salesman here—put it together."

"What did you call him? An *initiative?*"

"Initiate. We have, uh"—he tapped the stenciled letters on the glass door—"a Church that meets here, and some of the guys here are associated with it."

"Are any of the guys here now?"

The man frowned as if he would rather have had a customer at the moment than a new Initiate, but offered his hand. "My name is Eleazer Illuminati—pastor and founder of the Church. Unless I miss my guess, you're not really here to buy a television set, are you?"

"Not really, no."

"So—as a pastor—how can I help you, then?"

"Tell me about your Church."

"Are you interested in joining us, brother?"

"I'm interested . . . in checking it out."

Illuminati sighed. Not too promising a customer, really, but in the absence of any other—

They heard a scream.

Illuminati glanced in irritation down the mall's walkway, where a woman pushed a toddler in a stroller. "If we're going to talk theology," he said, straining to be heard above the child's tantrum, "we really ought to go inside."

Homer followed him into the store, where television sets in all shapes and sizes chattered on the walls, interspersed with videocassette recorders and minicams. The floor was carpeted in a rich ruby weave, and the walls behind the merchandise were papered in somber gray, which lent the place the tone of gravity Homer associated with a mortuary. Four glass counters had been arranged in a square in the center of the room to form a crystal castle around the cash register at their center. In the case facing the door, Homer saw a display of remote controls, laid out on burgundy velvet. The whole rear wall was covered with coaxial cables and connectors, rolls of antenna wire, and rabbit ears on elaborate silvery hooks stuck in a gray cork wall. In the dead center of the wall was an imposing door, of highly polished steel or aluminum, which had no knob or other device to open it from the front, but along the very top had been engraved in a spidery hand *Church of the Unflagging Eye.* A large peephole in the center of the door itself resembled a nearly human eyeball that would size up any visitor who knocked there—just as the visitor might size up his own reflection in the door.

There was no one else on the sales floor, and Homer asked, "No Initiates today?"

"They're all at the Hackensack store—a mall-wide sale today," Illuminati said with a frown, reaching over the counter filled with remote controls to press a hidden button alongside the register. A moment later, the steel door opened and a young man appeared in the frame, blinking at the light.

"Reverend?"

"Hold the door there, Ricky," said Illuminati.

"I'm still a Fred, sir."

"All right, Fred, just keep an eye on things, will you?"

"Alone?"

"You can call me if anything intimidating happens."

Fred held the door until the Reverend had caught it, then moved to the center of the glass counters, taking up his position behind the register with reverence. Illuminati made a sour face at him and then gestured for Homer to precede him through the door. As Homer crossed the threshold, Illuminati muttered, "Just amazing what I'm getting these days!"

Homer stepped through, the Reverend followed, and the steel door clanged shut behind them.

Inside was a dark room hung with heavy draperies, in front of which a series of identical nine-inch monitors stood on silver tables. On each monitor a candle burned, their flames trembling in precise unison from the tape-loop feed supplying them all. The carpet underfoot continued the color scheme from the selling floor, but here in the dimness the burgundy was burnished, taking on the hue of sacramental wine. The central area was filled with aluminum folding chairs in a slightly different shade of scarlet, arranged so that all could see a huge video projection screen at the front of the room, surrounded by garlands of flowers, and a rosewood rostrum beside it. There was a space between the first row of chairs and the rostrum, and Illuminati led Homer there, picking up a remote control from the rostrum and touching one of its buttons so that the video projector filled with images from the loop playing in the storefront window. Behind the screen and rostrum was another bank of monitors, which were not apparently connected to the same loop, because when the video projection screen showed sailing ships following signal flares, the banks of monitors behind them remained lit with nothing but random noise, twinkling electronic snow, which in its patternless patterns, Homer supposed, resembled the cosmos.

"So," said the Reverend resonantly, "what do you need to know about our worship?"

Something in the room—in the walls behind the curtains?—gave his voice a deeper, richer timbre. Homer took a moment to look around and gestured toward the monitors flickering behind the altar.

"Are those the Unflagging Eyes?"

Illuminati glanced at the screens behind him, and

shook his white mane. "The eye of God is the Unflagging One. These are but reflections of the Creation which is God's own production, a major release." Here he paused to allow the metaphor to resonate in Homer's apprehension. "Our job is to read backward, so to speak, from the production to the intention that lies behind it, the design it exemplifies—"

"You mean on the sets?"

"Everywhere! But, of course, the Creation is present on these machines as much as anywhere. And because we can record what we find there, and study it in detail"—and here he moved to the projector at the rear of the room, adjusting the color balance before returning to Homer—"we can do more than honor God's Creation as it appears before us. We can use this technology to break it down, analyze it, and better understand our Producer's plans for us."

Homer blinked at the network of fiber optics spreading across the video projector. Something to honor—and listen to—and learn from, too? "So all these . . . TV screens . . . are used as oracles and idols at once?"

"Haven't you ever seen people watching them? Gathered in a circle in the largest room of their home for hours and hours a night? Staring in silence, and listening intently, believing whatever it says to them?"

"But to God the Producer? Would that make the rest of us . . . Consumers?"

"God is the Consumer, too," Illuminati said, raising a crooked finger, "the Consumer of all things! Although we, of course, are created in His image."

"So," reasoned Greeley, "to fulfill ourselves as spiritual beings, we must learn to consume?"

Illuminati nodded sagely, almost sadly, as another disciple arrived at the inescapable truth. "That is why," he explained, "our Church has attracted devoted followers, true believers who practice our creed. In the beginning, it was religion, totems, and drums in the night, that sustained us. Then science declared redemption a hoax, and we were asked to believe in 'progress' instead—until the myth of science itself exploded, at Hiroshima. What has replaced science now for us to believe in? The answer shouts at us from every billboard, every radio and television set in the country. It's written on the sky in white smoke, sewn into our clothing, stamped into the food we serve our children in the mornings. We can buy our perfection! And what a relief to know we can! Join us, brother, stay with us, to study and revere the Lord's Creation."

Homer didn't know what to say, but the Reverend spared him the necessity of responding.

"Come."

He knelt in front of the video projector in the center of the altar, drawing Homer down by the shoulder beside him. "Lord who consumes all, favor us with your Creations! Permit us to view your productions with alacrity, reverence, and awe. Accept our prayers as they are intended, supplications that we might learn to see the subtle subtext of your plots, the hidden lines of characterization, the scrims and flats of your holy scenes." Illuminati took a paperback book off the altar, which Homer realized was a copy of *TV Guide* only when the Reverend opened it at random and began to read in a most solemn voice the listing for an episode of "MacGyver."

"Seven o'clock in the evening. USA. MacGyver. Adventure. Sixty minutes. Videocassette recording number 445777. 'Mac is asked by an old friend to save his daughter from a loan shark. Richard Dean Anderson.'"

The last three words were pronounced with special reverence, as if they named a saint in the Catholic panoply. When he had finished, he turned half-closed eyes to Greeley and waited, until Homer realized he was expected to intone some sort of response. "Amen," he said, and was rewarded by a nod from the Reverend, who stood and brushed off his knees.

"So?" he said. "What do you think?"

Homer brushed off his own knees even more carefully than the Reverend had done. "I dunno. What's the next step?"

"For New Believers? You might want to try a retreat at

our Training Camp in Sussex County. Instruction and contemplation, with swimming and boating, too."

"I'm not sure—"

"Lots of people go away unsure," the Reverend reassured him. "They're sure enough when they come back."

Illuminati had not said it ominously, but his memory of the clinic sent a chill up Homer's spine. "I'll have to give it some more reflection," he decided.

Illuminati nodded, perfectly understanding how personal these spiritual matters were. "Perhaps," he said helpfully, "it might help you to think it over in front of a new thirty-inch screen? As a personal discipline, I mean. There's a model just in from Sony, with three hundred programmed channels, that you really ought to look at while you're here."

"Let me think about it."

The Reverend shrugged. "Look into your heart then, at what you really believe inside. You'll find that you're one of us already. And you're not alone, my friend, not by a long shot! Our congregation may be small, by the count of official members, but when it comes right down to our principles and practices—we're the largest faith in the West."

12

SEVEN TIMES AROUND THE LAKE——THAT WAS THE INSTRUCTION, and Shelly was more than happy to follow it, since it allowed him some extra time alone with his thoughts, and didn't require any mind-bending mumbo jumbo, which he suspected the remainder of his Initiation might include. He wasn't sure how he would respond to that, how far to allow it to go, before his refusal cut him off from any further insight into the workings of the Church of the Unflagging Eye. There were six full-time New Believers living in the cabins, whose goal was to be True Believers by the end of their two-week session; Roger the Group Leader had suggested there were also others, who did not live in the cabins with the *Neeshes,* as the Initiates were called, but were part of advanced courses, moving up the ranks of the Church hierarchy. Roger was himself a *Ricky,* who had advanced from a *Fred* more than a year before; he had spoken of his *Lucy,* but Shelly could not determine if she were his superior, inferior, or equal in the eyes of the Church. From the way Roger referred to "Reverend El" there could not have been much distance from the top of the hierarchy to the bottom, and Roger had more than once alluded to the "democracy of the Church" as a salient selling point.

Shelly strode briskly around the lake's perimeter, as he

had been commanded to do, for his first three times
around; after that, he began to hear the lake lapping at
the granite along the pathway, and the sycamores and pin
oaks, maples and sweet gums rubbing their leaves in
anticipation, murmuring among themselves. He stopped
for a minute and watched the branches sway in a breeze
that was hardly a wind, passing rumors and forest gossip.
There was a sycamore on the landward side of the path
whose lower leaves had already begun to turn yellow,
through which Shelly saw something slanting in an
unnaturally straight line. It was a roof, brown shingles
over whitewashed pine wood, though the white had long
ago turned gray, overcome with black streaks of tar
carried down from the roof by rainwater. Through the
croaks of frogs, and the lapping of the lake, and the
hissing of the treetops around him, Shelly thought
he could make out another sound that came from the
direction of the shack—the cooing of a young girl trying
to put a baby to sleep.

Roger had made it plain: Shelly was not to leave the
path until he had completed seven revolutions around
the lake; but Shelly felt that three-and-a-half should have
earned some flexibility. He checked to make sure he was
not being watched by his brothers and sisters in faith,
and then sneaked off the path into Queen Anne's lace
and the tall grass behind it that was the straightest route
from the spot where he had been standing to the white
shack peeking out through the yellow sycamore.

As he approached, the cooing became louder, and the
squeak of his sandals on the insecure boards of the porch
set off a noisy flutter inside. Shelly knocked on the door,
received no answer, knocked again, and opened it,
blinking at the darkness beyond it. The room was
illuminated only by shafts of sunlight streaming in
between the boards of the walls; and the place stank of
straw and an odor stronger than straw, rather like chick-
ens, Shelly thought. There was a window, covered by a
warped orange shade, and as he crossed to open it, his
passage set off an awful squawking from dozens of

disturbed nests. He opened the shade and saw pigeons, thirty of them, squatting in straw-filled boxes rigged with an intricate network of red and blue plastic tubes, with a button inside each box. The boxes were dirty, the straw badly in need of replacement, and the pigeons strutted and clucked at him as if to express their indignation that he had so long neglected their care and feeding. And they were right—the food boxes were empty and the water bottles, hung upside down along the sides with a spout at the bottom, were almost dry. Whoever was responsible for the maintenance of these birds hadn't been up to snuff the last three or four days. Shelly saw a clipboard on a nail near the door, and took it down. The date on the top chart confirmed his estimate: The last recorded feeding had been three days earlier, according to the scrawled initials, *N.Z.*

He heard a step on the porch boards outside and returned the clipboard to its nail just as the coop door opened, and a figure stood framed against the daylight outside. Shelly searched for a reason he might give for snooping, for invading the privacy of the pigeons, but came up with nothing better than a bored guest's curiosity, when the figure in the doorway spoke his name.

"Mr. Lowenkopf?"

Shelly stepped forward, into the light, and only then could he make out the features of the speaker—which he recognized as belonging to the driver he had seen in the garage looking over Ralph Kotlowicz's shoulder.

"Eduardo?"

The driver raised his hand, and his fingertips sparkled like silver in the sunlight. Shelly blinked against the glare before he realized they were wrapped in new aluminum foil.

"You're wanted."

"Are you . . . one of them?"

Eduardo nodded. "And now you're about to become one of us, too," he said. "Congratulations."

"Right now?"

"Roger asked me to bring you to the Installation."

It made Shelly think of himself as a washing machine, which he preferred to put off for a while. "I haven't made it around the lake seven times yet."

"How many turns have you completed?"

"Three. And a half."

Eduardo shrugged. "That's enough. The ritual used to be called 'Around the Dial,' but who has dial controls anymore? Everything's digital, to start with, and remote controlled, too. The Reverend was talking about losing it, the other day, and I think he's right—as he is about everything else! Seven circles around is better, but three can give you the idea. I'll tell you what—if you don't tell Roger you wandered off course, I won't tell him either."

He winked, and Shelly understood he was being done a favor. He said, "Where are we going now?"

"To the Installation—where New-ies become True-ies, at your own level, and Ethels become Lucys at theirs. Believe me, it's better than 'Family Feud.'"

Shelly expected to be led back to the cabins, but Eduardo cut across to the hillside path near the dock, and climbed toward the ranch house. Before they had scaled halfway up the slope, he turned onto a bypath which wound around the curve of the hill, climbing again on the far side toward a familiar concrete bunker, at the sight of which Shelly stopped in his tracks.

"The Research Building? Is that where we're going?"

"They just call it that," said Eduardo.

"What do we call it?"

"We call it 'The House of Faith,'" Eduardo replied solemnly, missing Shelly's irony. The lack of a sense of humor seemed to be a prerequisite for cult membership. But there was nothing funny about what Shelly had so narrowly escaped in that barber chair in the Research Building.

"No electrodes?" he asked.

Eduardo smiled as if Shelly had accused them of branding new Initiates with hot irons. "You'll see."

There were already seven people gathered in the fourth-floor room when Eduardo led Shelly in, assembled in the traditional semicircle with a television screen at the open end. Before Shelly was invited to join them, Roger stood before him gravely and wrapped a hooded cloak around his shoulders, drawing the hood forward until it fell over Shelly's eyes, and tugging it back by pinching the peak over the crown of Shelly's head. Roger took Shelly's right hand in both of his own and inspected the fingertips carefully, stopping to dig out some pigeon shit from under Shelly's pinkie nail. Then he reached into the pocket of his own cowled cloak and produced a piece of smooth aluminum foil about four inches long by three inches wide, which he wrapped around Shelly's index finger with a single twist of his wrist. This was followed by nine more pieces of shiny foil, each twisted in similar fashion around a digit until all of Shelly's fingers were covered from the second knuckle to the tip in tight cones of foil. Roger held up Shelly's hands to inspect them by the blue light of the television screen, which provided the only illumination in the room, tightening the foil on Shelly's right thumb and his left ring finger. When he was satisfied, Roger held out both of Shelly's hands for the rest of the assembly to admire; they did in fact respond with the necessary nods, mumbling approvingly and checking one another to make sure their acquiescence was commonly shared. Shelly was led to a spot in the semicircle and helped by Roger to sit without the use of his hands. Roger reached into his pocket, wrapped ten silvery cones around his own fingertips, and took a seat directly across the semicircle from the place he had seated Shelly.

"Attitude check," he intoned.

Each of his listeners responded by striking a favorite TV-watching pose: stretching out full-length on the side with the head supported on an elbow; or lying on the back with the ankles crossed and the hands behind the head; or sitting in a ball with the knees pulled up in front and the fingers interlaced around the shins. Roger himself sat cross-legged, with his chin craned forward, gripping his balls, inspecting the attitudes of all of the other participants.

"Good," he said to each in turn.

One of the younger Initiates said, "Let's eat," and received stares for his impoliteness, but after the chastened young man hung his head, aluminum trays were indeed passed around, and when Shelly accepted his own, he recognized the aroma rising from the aluminum cover as that of a Swanson TV dinner. He had lived many years as a bachelor, between the day Ruth threw him out and the one Mordred moved in, during which time he had learned everything there was to know about the Swanson line. All of the others had left on the lid, so Shelly did the same, spreading a paper napkin on his lap and placing the tray on top of it, while Roger closed his eyes and began chanting in a contemplative voice, *"Well, I'll tell you all a story 'bout a man named Jed—"*

The rest of the semicircle supplied the next line: *"A poor mountaineer, barely kept his family fed—"*

And Roger led them in responsive reading through the entire introduction to the weekly episodes of "The Beverly Hillbillies." Shelly was amazed how easily the words came back to him, although he had not watched the show in—what was it?—fifteen years? He had forgotten most of what he'd studied in school, and wasn't sure he could remember all the words to the national anthem, but found himself singing, *"Black gold . . . Texas 'T' . . ."* along with the rest of them, earning from Roger an encouraging wink.

When they had finished the prayer of gratitude it was time to eat, and all of the Initiates tore off the aluminum lids from their trays with real anticipation. Underneath was a chopped meat patty Shelly remembered calling a Salisbury steak, with peas and carrots, mashed potatoes, and hot applesauce with cinnamon. The patty in its red sauce tasted exactly as Shelly remembered it tasting, as did the microwaved potatoes and vegetables—although the applesauce tasted different, a little more acidic, as if a new ingredient had been added to the cinnamon topping. Appetites were vigorous, and no one spoke, so the nine of them gobbled up their trays in seven or eight minutes. There was a moment during which Roger watched in silence as the empty trays were collected and small paper cups were passed around, each with a thimbleful of beer foaming inside. Then a toast—"Gilligan!"—and they all threw back their heads and downed their beers in a single gulp, crushing their paper cups and tossing them over their shoulders. The Initiates looked at each other, sharing the communal warmth, and tightened the semi-circle, scooting themselves in closer to the TV screen at their center. Roger leaned forward across his legs, which were crossed in a full lotus, and pointed his remote control at the front of the set, hitting the button with a single dramatic downthrust of his thumb; and the picture burst on, in a swirl of colors and audience applause.

This time it was not a tape, but random TV off the airwaves: a game show at first, three contestants behind booths, pressing buzzers to answer questions, followed by a commercial for what was called "feminine protection," followed by another for dietary chocolate pudding pops. Each image had just enough time to form, and one or two lines of dialogue to be exchanged, before Roger would hit the channel button, switching to another station in the middle of a sentence. "I'm sorry, Suzie," a man would say while the organ music swelled behind him, "but I'm going to have to tell my brother what you've been doing with—" And then the scene would switch to an audience shot, with Phil Donahue's white head making its way through the rows to shove a microphone under the nose of a woman in plaid, who said, "How do these people learn to do all these things? If I can get my husband to lie on his back, I think we're really out on the edge—"

Then a wildlife shot of two cougar cubs, followed by some black-and-white footage of an aircraft carrier, an episode of "Kojak," a discussion of facial cleaners featuring Cher, and the diamond deal of the century on Home Shopping Network. Roger never let the station linger on C-SPAN's coverage of the Senate Subcommittee on Appropriations or CNN's analysis of the latest change in the Middle East, which according to Church gospel were not really television at all. Instead, they devoted themselves to popular culture as television had defined it, which meant the networks on the first go-round and the local stations on reruns. After five or ten minutes of this, Shelly felt his head going woozy, and closed his eyes, but was forced to open them again as the first Initiate to the left of the set wiggled directly in front of the screen, leaning in toward the flickering light and pressing his aluminum-coated fingertips to the surface of the picture tube. There was a glimmering flash of static electricity or something else leaping between him and the set.

This blocked the view of the others, of course, but no one objected, and Shelly understood this was expected—and, gazing at the aluminum foil on his own fingers, realized it might well be expected of them all. The Initiate at the screen closed his eyes and rubbed his aluminum-capped fingers in hypnotic circles on the glass—as he did, he seemed to groan, caught up in some sensation communicated directly to him by the static electricity of the TV set itself. And then the voice of Roger boomed out, addressing the man at the set by name but speaking to all of them indirectly through him.

"Listen to it, Robbie—feel its vibrant message! The whole world passes through it, day by day . . . the only community of all people on Earth!

"What is it that separates us, person from person, we ask? And the answer is given to us, day after day, hour after hour! Our questions answered and more, the answers to questions we have not asked, have never dared to ask out loud . . .

"What is it that separates us? What is it that cuts us off from our neighbors, that isolates each of us and makes us feel lonely and alone, abandoned by friends and family, outcasts from the human race?

"All of us know the answers, don't we?

"We know that the esteem of our friends and family are important to us—and when there's a dirty ring around the collars of our shirts, when there are spots on the glasses we serve to our guests, when our children wear clothes that are dingy yellow, when our mouths are full of morning breath, when our lawns are overrun with weeds and our houses are gray with lack of paint—these things affect us, they touch us deeply, they make us feel we've disappointed the expectations of our loved ones and ourselves.

"Don't laugh, Samantha! Because that box—television—both reflects and shapes our consciousness as communal human beings. We all listen to it—is there anything else all of us attend to? And as we listen, we take in what it tells us and learn what we are all about. It supplies the physical forms of our dreams and our fears and the categories by which we judge personal success. It reminds us of the things we wish we had and the problems we're afraid of. But it also teaches us how to solve those disturbing problems.

"We learn that Wisk will clean our collars, and Calgon our glasses; Momma gets out sticky stains with *A-L-L*, and Clorox now treats colors, too. Ortho makes for healthy lawns, and Glidden will keep our houses painted for years. For each thing, for each genuine problem that afflicts us, we have been given a solution, if only we would open our eyes and ears, to see and hear what has been offered us!

"The answers are there, inside, offering themselves to us! Listen to it, Robbie, take it in, absorb it through your ears and your eyes and your fingers! Let the tips of your fingers tingle with it—the knowledge of all things that people want to know and all things we can imagine! Release the grip on yourself, the grip of your ego, and allow your mind to be carried off, down the mainstream of your culture . . . for what common values are left to us but the jingles of the living screen?

"We are what we consume; it becomes a part of us, the stuff we are made of. So we are each of us what we choose to buy, both in the exercise of our judgment, which is the crux of identity, and in its consequences—the things we eat, that become our cells, and the things we wear, that become our social selves, and the things we wrap ourselves in, our cars and our homes and the other extensions of our bodies and minds. Now it is also true that in America we can all buy anything—which means that your identity is your own to decide, to consider and compare, to select and to buy. Where do we find what we want to consume? There is only one venue really, where information on available goods is pumped out hour after hour, day after day, offering, offering, the goods of the Earth to each one of us . . .

"Grab it, Robbie! Hug it to your chest! Because there, at the tips of your fingers, is the answerer of answers, the voice in your head, the oracle in your living room. Let your body feel its power, let its wisdom enter you, warm you, and enlighten you; allow yourself to become one with it, with the humming voice of television—and you'll never be lonely again!"

As Shelly watched, Initiate Robbie did indeed seem to merge with the television set, crawling on top of it as if he would climb into the screen, if he could. His movements were licorice, languid and liquid, as if in a trance—and Shelly realized that he too felt his head spinning at the sound of Roger's words, the images on the screen behind Robbie running together as blobs of color, their shapes losing definition, blurring into a single tele-vision of a unified field, full of messages about the world and the lone individual's place in it, which all seemed to run together. Who did Shelly really want to be? It was easy enough, if he just believed he could buy it. He was making good money now, wasn't he? What was the point of resisting it?

He gripped his head by the temples.

Or was it Roger's words that made him feel so woozy, Shelly suddenly wondered. A sudden fear came over him, and he glanced about the room wildly, trying to find the trays. There was one in the corner, left behind when the others had been carted away. Shelly reached over, and fell backward onto the carpet, captured his balance and caught the edge of the tray. By the edge of his foiled fingers, he dragged it toward himself, bumping over carpet fibers, as Robbie sagged in a heap at the foot of the TV stand, and Roger spoke again, in his normal, softer voice.

"Very good, Robbie. Who's next?"

Shelly had the tray. He could barely focus both eyes in the flickering darkness, but managed to peer into the depressions in the aluminum where the food was held. This had been Roger's tray; he had shoved it into the corner to finish later when he began to prepare his monologue. There was still half a steak of cold chopped meat, and—as Shelly had suspected—an entire square of untouched applesauce.

"Opie?" said Roger. "Are you ready?"

It took Shelly a moment to remember that the name *Opie* had been given to him as his Initiate's cell-name, which would be known to the brothers and sisters of his Initiation Group but to no other members of the Church —with the exceptions, of course, of Roger and the Reverend himself. Shelly hadn't given it much thought at the time, but now, as Roger stared at him, his eyes flitting strangely to the tray in Shelly's hand, the name rang in Lowenkopf's mind as a giant warning gong. Roger's stern face swam before his eyes, and as he struggled to his feet, his breath and heart rate increased sufficiently to speed the drug through his system.

"It's in the applesauce, isn't it?"

Roger frowned. "Brother Opie does not seem up to his turn," he mumbled to the others in the circle. "Perhaps Cissy would like to worship next."

Shelly opened his mouth to say something to Cissy, lost his focus on her, and closed it. He wobbled for a moment while she crawled forward, kneeling before the box, and then turned himself toward the door. It seemed a long three steps in the flickering darkness to reach the knob, and two of the others looked at him, and then at Roger, who shook his head. Then Roger's voice boomed out again.

"Listen to it, Cissy! Feel it inside you . . ."

Lowenkopf grappled with the doorknob, and in a moment was free, tumbling to the hallway carpet outside the lab. The heavy door clanged shut behind him, and for a moment he worried that someone might come after him, but the door remained closed for a full minute as he lay facedown against the baseboard, and he knew Roger had let him go. There was nothing they had done that violated the law, and any surprises he found distasteful had been covered, no doubt, by the disclaimer he had signed on applying for Church membership. But someone should be responsible to see that this sort of brainwashing was stopped—and the only person he could think of who might care enough to stop it was the man in charge of everything, the whole clinic.

Harrison.

Shelly forced himself to his feet, and pushed himself off against the wall until he'd made his way to the elevators. They were on the opposite wall, of course, all the way across the width of the carpet, and it required a desperate lunge for him to throw himself across to the call button. He punched it three times with the flat of his hand, and the red button lit. By the time the car arrived, he was able to roll himself in, where he bounced off the rear wall, causing the car to tremble and strain against its supporting cables, but at last he ricocheted back toward the elevator buttons and stuck his thumb on the lobby sign before he sank to the floor.

When the door opened on the ground level, he sat in his place for a moment, and then managed to raise himself just when the doors began to close again. He stuck his arm between them and mercifully they opened. There was a broad stretch of open space that had to be crossed to the lobby door, but the strength was stealing back into his knees, which held without buckling. He burst through the door, and the fresh air revived him, though it also made his head feel like a blacksmith's anvil after four new shoes had been hammered on it. The hillside was a mountain's slope, in Switzerland by the pitch, an endless climb of slippery green grass boobytrapped with edelweiss. Or dandelions. The ranch house loomed above him, threatened to crack off its upper stories and send them tumbling down the hillside, on top of him. But the ranch house wobbled and held, and

Shelly did, too, and after years of struggling against the grass, his foot hit planks of wood. The porch steps. From there his arms could haul him up the stairs, with enough force to cross the lobby, in spite of the sentry receptionist, and throw himself up the staircase to the Doctor's personal office on the third floor.

"You c-c-can't go up there!" she said.

Shelly accepted it as a prediction, and thought she might be right; but by the second landing, he knew he would make it, and saw that she wasn't after him. He slowed his progress, trying to catch his breath and take the giant steps one huge leap forward at a time.

It was a two-room suite, with an outer reception room and Harrison's inner sanctum. In the outer room, Howard Davenport sat at the secretary's desk, collating two stacks of papers into a single two-sheet memorandum. Harrison's secretary was nowhere in sight, which suited Shelly fine. He crossed the room, full of purpose, heading straight for the door to Harrison's private office as if he were expected. But Davenport looked up and shook his head, sadly, as if it pained him to have to insist, "Sorry. You can't go in there."

Shelly studied the door. "Why not?"

"Doctor Harrison is with Joseph now. He can't be disturbed when he's with Joseph."

"The monkey?"

"Even Dr. Kaufman respected that. She came back here a few minutes ago, really steamed up. But when I reminded her he was with Joseph, she said she'd come back to see him later."

There was a *whack!* from inside the room, and then another *whack!* and a *clang!*

"What's going on in there?"

Davenport shrugged. "They've been making those noises for almost ten minutes now. Some new kind of training. For his research, I guess."

Shelly didn't like the sound of that *whack!*—but what he saw next, he liked even less. Because from under the Doctor's big engraved door, a thin line of red liquid ran out, crossing wooden floorbeams until it reached the Persian rug, staining the edge a reddish brown. Davenport saw it, too—his eyes widened and he made no further objection when Shelly grabbed the brass doorknob and said, "I'm going in, anyway."

The door was unlocked—it opened easily. What Shelly saw on the other side was much harder to manage. It was a square room at the top of the house, with windows on three sides, all covered with wrought-iron bars. Between the windows were bookcases and file cabinets; in front of the bookcases was a big rosewood desk, and in front of the desk, in the center of the room, was a cage in which stood Joseph, Henry Harrison's acclaimed chimpanzee, while around the outside of the cage a white pigeon with a gray head scampered, losing feathers. Harrison himself was everywhere—his head lay on the desk as if he were sleeping, while his feet stuck out at an awkward angle from underneath the desk drawers. But his left arm was by the window, and his right arm near the door; the bloody remains of his trunk lay hacked to pieces between the desk and Joseph's cage, a longhandled ax sticking out of its back like the tree stump next to a woodpile. It was an unusual ax, double-headed in bronze, the sort of ceremonial weapon found on Crete in museum collections of the Minoan age. The end of its long handle wobbled close to the cage—where Joseph was still imprisoned, gripping the padlocked door with both of his hands, rattling the latch against the unyielding lock, staring at the disassembled components of the Doctor strewn in every part of the office around him.

Joseph looked up, noticed Shelly, and grinned at the mayhem, at the horror, baring his teeth, primate to primate. Then the corners of his mouth fell, and his brow wrinkled in a shockingly human expression of grief and personal loss. He shook it back and forth a few times, dragging his long, narrow hand across his eyes as if trying to wipe out the memory of what he had witnessed. Lowenkopf reached out in sympathy toward him. Joseph pointed at the floor near Lowenkopf's foot, where

Harrison's right hand had fallen. Still gripped in the fist was a silver whistle on a ring that also held a small key, like a mailbox key. It was the key to the padlock on the chimpanzee's cage door. Lowenkopf squatted down and studied it in the dead man's hand. And Joseph began to scream and scream and scream.

13

JERSEY POLICE WERE A BREED UNTO THEMSELVES, SHELLY HAD always felt, and the two officers sent out from the Sussex City Police Department proved no exceptions to his rule. Detective Foley was senior, well into his fifties, with a square jaw that dominated the lower half of his face, particularly since the muscles could be seen at ear-level sliding his gritted teeth back and forth. His nose was flat, and his eyes were two dark brown beads set in a sea of wrinkles that receded like a topographical map to the plain of his forehead above and the compressed fault line below that served as his mouth. Only the center of his lips opened when he spoke, as if the downturned edges were occupied holding his face together. Fortunately, he didn't talk much, that job having been left to Detective Stohler, in his early thirties with a thick, toothbrush mustache which failed to distract the eye sufficiently from his prematurely balding head. A broad expanse of forehead ended suddenly in overgrown eyebrows which met at the top of his nose, under which pale blue eyes were washed almost continuously by frequently blinking eyelids. It took Shelly some time to realize he was not blinking in incredulity at the story Howard Davenport told, but out of a nervous habit that seemed to accompany any impression he thought noteworthy enough to jot down in his black leather notebook. When a point seemed especially significant to him, he pressed his lower lip more firmly against his upper, causing the toothbrush mustache to spring forward, as if the hairs that composed it were standing on end. It was an effective interrogative device, Shelly decided, if an involuntary one, since it forced the person he was interviewing to wonder whether something said carried an unintended implication. In an attempt to clarify the meaning of a statement already recorded, a witness will volunteer all sorts of information he would never have supplied in response to a direct question. And so the ticks of the two Jersey plainclothesmen made a good team: Foley's jaw made him look as if he doubted every word and was growing angrier at the witness moment by moment, while Stohler's bristling upper lip suggested there might be some truth to the statement that the witness had just delivered, and he might even bring it out—with a little further clarification.

Unless, of course, the witness was Shelly Lowenkopf, who had not only conducted his own homicide investigations as a detective in the Bronx, but had done so by his own rather individual mode of analysis. While Homer had tracked down the physical evidence, the minute signs of passage recorded in stains on tenement stairs and the ashes dropped from a cigarette, Shelly had concentrated on motive, who had done what to whom for what purpose, guided for the most part by his sense of the contradictions of human nature. In this case, however, his approach looked as if it might have been equally stymied, since no one seemed to have been able to do what had been done to Henry Harrison.

"Now you were the one who actually found the body," Stohler said, glancing from his pad to Shelly.

"That's right."

"Was he still alive when you found him?"

"Alive?"

"Did he say anything at all to you? Any last words?"

"He was in pieces, Detective."

"Right. Then I take it that he didn't."

"That's correct."

"Just checking out all the bases, here. Covering all the corners."

They were supposed to be *covering all the bases* and *checking out all the corners,* but Shelly said nothing. This was not his investigation, and he was hoping for all the cooperation he could wheedle out of these two.

"Were you alone?"

"When I entered the room? Yes. Mr. Davenport was still at the desk, behind me."

"That would be you," Stohler said to Howard.

"I know," Howard replied.

"Yes, well. We'll get to you later. You were the one who was staffing the desk while the secretary—"

"Was out to lunch," broke in a squat orange-haired woman in her early fifties. She had a wide mouth with no lips to speak of, a pinched nose, and eyes that touched off a chain reaction of creases and wrinkles whenever she frowned, which was often. She wore a blouse that was printed with flowers and tied in a bow at her throat, and a pleated pink skirt that ended above her knee but should have run longer. Her small hands were already balled into fists, scarlet nails digging into her flesh, ready to fight. "I mean, a person's entitled to an hour for lunch, isn't she?"

"At one-thirty?" asked Stohler. His mustache ends bristled forward and Foley's jaw clenched.

"I didn't want to wait so long!" she shouted. "It was Henry who made me stay—Dr. Harrison. I was packing up my purse to go when he came out to greet Helen Kaufman. He showed her in but stalled a minute outside, to speak to me. 'Hang around, Doris,' he said. 'I think I'm gonna need you.' "

"To handle Dr. Kaufman?"

"Henry could handle anyone himself, thank you! No, it was afterward, when she had left in a huff, that he came out to talk to me again. To give me a job."

"What sort of job?"

"It's confidential. Personnel policy."

Foley broke in to shake his big dog's head. "Nothing is

confidential now," he said, glancing toward the door that closed off the inner office, where members of the Crime Scene Unit were still on their hands and knees, dusting the shiny surfaces and poking into the fibers of the carpet with tweezers.

Doris shuddered.

"What sort of policy?" Stohler prodded.

She looked from Stohler to Foley, at Davenport, and finally settled on Shelly. "Termination."

"You mean he fired somebody?" Stohler asked her.

Doris nodded. "He fired her. And he should have, the way she was yelling at him. I could hear it through the door! There is never a reason to raise your voice like that."

"They had a fight?" asked Foley. In his enthusiasm, he had forgotten himself and spoken twice in as many minutes. Stohler looked at him, hurt, and Foley leaned back against the edge of Doris's desk, toppling a Styrofoam cup with a few pencils in it. But she was too indignant to notice.

"*She* had a fight. He was a gentleman. She evidently did not like what he had to say to her. And she let her displeasure be overheard."

"What did she say?" Stohler asked.

"I couldn't make out most of it—just heard the shrieking. But I did hear her say, 'The girl almost died!' a few times, like she couldn't believe it. As if what happened to Neela Zapotnik was his fault! Really—"

"Who's Neela Zapotnik?"

"A girl who attempted suicide here three days ago," Shelly said. "A graduate intern."

"Helen was her advisor, after all," Doris said. "If anyone should've known what she was up to, Helen should have. That's probably why he fired her, if you ask me. They're all supposed to be therapists, aren't they? So insightful! Then one of their own students tries something like this, and there's nothing they can do but blame each other."

She has a point, Shelly thought. But Stohler was obviously thinking about it from another angle.

"She was screaming at him about it? Blaming him?"

"That's what it sounded like to me. From what I couldn't help overhearing."

"And she left in the same mood?"

"Definitely pissed."

"And then he came out to you . . . and told you to start doing the paperwork necessary to fire her?"

"I said, 'Dr. Harrison, I still haven't taken lunch yet. So if it's all right with you, I'll do this when I get back from my sandwich and apple.' It wasn't really all right with him, you could see that in his eyes, but what could he say? A person's got to eat, doesn't she? I had already kept Howard waiting more than twenty minutes to relieve me."

"You heard all this, too?" Stohler asked Davenport.

"I heard . . . voices," Howard said. "I'm not so sure what it was exactly they were saying."

"I was closer to the door," Doris explained hastily.

"A lot closer," said Davenport.

Doris frowned at him.

"Do either one of you think Helen Kaufman might have been angry enough at Dr. Harrison—for neglecting Neela Zapotnik, say, or maybe even for firing her—that she might have done what we saw in there?"

Howard and Doris looked at each other.

"She's not that sort," Davenport said finally.

"She was plenty mad," observed Doris.

"Wait a minute," said Shelly, unable to restrain himself any longer. "You saw her leave the office, didn't you?"

"Uh-huh." From Doris, suspiciously, wondering just what he was trying to prove.

"Did you see her go down the stairs?"

"I did," said Howard.

"Did she ever come back? Either while you were still here, Doris?"—and when Doris shook her head—"or afterward, while you were alone at the desk, Howard?"

Davenport thought about it and nodded slowly, his eyes wide. "Yes. She did."

Stohler drew up a chair close to Howard and asked quietly, "Tell us about it."

"About Dr. Kaufman's coming back?"

"Why don't you just give us everything," Stohler suggested, "while you're at it? A full account of what happened during the time you were responsible for the office. Think you could handle that?"

Howard's demeanor slipped, and he cast a desperate glance at Lowenkopf, who tried to offer him a reassuring nod in return.

"I suppose," Davenport said unsteadily.

Stohler smiled and cocked his head at an angle to listen more carefully.

"Mrs. Juniper—Doris—told me to cover for her at twelve-thirty, when she was planning to step out for lunch. But Henry—Dr. Harrison—wouldn't let her go. So it wasn't until after one that she actually got a chance to eat."

He said it with sympathy, glancing at Doris, who thrust out her ample chest at this account of her institutional suffering. "Happens all the time," she murmured bravely and turned to Foley, who did not cluck in admiration.

"And when she did?" prompted Stohler.

"From the time I took over the helm," Howard said, "no one came to see Harrison except Helen Kaufman and Mr. Lowenkopf here. Henry had given strict instructions to Doris, in front of me, that he was not to be *disturbed* while he was working with Joseph. From the way he said *disturbed* like that, looking at me, the message was pretty clear—I was not to bother him with questions about phone calls and other business of the desk. The truth is, he looked annoyed Doris was going at all. If it was up to him, she would never go to lunch. Ever."

Shelly began to wonder if there was anything more than staff sympathy between Howard and Doris.

"So I never did. There were two or three calls for him, but I told them all he could not be interrupted. And when those . . . sounds . . . starting coming out of the inner office, I didn't think of interrupting him."

"What sounds?" said Foley. Stohler looked as if he would rather not have had the recitation interrupted, but his partner's question was the one Lowenkopf wanted answered as well.

"Sounds," said Davenport. "I heard Joseph rattling around the bars of his cage, now and then. I heard the pigeon, too, sometimes, cooing fast and loud, on the other side of the door. And I heard these . . . thumps, you know? Whacks, like."

"Like what?" asked Stohler, when it became clear Davenport would not go on until he was sure they understood the sort of noise he remembered.

"Like an ax?" suggested Lowenkopf.

Howard thought back for a moment. "Could've been."

Foley jotted down the answer, but Stohler frowned as if he felt control of his interrogation was slipping away from him. "Did Harrison say anything?"

"Not that I heard. The walls in this place aren't thick. Sometimes I've heard music, or his whistle, coming through. But this time, only the whacks."

"Did he scream?"

"No. I'd have heard that, for sure. They just clanged the cage and whacked, happy as clams."

Stohler didn't like that—what sort of man doesn't scream when he's attacked with an ax? He made a terrible face and said, "And then?"

"And then what?"

"What happened next?"

"Nothing happened next. Until Helen Kaufman showed up with a few choice words she'd forgotten to share with Henry. I told her he was with Joseph, and she understood that all right—as one psychologist to another, I guess. She asked me to tell him she wanted to see him one last time."

" 'One last time'? She said those words?"

"Uh-huh."

Foley was scribbling happily now, licking the tip of his stubby pencil to maintain the flow. Stohler was nodding with a satisfied smile, pleased with the success of his cool investigative technique. Lowenkopf hated to interfere with such an effective interrogation, except that it seemed to be leading in the wrong direction. He realized he should keep his mouth shut; they were not interested in his opinion; they would only resent his contribution, even if successful, as an intrusion. Then he leaned toward Stohler's shoulder and murmured, "Mind if I ask a question?"

Stohler stared at him for a moment. "Is there something you can add to what we've heard?"

"Maybe."

"This is an official police investigation."

"I can see that. But I, ah, used to be a policeman myself, and, since I was on the scene . . ."

"You were a cop?"

"Detective Sergeant with the Allerton Avenue Precinct, in the Bronx. Working homicides."

Stohler's face revealed that this was not what he was hoping to hear; but he didn't see how Lowenkopf could screw things up now, anyway. He shrugged. "Go ahead."

Shelly turned to face Davenport. "Howard, you said that Dr. Kaufman came back to see Harrison when you were manning the desk alone—after their argument. Isn't that right?"

Davenport nodded.

"But you told her that Henry was working with Joseph, and she understood that?"

"I just had to tell her once."

"And she left, without seeing him?"

"That's right."

"Not even for a second? Not for one word?"

"She never got through the door."

"So if it was Helen who killed Henry, she would have had to do it earlier—before Doris went to lunch, wouldn't she?"

Howard blinked at him. "I guess."

"So what?" said Foley. "What difference does it make when she killed him?"

Lowenkopf addressed his response to Stohler. "Her

motive is not going to help us out much, if she never had a chance to act on it. Harrison's office is an add-on, the only one on the third floor, accessible only from this one, and the stairs leading up here. Building code probably required an escape route through a window, but Harrison must have had bars put on them all after inspection —to prevent any escapes from his animal subjects, I'd guess." He looked at Doris, who gave him a grudging confirmation on that point. "So the killer had to come in and go out through this staircase here."

The two policemen exchanged a silent glance, which meant, on Foley's side, *Can't we shut this guy up?* and, on Stohler's side, *Not yet.* Lowenkopf knew what their glances meant, and knew the only response he could make was to score his point, to strike pay dirt before they pulled his spade. He concentrated on the other two witnesses.

"Helen Kaufman left the office in front of both of you the first time. Isn't that what you said?"

Doris didn't reply, trying to work out the consequences of an affirmative response. But Howard nodded.

Shelly persevered. "And you're sure that Harrison was still alive when she left?"

At that, they both nodded. "He came out to give me the job, I told you," Doris complained to the officers. "He couldn't have done that if he was dead already, now could he?"

"No, he couldn't," Shelly agreed. "So Helen Kaufman couldn't have killed him, then. And since she never got a chance to see him later, she couldn't have killed him, ever."

There was a dead silence in which the two cops stared at him and then at one another, while Doris and Howard waited to see if Foley or Stohler could come up with an objection that hadn't occurred to them. After a long pause, Stohler drew a breath and said, "Not necessarily."

It took Foley a second longer to find the possible hole, but find it he did, nodding in solidarity with his partner.

"Not alone, maybe."

And he cast an ugly glance at Howard, who quailed under his scrutiny. "Me?"

"You're the only one who could have, aren't you?"

Lowenkopf understood their reasoning. They were obviously sorry to lose Kaufman as their suspect, since that explanation would have made their jobs so much simpler—a clear motive and a pair of witnesses to place her at the scene of the crime. But the timing created a problem, which could only be overcome if she had in fact reentered by the only access to Harrison's office. Which meant that Kaufman could only continue to be their leading suspect if one or both of their witnesses were lying about her failure to return.

If she had in fact come back before Doris went to lunch, both witnesses would have to be lying about it. But if she came back after Doris left—returning, say, to speak her mind after stewing about it for a while—only Howard would have to be lying, about her walking away from the office, unheard. Since Howard would have to be lying in either case, it made sense to wonder whether Howard could be fitted for a role as accomplice at least. He was, after all, a patient at a psychological clinic, which they probably thought of as a mental hospital anyway. And if the two detectives had to take on one or the other of the witnesses, Howard Davenport seemed a lot easier to tackle than Doris, whose grim visage spoke of many hours turning down applicants for positions, reporters with questions, and all kinds of oddballs seeking wisdom from the great guru of behaviorist training. Joseph had made Harrison's name famous around the psychological world, and who didn't have a few monkeys on his or her back badly in need of retraining?

"I didn't do it," grunted Davenport.

Stohler contemplated his suspect serenely. "Was Dr. Kaufman the only person to enter this office after Mrs. Juniper left you in charge?"

"Except for Mr. Lowenkopf."

"But Dr. Harrison was dead by then?"

"Yes."

"And you say that Kaufman left again without ever seeing Harrison?"

"Uh-huh."

He turned to Doris. "And you know for a fact that your boss was alive when you went to lunch?"

"Absolutely."

"Then I don't see any alternative," Stohler concluded as he reached behind his back for the handcuffs at the rear of his belt, "but to arrest you for the murder of Henry Harrison. For aiding and abetting, at least. Detective Foley—read him his rights, please."

Stohler clasped the bracelets on Davenport, who shifted his eyes to the bigger cop as he began to recite, "You have the right to remain silent . . ."

"Wait," said Shelly, "That's not right—"

Stohler patted him on the arm. "Thank you, Mr. Lowenkopf, for your assistance. Me and Foley—we never would have worked it through so quickly on our own. But I think we can handle this part without you."

14

"YOU MEAN WE'VE GOT A CLIENT AFTER ALL?" HOMER ASKED Shelly in the gravel parking lot outside the ranch house, when the blond detective finally arrived at the clinic in a baby-blue Mustang, with his report on the Reverend Eleazer Illuminati and the Church of the Unflagging Eye in the Paramus mall. On the ride out, he had sorted out the details he would report to Shelly from those he would not—there was no reason to reveal, for example, that he had knelt before an altar of television sets while the Reverend had prayed to MacGyver. But by the time he reached the clinic's grounds in Sussex County, Shelly had lost all interest in the Church. As soon as Homer had pulled into the drive, before the Mustang was parked, Shelly was shouting over the convertible's side about a murder—about Harrison—and about their own overaged Peter Pan, the insufferable Howard Davenport.

"They've taken him away," said Shelly, and not for the first time, as Homer cut his engine and the roar of the V-8 engine died away among the crickets of the Jersey countryside. There was a sweet smell of cut grass from the lawn sloping down to the highway.

"Who?" said Homer. "Harrison?"

"They've taken him away, too," Shelly said, dropping his volume, "in a box."

"Dead?"

Shelly nodded. "Chopped to pieces."

"Not a suicide, then."

"Murder. The local police have just come and gone. And who do you think is on their hook for it?"

Homer thought immediately of Adrienne Paglia. But there was no way for Shelly to know her. The only one his partner might have cared so much about was . . .

"Our client?"

"Howard Davenport."

"So maybe we do have a case out here, after all."

Shelly nodded. "We need to see the interim director and get her permission to poke around the place."

"Her?"

"An M.D. named Marsha Mullens. I met her once, at the scene of the accident. When Ray Singh was hit. Although it doesn't seem like much of an accident now, does it?"

"Was Harrison there?"

"He had been, moments before. Someone could've started up the truck with him in mind."

"Any idea who?"

"Plenty. From what I've seen so far, Harrison was less than a marvelous human being."

Homer closed the car door smartly behind him, and rubbed an invisible smudge from the silvery handle. "She's got to be in the ranch house, right? So what are we waiting for?"

"I was waiting for you."

They climbed the steps of the ranch-house porch in unison, the first time they had acted together in days. It was another thing Homer didn't like about this business —they were always splitting up now, taking care of clients, instead of working hand in hand, which is what they had always done best. They needed a good little murder to bring them together, lately. Fortunately, Mrs. Davenport's missing person had become a murder suspect—just the kind of motivation that brought out the best in them.

"Let's try the second floor," said Shelly. "The top floor

was Harrison's own, higher than anyone else's. That's where I found him, diced."

"You found him yourself?"

"On my way to complain about professional impropriety in the Church initiations."

"Prayers to MacGyver?"

"What? No. Brainwashing."

This conversation mercifully was cut short when the door to an office on the second floor opened and Doris Juniper's whine spilled out, archly overpolite.

"I understand what you're asking, Dr. Mullens, but Henry didn't want it arranged that way."

"Alphabetically?" asked Mullens, running slender fingers through her black and gray hair. Five-seven, about one-thirty, in an understated blue Chanel suit with elegant pearl buttons. "He didn't want his files reflecting the alphabet?"

"He didn't want his files reflecting anything I ever heard of," Doris insisted. "He didn't want me filing anything in those drawers, and never saw fit to explain to me just how he was going about it. I offered—it wasn't that he didn't think I could do it. But he was, well, a private man. You know that, better than anyone."

The last line was delivered like a letter opener in the hands of a skilled receptionist, tearing through the outer paper to get at the stuff inside. At this unsolicited commentary on her personal relationship with the deceased, Dr. Mullens looked up through burning hazel eyes and saw Shelly and Homer in the hallway, listening through the half-open door, the knob of which was still grasped in Doris's sweaty hand.

"Can I help you?" asked Mullens, the icy professional.

"Dr. Mullens?"

She nodded. "You're the man who helped me carry Ray Singh, aren't you?"

"He's also the one who found Henry," added Doris. "Mr. Lowen-something, Lowenberg—"

"Lowenkopf," supplied Shelly.

"Sounds like you've been having a busy time at the clinic," Mullens said. From the flatness of her voice, she might have liked to drive him out of the building. But she reached across Doris to grab the door a foot above the knob and opened it wider. "Why don't you step in and talk about it."

Shelly edged sideways through the door, passing Doris, who hadn't budged. Then came Homer, before whose grim countenance Doris gave way.

"Who're you?"

Shelly addressed the answer to Dr. Mullens. "This is Homer Greeley. My partner."

"Partner in what?" asked Mullens. From the dismay on her face, she was obviously thinking *lawyers.*

"We're private investigators," Shelly said, and for the first time ever, heard:

"Thank God," from Mullens.

"We're happy to know you feel that way," Shelly told her. "Most people don't."

Mullens sighed. "I'm a physician. I've never administered anything bigger than my own grants before. And now Henry is gone . . . and before I can deal with my own grief, I've got to make sure this whole place keeps running—and you have no idea the shape in which they've left it . . ."

"The police," explained Doris quickly, to make sure they didn't think Mullens had meant she and Henry had left it in any sort of mess.

"The police can be terribly disruptive," Shelly said with sympathy, frowning at the papers and files strewn all around the office. Doris held a stack in the crook of her arm, which she twisted away from Shelly when he glanced down.

"P.I.'s," Doris said, snorting, "are worse."

"Has . . . someone . . . hired you?" asked Marsha Mullens suddenly, casting a wary eye over the files as if that information might also be in one of them.

"You haven't, if that's what you mean," Shelly replied gently. "We don't represent the clinic. The wife of one of your patients became concerned over his absence. So she asked us to look in on him."

"Roberta Davenport."

"That's right. How did you know?"

"Henry's brought it up in staff, from time to time. As a question for us to wrestle with. Should we address family issues as a clinic, or shouldn't we?"

"Did you?"

"No. I was in favor of doing so, I seem to remember, but Henry overruled me."

"Why did he bother bringing it up," asked Homer, "if he was just going to decide for himself?"

Mullens sighed again and her eyelids reddened with tears. "That was Henry. The most exasperating man on the planet—take it from me! But also the most brilliant. Safely one of them."

"You knew him well?"

Mullens frowned at Doris as if to say, *You revealed too much and they heard it!* But she said, "We were colleagues together, Mr. Lowenkopf. We shared many hours on research projects working side by side. You get to know a person under those conditions—struggling with a problem together, sometimes around the clock, under stress from granting agencies and ethical review boards and public health inspectors—"

"Were you under investigation?"

"Nothing like that! Henry was always out in front of his field, inspiring both admiration and jealousy, and there is never a shortage of red tape that can be shoved in your way, if anyone is so inclined. We've been inspected by every branch of the NIMH and found to be perfectly professional. So whatever else they accuse him of, and I'm sure his academic competitors will, there was no impropriety in his current research."

"I've just come from an Initiation rite of the Church of the Unflagging Eye, in your Research Building. Have you any idea what goes on?"

She waved her arm in the air as if to dismiss the whole enterprise. "That's not research! Henry tolerated those fringe groups to pay the rent on this place. What difference does it make, he used to ask, if they do their mumbo jumbo here, where we can at least keep the circuits from frying them crisp, or if they're forced to do it in some dark cellar that was never wired to support twenty-five television monitors? I know what you're talking about—I've argued with Henry about them, too, but he felt he needed them to keep the doors open. Now we'll have to see if that's enough."

"It's not going to help if one of your patients is convicted of murder, is it?"

The thought had occurred to her, clearly, but so had her response. "I can't help that, can I?"

"Perhaps we can," Shelly said.

She scrutinized him carefully. Was this man going to help her keep the place afloat? Or was he another one of those who had his own agenda, which included the end of their work at the clinic, the end of her own research and Henry Harrison's legacy? Casting in her own lot with Harrison had been a risky move for a psychiatrist: The medical profession tended to trust their own exclusively, and a clinic that was not run by an M.D. was hardly a true medical facility. But she had believed in Henry, and her faith had been in part borne out by the tremendous reputation his work had acquired. She was determined not to allow it to fall apart now.

"What do you need from me?"

"First, permission. To follow our leads where they take us, in and around the clinic."

"You have leads?"

"Maybe. Do we have your permission?"

Mullens hesitated, glanced at Doris, then shrugged. "Why not? Anything you find can only help the police. And if by chance it helps poor Howard at the same time, it won't hurt the clinic any."

"Thanks. I'm glad you see it that way."

"I hope I do when you're done." She started to gather up some of the files on the floor, and Homer stooped to help her. Shelly picked up one file and read the name HOLZMAN, inscribed in childish block letters on its stick-on label. Doris snatched it away from him.

"Those are confidential files," she said, sniffing.

"What were they looking for?"

"Something provocative," Mullens told Homer. "Henry locked personal records in his office, if the material they contained was of a certain kind."

"Incriminating?"

Mullens shook her head. "You're in a different business, Mr. Lowenkopf. People come here with all sorts of problems they can't handle on their own—alcoholism and drug dependency, even an occasional kleptomania. Henry felt security was an issue when these things were involved, so he kept the relevant files where he could keep an eye on them."

"Compromising stuff, huh?"

"You could call it that, I suppose," agreed Mullens. "But I don't see how they're relevant."

Shelly shrugged. "The police did."

"You do seem to think alike," observed Mullens with a smile that conveyed no warmth. "I hope you don't plan to do to our clinic what they did to our files."

"Did they find it?" Shelly asked Doris.

"What?"

"The file on Howard Davenport."

She knew—they could all see that from the way she struggled to say nothing. Finally, Mullens said, "It wouldn't compromise our ethics, Doris, to answer that question honestly."

"Henry wouldn't've."

"Perhaps not. But I'm in charge now."

The wind had changed; Doris could swing her sails around or abandon ship. Something passed behind her eyes—her mortgage, maybe, or the shiny black Lexus parked in her personal spot. She said slowly, "We had two files in here on Davenport—thick ones. The police took 'em both."

Doris looked at Mullens, who nodded approvingly, and then at Lowenkopf, who nodded differently. "Did you happen to see those files go?"

"I wouldn't've let them out if I saw them, sir! But they're not here anymore."

"You said Dr. Harrison never let you near them."

"I have to touch them now, don't I? To put them all back where they belong."

"But then how do you know what's missing?"

It was a question she was not prepared to answer yet, and she turned to Mullens, half expecting to be bailed out—but Mullens was not Henry Harrison.

"Answer the question, please, Doris."

Shelly waited.

Doris turned to Homer in desperation. He saw her cheeks fall into jowls as her mouth trembled and the wrinkles beneath her lower lip quadrupled. But there was nothing he felt like saying to her, in comfort or accusation. She stared for a moment into his untroubled eyes, and then turned back to her main inquisitor, that man Lowenkopf.

"He told me about them, that's how! He used to . . . have me copy a page, now and then, and send it in a clean white envelope to Davenport, without even a note. 'He'll know what it means' is all Henry ever said—and he was right about that, too, because whenever we sent one, Howard came to see us, awful fast. How do you think I got to know him so well? To use him to cover my desk for me? He would come in and talk with Henry, plead with him, really. In the end Henry might say, 'You'll have to find a way, then, won't you?' It was about money, of course. Howard had used up all that he had and needed a way to stay here. So he came to me for staff support work."

"Did you ever get the impression . . . he was forced to?"

"His wife wasn't gonna help him. Everybody knew that."

"Did you ever think that Dr. Harrison might've had something on him?"

"You mean dirt?"

"Anything."

"Hell, yes! He came here at first to be treated for cocaine dependency—him an accountant! That gave Henry an edge on him, wouldn't you say?"

148

Mullens paled. "But Henry would never have ever *used* an edge of that sort."

"Whatever was necessary," Doris said cheerfully, confident in her ground. "That was his motto, as an administrator and a therapist. If he needed a hand to squeeze Howard to do something he wanted? Sure, he'd use it."

"And the rest of these?" Mullens asked hoarsely, passing a wavering hand over the files on the floor as if to exorcise any demons that might remain in them. "Did he use all of them . . . the same way, too?"

Doris noticed her new boss's expression now, and hesitated, reconsidering. "You'll have to ask the people involved for that information, I guess."

"I'm asking you," said Mullens.

Doris struggled between vanity and necessity for a moment, then gave up the struggle and beamed defiantly. "Henry Harrison used every advantage God ever gave him," she said with pride. "That's how he built this place. And that's the only way anyone will keep it going."

They heard Mullens's jaw click. "We'll see about that, won't we? Or one of us will."

Doris glared at the opposite wall.

There was a private battle there between Doris and Mullens, and the two detectives looked away, allowing them their privacy. In the glance from Shelly, Homer saw his own train of thought reflected back to him: If Harrison was blackmailing Davenport, he had a reason for wanting the psychologist dead. Which meant the police now had both motive and opportunity; if they nailed down a method, Davenport was dead. His only hope was if someone else—perhaps someone in these files—had an equally strong or stronger reason to kill Harrison.

There was a yellow square of cardboard sticking out from under a cabinet. Homer bent down and fished out a file, at once snapped away by Doris. But before she had quite managed to wrest it from his hands, he had caught the first half of the name at the top, which, since it was written last-name-first, was in fact the last name of the client it represented. But the single name was enough to send a chill up his spine—a name he loathed to find there, and almost kept to himself.

PAGLIA.

15

HOMER GREELEY AND SHELLY LOWENKOPF HAD TWO DIFFER-
ent ideas about whom they needed to interview next.
Shelly wanted to interview Helen Kaufman, and his
rationale made a great deal of sense, from a private
investigator's point of view. The local police were holding Howard Davenport because they felt he had to be
involved with the homicide in some way, either as the
perp himself or as an accomplice covering up for the
perpetrator. Their plan would be to sweat Davenport, to
lean on him, to hang him out to dry for a while. If he was
simply an accomplice after the fact, they would offer him
a deal, in which his testimony against the killer could
offset the penalty he would face for his own part in the
crime. Davenport did not seem to Homer a man who
could resist that sort of inducement; nobody likes to pay
the entire bill for somebody else's crime. If he refused
their deal, his silence itself would persuade them that
Davenport had indeed acted alone in murdering Henry
Harrison.

Shelly did not seem to think that Davenport had acted
alone. Homer wondered whether his partner's conviction came from their role as private investigators in
Davenport's employ, or from his usually sensitive assessment of the man's capabilities. Shelly was a fairly good

judge of what people could do and then cover up convincingly, the coverup being the hardest part of a murder committed in a burst of passion.

"Anyone can kill somebody," Shelly once told him. "But it takes a strong stomach to sit over it afterward, to watch the police come and go, asking questions, and not blurt out in horror what you've done, or bury your head in the bedding, hoping it'll all go away." Shelly had a good bullshit detector built into him which he used to measure the strain on a suspect who was either telling the truth or covering up. To lie and lie and lie to the law requires guts. Davenport might have worked himself up to hack away at Harrison, but the sustained stomach needed to keep a straight face afterward was more than Shelly believed Davenport could muster.

That left only the possibility that he had acted as an accomplice, lying to the police about a guest who passed through after Doris had gone to lunch. If there was such a guest, and Howard was lying, the police would get it out of him. The name at the top of their list, for the moment, was Helen Kaufman's, so it made sense that Shelly and Homer should go talk to her first. But Homer didn't want to talk to Kaufman first. He couldn't have explained why, but he felt a compelling urgency to talk first to the patient whose file he had recovered from under the cabinet in Mullens's office—a patient who might have been blackmailed by Harrison before his death. He wanted to get her out of the way, he told himself, to eliminate her from their list of possible suspects, since the very idea she might be involved made Homer's own stomach queasy.

He wanted to talk to Adrienne Paglia.

The fact that he wanted to made him uneasy; it was usually Shelly who allowed his judgment to be influenced by impulses, while Homer had always maintained a detachment that permitted him to follow a trail of hard evidence. Once you started paying attention to *feelings,* you were bound to find yourself sloshing through a swamp that stretched for miles and miles, like the

Everglades. There was an image that occurred to Homer whenever he thought about his emotions, a dream in which he was an escaped convict, lost among the cypresses, his chained feet disappearing in the white mist rising from the bog on all sides. Better not to dwell on it much, he decided, as he usually did. But he also wandered over to the ranch-house porch, where he had last found Adrienne Paglia.

She wasn't there, of course, but the receptionist at the desk was able to tell him that Ms. Paglia did in fact have a room in the original ranch house, which was now the eastern wing of the enlarged structure's first floor. Homer strolled through the airy central section of the building, where the lobby, staircase, and meeting rooms had been stocked with soda and candy machines and hidden wiring to accommodate the clinic's needs. He followed arrows to an older section of the building, identified simply as *Wing C* on the small lettered signs posted discreetly at corners and diverging hallways. Homer passed through a glass portal, and entered a humbler hallway of forest-green doors and plain wooden floors, lit by simple fixtures of frosted glass attached directly to the ceiling. This had once been the entire "ranch house," so named in acknowledgment of its architectural style rather than its function. As far as Homer could tell, there had never been a ranch on the grounds of the clinic, although the connotations of "ranch living" provided a motif Harrison had played up for all it was worth. You could induce people to live in quarters far less comfortable than their own bedrooms if they believed they were *roughing it*—especially when a promise of spiritual or emotional redemption resulted from the sacrifice. The clinic was a slick operation, at the very least, which Homer couldn't help admiring as he found his way to Adrienne's room.

She wasn't in it. He knocked on the door of 103, the room next door, even though a rolled magazine had been squeezed between the knob and the frame, the September issue of *Psychology Today*. No one answered—of course, Homer realized, when he saw that the mailing label read *N. Zapotnik*. But at the end of the hall, just before the tiny back porch at the exit, was a picture window overlooking a patch of tall grass that did not seem to interest the team of groundskeepers who kept most of the site manicured and in flower. In the tall grass was a blue-and-white checkered tablecloth or blanket, and on the cloth was a slender blonde in shiny red toreador pants and a sleeveless blouse, stretched out on her stomach, one knee bent behind her, eating a chocolate éclair and reading a book. On the grass beside her was her wind-up Victrola, which was playing an old red 78 that Homer could not hear; but a bird evidently could. It crept out of the tall grass and hopped up to the edge of her blue-and-white checked blanket. It was a house sparrow—a male, by the wing bars and black patches on his brown breast and throat. Adrienne did not seem to notice her winged visitor, but tossed a pinch of yellow cake from her éclair over her shoulder, which landed a foot in front of the bird. He hopped forward, poked at it, and retreated, cautious of her. But she didn't even glance his way, and he skittered in to claim it. Only then did Adrienne seem to notice him, tilting her head to one side, watching him through glittering eyes. Framed in the window, she seemed to Homer a fairy-tale princess, young and pretty, and at peace with the world around her.

He must have stirred with longing himself, because the next moment she looked his way, saw him behind the glass, and smiled, waving at him. There seemed to be no way to make her stop, short of waving back; and when he did, she gestured toward the exit at the end of the hallway, for him to go around and join her. Homer shook his head, but she nodded more vigorously, and again he saw no alternative but to do as she demanded. When he passed through the exit door, he heard the music from her phonograph. It was the "Sleeping Beauty Waltz," which had been playing the last time he saw her, on the porch. He walked over to the stack of records beside the

Victrola and found that, yes, they were indeed all Disney soundtracks.

"Quite a collection you have here."

"Thank you," she said, beaming sunlight. She swung her foot a couple of times in the sweet-smelling air. "They don't really sound right without the scratches from these old machines."

He listened and thought he agreed with her—the hissing of the old 78 made the music more distant, nostalgic, and magical. Although the effect of the girl herself might have contributed to that also. He took a deep breath and let it out.

"This is a pretty spot."

"I like it. They put most guests in the cabins, so no one's around most of the time to bother you."

"Who uses the other rooms?"

"Staff, mostly. Neela was next door. Some guests who come back often, or stay for long periods of time."

"Which one are you?"

She shrugged. "I'm in for the stretch. My father thinks it's summer camp."

Homer wondered what horrible secret could be hidden in the file he had found among Harrison's private collection—could this girl really have developed a compromising secret already? Then he noticed her wrists as she slipped a stalk of yellow grass into her book to hold her place, and knew at least what her secret must include.

"Are they helping you any?"

She blinked and looked away for an instant, taken unaware by this rather indelicate advance. But she recovered and even managed to meet his eyes again a few brief flutters later. "Who am I to say? They zap me with their machines, and I lie in the sun. Which one do you think makes me feel better?"

Homer looked up, letting the afternoon sun fall on his face, watching it play off the shuttered windows of the rooms lining the eastern wing of the ranch house. He blinked a few times but felt its warmth on his cheeks. A breeze blew through the tall grass, and one of the birds peeked out from between the stalks in which it had taken refuge upon his arrival. Homer knelt, picked up an uneaten morsel of éclair, and tossed it.

The bird fled back into the stalks, and Adrienne laughed. "You've got the right idea," she said, "but not the touch." She pushed another chunk of yellow cake between his fingertips, took his hand by the knuckles, and swung it so that the released cake landed a foot in front of the spot where the bird had disappeared. A moment later, it reappeared, tilting its head sideways to keep an eye on Homer, and then snatched up the piece of cake, bearing it off into the grass.

"I think I've got the hang of it now," said Homer, swinging his arm in the arc she had used, like a rookie pitcher taking instruction from an experienced coach.

But she didn't offer him another piece of éclair, stuffing the remaining end, about an inch and a half long, into her mouth, where it filled her cheeks until she chewed it and swallowed it down. She patted her mouth delicately with a cloth napkin which matched the blue-and-white checked blanket, and then opened her eyes in surprise as a silent, ladylike belch escaped her.

"Excuse me!"

The thought of it might have repelled him, but the sight of it enchanted him, and Homer smiled, forgiving her, as the bird reappeared from under its stalk. The movement of Adrienne's head as she turned toward the bullfinch made her short blond curls bounce, and when she looked back at Homer and grinned, the light played among them so invitingly he nearly reached his own hand in, too. But there was something about her that prevented him, a frailty that was more than the skinniness of her limbs and torso. He felt as if she were a cartoon, or a reflection in water, which might dissolve into rings of color and light if he reached over and actually touched her. He wanted to avoid doing anything that might disrupt their moment together. But he remembered his job, the purpose of his visit, and the corners of his mouth must have strained.

"What is it?" she asked.

"It's the reason I'm here," he said glumly. It was supposed to serve as a warning to her, of what might be coming next. But she didn't notice or ignored the threat, and plunged ahead just as gaily.

"Aren't you here to see me?"

"In a way."

"What sort of way?"

He would have liked to reply that the thought of her had stuck in his mind since Wednesday, and that he had come back to find out who she was—who this magical creature might be. But that would not have allowed for the kind of questions he felt he needed to ask. So Homer dropped the big word, which broke the fine skin of their shining moment as he knew it would.

"A professional way."

She sat up, shielding her eyes. "Investigating . . . what? The willful misrepresentation of medical science?"

"Looking into a murder."

"Here?"

It seemed ridiculous to him, too. "Dr. Harrison. I'm afraid he's been killed. And the police believe—"

"Oh, him!" cried Adrienne, resettling herself with a burst of relief and disinterest. "Well, of course, he was murdered! The only surprise is that it took someone so long."

Homer waited for her to explain, but she had apparently said all she intended to say. He squatted alongside her blanket and asked, "You expected this to happen?"

"If you knew Henry Harrison, you'd have expected it, too," she replied. "The man was a beast to everyone who knew him. It's time somebody let him know."

"I doubt he knows anything, now."

"Do you?" she asked with more interest. "I don't understand why people are willing to *doubt* the existence of life after death, on no more evidence than there is to prove that *there is* life after death. I mean, you're pretty certain you doubt it, aren't you?"

"Until somebody shows me otherwise."

"But nobody has to show you that there *isn't* anything after death, do they? You're willing to take that on faith."

"I don't take too much on faith," Homer admitted slowly. "That's really why I'm here. I have a few questions to ask you. About a file of yours that was found among Harrison's private papers."

"Of mine?"

"That's right."

"Oh," she said, and then again more quietly. "Oh."

"I'm sorry," he said.

"All right." A pause. "Go ahead then."

"You were Harrison's private patient?"

"For a day. My father knows him and sent me for a consult. What an awful hour that was! Not a single question about what I was feeling—only whether I ate grains for breakfast, and how many times a week I relieve my bowels. I couldn't stand the man, but Daddy sure liked what he heard—which shouldn't have been anything at all if Harrison had respected confidentiality, right? But he didn't, of course. My father had to go to Europe again on business this summer, and didn't know what to do with me—as he so charmingly informed me. So when Harrison said he'd 'admit' me here, and keep me alive this summer, Daddy wrote him a nice fat check—the solution to most crises in Harrison's discipline. And the dirty deed was done."

"You're . . . what? Twenty-four?"

"Six. Sweet man."

"So why did your father have anything to say—" He didn't know how to phrase it exactly.

"About where I spent the summer? Because when I did this"—she turned her wrists so the inside showed—"I was released from the hospital under his supervision. There's probably a legal way to challenge it, but he's the one with all the lawyers anyway. What would I use to hire one? It's not as if I had any big plans of my own for the summer."

"Did Harrison ever threaten to use your suicide attempts against you?"

"Why would he need to?" She laughed bitterly. "I've been a very good girl since I'm here. And Daddy's already written the big check, so what else could he have wanted from me?" Homer did not respond verbally, but she met his gaze and said, "Nothing like that. Ever. His lust was for power over people, control of their minds. If he'd ever asked, I might have done it, just to get something to hold over him. But he never did, and I'd never have suggested the idea myself."

Her answer reassured Homer, more than he could explain by the details of the case. But he wanted to be absolutely sure. "And there's no other reason anyone might find why you would want Harrison dead."

"I can think of several reasons."

"You can?"

"I told you. He was a miserable human being. He treated his staff like Malificent . . . Cruella De Vil . . . or Count Dracula. Those staffers are my friends."

"But you wouldn't kill for them?"

"Wouldn't I? My father would be happy to hear that." The idea seemed to appeal to her, as a step up from suicide. "How exactly did I manage it?"

"You're not a suspect yet."

"Then why are you asking these questions?"

It was the one Homer hadn't answered yet, for himself or for anyone else. He felt he couldn't go into the details of their investigation thus far, and felt even queasier about the idea of exploring his own motivation. She seemed to sense this, and it inspired her.

"Is it just me?"

"I'm sure you're innocent."

"I wouldn't go that far, myself."

"Adrienne," he said finally, "just tell me . . . you didn't have anything to do with the murder."

159

He watched her in silence as she gathered her things and went back toward her room. She clomped up the wooden back steps, and turned to him at the door, where she gave him a soft, wry smile. "I didn't have anything to do with the murder."

It was only after she went in that he realized she had said precisely what he had asked her to say.

16

SHELLY LOWENKOPF HAD STARTED IN A DIFFERENT PLACE IN HIS analysis of whom to see next. Their problem, he felt, centered on *opportunity:* Nobody but Howard Davenport seemed to have had the chance to murder Henry Harrison. This was a serious problem, Shelly recognized, carrying lots of weight with the police, who would reason, quite reasonably, that if all other possibilities are eliminated, whatever remains, no matter how unlikely, must be the truth. Since no one could have entered the Doctor's private office without Davenport's acquiescence, their client had to be guilty of conspiracy at least. It was possible he acted alone to commit the crime: If Harrison was blackmailing him, Davenport certainly had a motive. And motive, opportunity, and method were all the police required. The fact that Harrison kept a Minoan ax in his office supplied sufficient method. Howard's easy access to the Doctor's private office, together with a threat of blackmail hanging over his head, meant the police had a neat case waiting for the prosecutor to bring before a court.

The only ones who had reason to doubt it, in fact, were Shelly and Homer, and not because of any inconsistency among the facts. They had a client in Davenport, and that relationship itself gave them cause to champion his innocence. They did not know for sure that he was free of culpability for the murder, but their prior arrangement supplied a reason for them to look into the matter more skeptically. This was quite different from their usual procedure on the force—it made them uneasy to be working this way. But they had confidence in one another, and their own determination to discover the truth, and neither of them ever doubted that the other would come forward with whatever evidence he uncovered, damning or exonerating. It was just that they gave a special emphasis to any effort that might uncover the latter, although they each had different ideas where this evidence might be found.

The names of clients in Harrison's special file would have made an excellent place to start, but Marsha Mullens was not willing to divulge this information, and Doris Juniper planned to make sure those instructions were respected. Homer had caught a single name on a file under the cabinet and felt they should pursue that clue immediately. Shelly, for his part, had gone to considerable lengths to persuade the police that Helen Kaufman could not have committed the murder, and now felt an urgency to convince himself. For that reason, when Homer went off to follow his sneak-a-peek clue, Shelly headed off in another direction, hoping to confirm his own argument.

He marshalled his questions as he headed for Dr. Kaufman's office, in a bungalow that had been joined with another one like it to make a suite of two consulting rooms with a common waiting area. There were a couch and two armchairs and tables provided with magazines —one magazine to a table, with pictures of houses with ferns on the covers. There was a desk in the waiting room, but no secretary or receptionist; instead, a looseleaf notebook sat on the desk, open to a blank page, with a white card standing behind it on which a neat, feminine hand had printed, *Please sign in and be seated. Thank you.* Shelly thought this instruction was intended for patients, but did not wish to lose his place. So he signed the book, found a seat and a copy of *Outdoor Decorating,* and waited.

And waited. Neither door opened in the first half hour, and he thought he might have come in at the wrong moment—there were still twenty minutes to the hour. But thirty minutes later, when the hour had expired and ten minutes more besides, and still no one had emerged from the inner offices, Lowenkopf stood, walked over to the one with the nameplate reading *Kaufman,* and rolled a fist to knock . . . but hesitated, reluctant to disturb the session beyond the severe white door—

When a cheerful voice from the doorway behind him boomed, "Nobody's home."

Shelly turned and saw a young woman in a gray sweat shirt that read *CCNY* and matching sweat pants, with straight blond hair pulled back in a rubber-banded ponytail, and a pair of fat textbooks under one arm. She walked right past him and opened Dr. Kaufman's office door without pausing to knock. When Shelly peeked in behind her, he saw a comfortable couch against one wall, two overstuffed armchairs in brocaded florals, a desk and coffee table in matching shades of pale blond wood. But there was no patient lying on the couch or sitting up in angst in either chair, and Kaufman herself was nowhere in sight.

The girl with the ponytail dumped the two books in a pile at the foot of Kaufman's bookcase, and walked past Lowenkopf once again on her way out the door. Before she had crossed the outer office, Shelly called after her.

"Where is she?"

"Dr. Kaufman? Or Dr. Mullens?"

"Mullens is in the ranch house, isn't she? A big office on the second floor?"

"They moved her already? I didn't know that." And the girl with the ponytail pushed open the other door, to the adjoining office. It was more richly appointed, with a better carpet on the floor and heavier wood furnishings. The windows had curtains instead of blinds, and the titles of the books included the word *pharmacology* more often than *personality.* But Mullens's office was clearly in a state of transition, with half-filled cartons all over the floor, and the desk top missing its blotter.

"Looks like it."

"They don't waste time with the big cheese, do they? It's another story with us mice. I've been waiting for a window shade in my room for two weeks already and they haven't managed to get around to that."

"What about Kaufman?"

The girl laughed, and her ponytail bobbed behind her head. "They couldn't have moved her out already."

"Why would they want to . . . move her out?"

"You haven't heard?"

"Why don't you tell me?"

"I think I'll let her tell you herself. That way, I won't be passing any misinformation."

"I'll take whatever kind of information I can get."

"Not from me," she said, grinning, and was gone.

Shelly stepped out onto the porch and watched her bob back up the hill. *An intern,* he decided—under Kaufman's supervision. But she never said where Helen was, did she? She knew she wasn't in the office, which meant she probably wasn't coming in; Shelly sighed and began the trudge up the hill to the ranch house. He could see how people lost weight at this clinic, treatment or no: trudging up and down the hill from the Research Building to the ranch house would take a few pounds off anyone. And if the diet they fed you was low in fat, and the program kept you moving, it didn't take a behaviorist genius to accomplish a little reduction in the waistline. It was in the lungs that he felt it himself—from his cigars, no doubt. But he hadn't had one of those since arriving, had he?

He didn't fare much better at Kaufman's private room. It took him ten minutes and a call to Mullens to convince the clerk at the registration desk that she could in fact reveal to him Helen Kaufman's private room number in the ranch house. But when he found it, and knocked on the door, there was no answer there, either. He stood in the hallway for a moment, working out the pattern in the carpet, reluctant to go back downstairs and face the receptionist again, who had made it quite plain the first time that her shift was about to end. Nor did he relish the idea of trooping down the hill again, to see if she kept a lab in the Research Building as well. There had to be some place at the clinic where all the staff schedules were kept; that place was most likely to be in the ranch house. So Shelly decided to spare himself a trip down the stairs again, and wandered over to the office in which they had found Marsha Mullens earlier in the day. He was in luck—the door was open. But Marsha Mullens was not inside. Instead, he found the girl with the ponytail again, in front of a glowing terminal, studying the screen. He rapped on the open door.

"Remember me?"

She looked up and nodded. "Sure. From Helen's office."

"And from her room. Where she also isn't."

"Can't find her, huh?"

"Not by myself. I'm Shelly Lowenkopf. I'm sort of looking into things for Dr. Mullens."

"A spy?"

"An investigator."

"Too bad," said the blonde. "I liked the sound of a spy. They're all *investigators* around here."

"Really? What do the others investigate?"

"Anything they can get a grant for," she said with a frown that lit up her face nonetheless.

"What's your name?" Shelly asked her.

"Elizabeth Gunnarson."

"Liz?"

"I like Liza. But I'll answer to anything in the ballpark —Lisa, Lizzie, Eliza, even Betty. If you're nice."

He was trying to be. "You an intern?"

"Even worse—a staff aide. That's a full-time job somewhere below grub in the pecking order."

"What do you have to do?"

"Whatever the shrinks tell me to do. Return books to their shelves. Delete personal files."

"When somebody's checking out?"

"I can't tell you about that, remember? Ask Helen."

"I would if I could find her."

She breathed an exasperated sigh, which set her pony-tail bobbing. "You don't know *anything,* do you?"

"Anything like what?"

"Like what everyone else knows."

"If everyone really knows it, it can't be a secret, can it? Tell me."

"Everyone knows where Helen goes . . . lunchtime, for instance. And on nights when she can't sleep."

"Where's that?"

"To the lake."

"You think she's there now? At the lake?"

"Not at the lake. *At the lake.*"

"Which means?"

"At Ralph Kotlowicz's cabin."

This information did not come from Liza, but was delivered in a deeper voice by Marsha Mullens herself, who arrived at that moment with an armload of files from the staircase to the third floor. She moved past Shelly and the girl and dropped the files on her new desk, sinking into the springs of her new chair with a moan of fatigue and disgust. She laid a heavy hand on the top file, and then cast a sidelong glance at Lowenkopf that seemed to ask, *If you can't find Helen Kaufman, how on earth will you find Henry's killer?* But she never put the question into words, or he never gave her the chance, because with a nod for Liza Gunnarson and an uneasy glance at Mullens, Shelly found his way out the door.

By the time he found the cabin, he knew that all the rumormongers had been right on target. Even before he entered, he knew that Helen was inside. A dolly loaded with taped-up cartons leaned crookedly on the roots of a tree that broke through the ground in front of the cabin. The cartons were labeled in black laundry marker: *Files, Tapes,* and more *Files.* From inside the cabin he heard a woman's voice rise to meet an objection.

"No! There is no way for me to continue living here now. I'm sorry, but there isn't."

"It's just a job," a male voice responded, with inexorable logic. "You wouldn't be moving out on me if you were leaving any other job, would you?"

"It's not any other job, Ralph."

Shelly hesitated to knock on the door. He didn't want to disturb them in the middle of a fight, but he didn't want to seem to be eavesdropping either. The eavesdropping itself, however, didn't bother him, so he waited, trying to make up his mind about knocking, while he listened.

"I know—it's a very important position. But in the end, Helen, it's just the way you make your living. And that should never be allowed to interfere—"

"It's not just a living, Ralph."

"A career, then."

"A commitment. I'm responsible for the careers and fragile egos of a dozen interns in this place. Who, like it or not, view me as something of a role model."

"So . . . what're you saying, now? There's something wrong with living with me?"

"We've been through all that, Ralph. And it's not relevant here. All I'm trying to suggest is that it wouldn't help their professional development to watch me try to hang on somewhere I'm no longer wanted."

"Damn their professional development!"

"How could I?"

"Then I'll quit, too."

"I didn't quit. And you can't. Where on earth would you ever find another arrangement like this? It suits you to a tee, you told me, and I always thought you were right. I'd never be able to forgive myself if I cost you this life."

"Then stay with me here."

"I can't! I can't continue to live on these grounds now. I'm sorry."

A pause. She had him coming and going—limited by all the restraints she felt on her personal and professional options. Which were not all that separate, it seemed to Ralph. He said, "I'm sorry, too. Because I thought what we had between us was more important than Harrison—

or anyone—yes, even more important than your damned position. Forgive me if I took you at your word. Even if it was one you delivered only at night, and only just before climax."

A mean shot—and she felt it. "I never meant to hurt you by it," she said quietly.

At that moment the door opened suddenly in Lowenkopf's face, leaving him to confront the angry countenance of Ralph Kotlowicz. The maintenance director's eyes narrowed as if to say, *What do you want here?* But he knew that Shelly wanted Helen, just as everyone had always wanted Helen since the beginning of his love affair with her. Ralph just frowned and muttered to Shelly as he elbowed past him, "She's in there. For now."

Dr. Kaufman was staring at him as he entered, tilting back her head so that the tears could not escape her lids and run down her fine cheekbones. She was wearing a pleated navy skirt with matching short jacket and a pale ivory shirt beneath it; discreet pearls were pinned to her ears, and she wore a gold band with a pearl in it on her marriage finger, which she now studied, and rotated, so the pearl disappeared into the underside of her hand, and then reappeared again. *From Ralph?* Lowenkopf wondered and felt sorry for her. She must have picked up his sympathy on her therapist's radar, because she dropped her left hand to her side, concealing the ring in a pleat of her skirt, and straightened her back to face him with her professional posture and expression. He was wearing the name-pin from his registration packet, and she scrutinized the red lettering on the plastic gold plaque before speaking.

"Mr. Lowenkopf? Is there something I can do for you here?"

"Do I understand you're leaving the clinic?"

"That's not something I can discuss with a patient at the clinic, I'm afraid."

"Don't be afraid. I'm not really a patient here."

"No? What are you? A therapist?"

"I'm a private investigator. Dr. Mullens has author-ized me to look into the death of Henry Harrison."

She paled. "Henry's . . . dead?"

"Didn't you know?"

"How could I?"

"The police have come and gone. So has the coroner. It's all over the grounds by now."

"I've been caught up in my own tragedy, today. I haven't been paying attention to that sort of news."

"What about Ralph?"

"He never tolerates gossip."

"Take it from me officially, Doctor. Your boss is dead."

Kaufman blinked—and then a grim expression worked its way across her face. "He isn't my boss anymore."

Shelly nodded. "He's nobody's nothing, now."

"That isn't what I meant. As of this morning, I'm no longer an employee of the Care Clinic."

"I couldn't help overhearing something about that. You've resigned your post?"

She shook her head. "I was fired."

"By Harrison?"

"About three hours ago."

Just before he was murdered. "That may have been his last act as a human being."

"He was never one of those, Mr. Lowenkopf."

"Never?"

"You're right, I shouldn't say that. He must've been human once—as a boy, probably. By the time I met him, it had all been drained from him. Programmed out, he would have said—proudly! There must have been some awful withholding in the Harrison house in the bad old days."

"He treated you badly? As an administrator?"

"He treated everyone badly. As a person! And like most true bastards, he was hardest on people with the least ability to defend themselves."

"Interns?"

"Including them, yes. But not restricted to them. It

could have been anyone he had a little power over. If you had a flat tire at the side of the road, and couldn't find a jack in your trunk, and Henry came tooling by in his Porsche, he'd stop beside you, and give you a grin—ever see his smile? But he'd keep his engine running. And when you'd got through the pleasantries, and worked around to asking to borrow his jack—that's when he'd shake his head sadly, and say he'd like to help you, but couldn't spare his valuable time on your petty problems, sorry. And he'd make sure you ate his dust."

"Is that a metaphor? Or a true story?"

"Who knows? It didn't happen to me, if that's what you're asking. He tells it himself, about himself—again, proudly. To let you know what you're dealing with."

Shelly noticed her use of the present tense, but chose not to call it to her attention. "But you didn't run when you heard that story the first time?"

"He doesn't reveal himself the first time, Mr. Lowenkopf—not if he wants something from you. And at the time he recruited me to work in this place, he wanted something from me. I had earned a reputation as a clinical supervisor, and had excellent connections at the best local schools—the ones with the sharpest students looking for clinical internships. He wanted to use my reputation to establish this place, along with his own well-known research. So he wooed me, and I came. The formula worked—we soon had all the interns we could handle. I was supervising them all, in their clinical practice as well as their research, they were told, although I had only agreed to take on the clinical end. Some of them managed to find mentors themselves for their research projects—Ray Singh was always willing to lend a hand with statistics, and a few of them even worked up the temerity to approach the Medical Medea."

"Who?"

"Marsha Mullens. Who feels research on human subjects should be done by M.D.'s exclusively, but would deign every now and then to show a poor psychology student how a medical student would be expected to perform."

"You know this from—what? Personal experience? Reports from your interns?"

"Adjacent offices, with a waiting room in common. You can learn an awful lot about a person from watching her patients wait for her."

"And Dr. Harrison?"

"He never showed the slightest interest in anybody else's research. Except that it be done, of course, and published in the right journals, so that the reputation of the clinic was continually renewed. But as far as helping anyone—and I mean residents and other members of the full-time staff as well as interns—forget it."

"He took an interest in one girl, didn't he? What was that, a sexual conquest?"

"I can't imagine who you mean."

"The girl who threw herself into the lake last week."

"Neela Zapotnik?"

"I think that's her name."

Kaufman smiled, the thought a genuine relief from the cares that crowded her thinking.

"There was nothing going on between Neela and Henry! You can take that, officially, from me. She's a sweet girl, very bright and careful in her work, but she hasn't got what it takes to interest Henry Harrison! He likes women . . . with presence," and she threw back her shoulders and rotated them, to suggest the kind of physical presence she meant to suggest. "Cheap, I'd say, but sure to provoke a response. Just like Henry himself."

"Then why did he invite Zapotnik to lunch?"

"You heard about that?"

He nodded. Ralph might have turned a deaf ear to the gossip that swirls around any small community, but Lowenkopf knew better than to ignore it. "You were there, too, weren't you?"

"I was there for the public part of the lunch, when Henry put on a show of manners. I was not there for the personal part, when he did what he really intended."

"Which was?"

She hesitated, then said in disgust, "You want the truth?"

He shrugged. *What else?*

Her mouth twisted in a violent scowl of pity and hatred. "To tear the poor girl to pieces."

172

17

"ARE YOU TELLING ME," LOWENKOPF ASKED HELEN KAUF-man, "that Harrison invited Neela Zapotnik out to his personal gazebo for lunch last week—just to browbeat her after you'd left them alone together?"

"Let me show you something," Helen said, instead of replying to his question. She searched among the three cartons of books and personal belongings she had packed in Ralph's cabin until she found a hand-embroidered sampler in a plain frame of brown wood and reflecting glass. It read: *The office of the scholar is to cheer, to raise, and to guide men by showing them facts amid appearances. Ralph Waldo Emerson, The American Scholar.*"

"Inspiring," Shelly said.

"It was a gift," Helen told him, "intended I think to help me fight the good fight when it came to our treatment of interns around here. I showed this to Henry once, in a fit of absolute frustration. Do you know what he said to me?"

She paused as if really expecting an answer.

"No," he said.

"'I'm no scholar, then'—which were the truest four words he ever uttered, in print or in person. But you see, that had always been an obsession with me."

"Scholarship?"

"In Emerson's sense—enlightening the world. I'd rather he said *men and women* instead of just *men,* but the basic idea is right to the point: We're supposed to help people by banishing the fears that lead to biases, by discovering the truth. To me, that includes protecting the next generation of scholars, too, guiding and cheering them on. But Henry—well, he was just what they need protection *from.*"

"What's that?"

"The exercise of authority in the service of vanity. The abuse of power to gratify the ego of the supposed scholar, at the expense of his students."

Shelly gave her a moment to be more specific, but when she refrained from explicating herself, he asked, "What exactly did Harrison do to her over lunch?"

"He talked about the prospects of her career."

"Were they really that grim?"

"No," she said with animation, "they weren't, really. She's not the sort of intern we usually get here, Mr. Lowenkopf, that much is true—not the top one percent of her class in a major research university. Neela is a local girl, who grew up in the area and used to see the clinic when she came to bring her mother lunches and messages from home."

"Her mother was a patient here?"

"A member of the staff. Who was very proud of her daughter, when Neela applied for an internship and was accepted here. I had to convince Henry to take her in, despite her school and academic standing. I succeeded only because of the incredibly high regard in which she held him personally—her project was a replication of his research, you know, the business with birds in the first chapter of his book on Joseph. But he never liked her, and once he saw her, his biases returned in full force. He wanted to get rid of her all along, and I guess the opportunity finally presented itself when I had to leave them alone to go lead a supervisory group."

That was her guilt talking, Shelly suspected, from the way her eyes looked down and up at him when she spoke about their lunch. "What exactly did he say?"

"They had a discussion, apparently, about her research project, which was modeled on some early work of Henry's—never a great idea, but she *admired* him so, and I guess this was her way of emulating him. And he responded in typical Harrison fashion. According to what I have heard, he told her that her design was hopelessly flawed—beyond repair. And he didn't stop there. He decided to use the occasion to tell her what he thought of her talents as a researcher and as a clinician in other respects. He told her the report he was planning to submit on her work at the clinic would recommend against allowing her to continue on to the doctorate; he said she had none of the necessary instincts, or intelligence, or habits of mind that were essential to success in his discipline. He said, in short, that she would never make a good psychologist, or even a middling one, since she would never be able to complete a decent training program."

Shelly whistled. "Are your student evaluations always so brutally honest?"

"This was not a regular evaluation! She wasn't due to be assessed for another month at least, and Henry is not the person responsible for making evaluations!"

She bit her lip.

Shelly said, "As director of internships, wouldn't that have been your job?"

"You bet it would! And he knew it—Henry and I had been all over that ground. I won't debate whether his judgments were accurate, or even fair—let's take the high road and assume they were his genuinely honest opinions. It was still absolutely reprehensible of him to make them without consultation, and to deliver them to unsuspecting Neela over lunch!"

"Without giving her a chance to prepare herself?"

" 'How could she have prepared herself?' That's what Henry asked me, when I went to see him about it. So he knew the effect he would have on her, he understood what he was doing to her. Imagine if you can, Mr. Lowenkopf, hearing those words from a man you've admired since you were a little girl. From a man whose judgment you've revered!"

She shook her head, still disgusted, and Shelly imagined the mood in which she must have approached Harrison when she heard what he had done to Neela. No wonder the poor girl threw herself into the lake! Helen must have drawn the same conclusion and gone to accuse Harrison of—what? Negligence? Or something worse? Shelly wondered just how far Helen Kaufman would be willing to go to protect her interns.

"Sounds like a son of a bitch," he said.

"He was that and more. The man was incapable of feeling for anyone beyond himself. And I mean *anyone,* period. Have you heard about his son?"

"Harrison's son? I didn't know he had one."

"That's just what the boy is hoping for! He works as a laborer in those oil tanks stretching out for miles near Bayonne. Trying to make his face black enough so that no one notices the family resemblance! He's tried everything he can think of to get away from his father—wouldn't take a penny from him. But his old man stuck it to him, anyway."

"Stuck what to him?"

"Who do you think is going to inherit this place?"

"I didn't know anyone inherited a clinic," he said. "Don't they belong to corporations or something?"

"And corporations belong to their stockholders, and who do you think held the lion's share of stock in this one? Henry Harrison, of course. So now that he's gone, that stock will pass into the hands of his heir, which will doubtlessly be his son. Because if Henry took the trouble to write a will, it would only have been to make sure his ex-wife's family doesn't get a penny of it back."

"Back?"

"Who do you think had the money to open this place? Not an academic psychologist at a state university."

"Harrison's wife staked him? Or her family?"

"Neither, willingly. My understanding is that she refused. As long as she was alive."

"She's dead?"

"By thirty-eight Seconals. From his laboratory. Must've forgotten to lock up one night, huh? Or secure the safety cap."

"You're not suggesting Harrison might have—"

"I'm not suggesting anything," she said. "He didn't mash them into her mashed potatoes or anything. But there are lots of ways of killing somebody, aren't there?"

"Unhappy marriage?"

"After what I've told you—what do you think?"

"You can never tell."

"Sometimes you can tell. As soon as she got to know him, Susan sunk into a deep depression. It was in trying to bring her around, without having to confront any of his own emotional baggage, that Henry discovered behaviorism. Not that it helped her any."

"You've got to feel sorry for him on that score."

"Of course you do. And I did—we all did. That was when he did his most effective recruiting. He wore his grief on his professional sleeve, Mr. Lowenkopf. Turning down his offer meant twisting the knife of his wife's suicide. He played it for all it was worth, believe me."

"You don't think he loved her?"

Helen sighed deeply, and cast an eye in the direction of the door through which Ralph Kotlowicz had passed. "Who knows what that man was capable of feeling? I'll tell you what he would've said to your question. He would have stuck out his chest and insisted, 'Certainly not.'"

Shelly thought fleetingly of Ruth, his residual feelings for his first wife, beneath the years of later resentment; and he pressed his question in disbelief. "He would have denied *ever* loving his wife?"

Helen's thoughts were evidently with Ralph already; she had to call herself back to respond to Shelly's follow-up question. "He would have considered it a meaningless issue. Henry Harrison did not believe in love."

"Of anyone? For anyone?"

"You'd have to ask Marsha about that."

"Dr. Mullens? And Henry Harrison? Was there something between them?"

"I told you," said Helen. "You learn a lot about somebody, watching her waiting room."

Ralph Kotlowicz believed in love—as he believed in all of the feelings in his gut. *What else do we have to guide us?* he thought. Hadn't Emerson in *Self-Reliance* encouraged him to "Trust thyself; every heart vibrates to that iron string"? And the strings of Ralph's heart sang out one song—Helen!—in a clear and constant harmony. What did all of her analyses measure up to, when set beside the thumping of his ancient heart whenever she walked into a room? "Trust your emotion," Emerson advised him. "Leave your theory as Joseph left his coat in the hand of the harlot, and flee." He couldn't find the harlot in their situation, but Helen was fleeing, wasn't she? Yet fleeing from him, not toward him—there was her mistake. She was too susceptible to anticipated consequences, the opinions of her professional colleagues. What difference did it make if all of her psychologists disapproved, so long as they loved one another with passion and consideration? He and Helen belonged together—Ralph knew it in his heart, and wasn't that the only place that counted?

He grunted, straining against the wrench.

And yet he couldn't shake the memory of a line from a later essay, *Experience,* in which Emerson acknowledged the value of collective wisdom, in observing that "The individual is always mistaken." So what was Ralph to believe here? Trust in himself, in his own emotion, his undeniable feelings for her? Or accept the judgment of Helen's colleagues, privileged as it seemed to be by the older and wiser Ralph W.?

It was with these thoughts that Ralph occupied the main part of his attention, whistling while he worked to free a lug nut on the underside of the boat dock. The nut held in place a rotting board that had lost most of its central section, so that small heels would slip from time to time on its slippery surface into the space between the boards on either side of it. He had tried to pry it loose when he first noticed it, but the lug nut had rusted like a red-brown bathing cap over the bolt that held the board in place; it was a job that required his biggest wrenches, and one that would require him to wade in hip-deep under the creaky pier, keeping his wrench out of the water lapping at his elbows. He had put it off until now, when he had enough on his mind to keep him from minding the chill, and he could take out his frustration on that damned nut.

His biggest wrench was too big for it and the smallest of the three Eduardo had brought him was too small, but the middle-size wrench fit just right, and he left the two spares on the grass at the foot of the pier as he strained against the rusted nut overhead, both hands gripping the long shaft just below the opposite head, pulling toward himself with gratifying effort. He was a handyman, not a maintenance director—another bullshit title! In the summer of 1842, Thoreau had worked as Emerson's handyman in Concord, and Ralph reaffirmed his affinity for that unsociable man. Like Thoreau, Kotlowicz disapproved of much of what he saw around him, and particularly of the extent to which his own happiness seemed to depend on the men and women of the clinic's professional ranks. Why did their opinions matter so much to Helen? "Who likes to have a dapper phrenologist pronouncing on his fortunes?" Emerson had asked in *Fate,* and Ralph considered the head-bump readers of the nineteenth century as the unacknowledged great-grandfathers of the shock-zappers, pill-pushers, and all-around licensed brain-fuckers whose misused machines he unplugged and rewired day after day.

He was starting to resent the place, he admitted to himself, and wondered how much of that feeling had been buried while he and Helen had made a little piece of heaven for themselves in the rural backyard of New Jersey. It made no sense that Harrison's firing of her would stick even after his death—Doris would have begun the paperwork, and notified Marsha Mullens, but how clear was it really that Mullens would in fact be appointed director of the clinic, and choose to respect Harrison's emotionally charged decision? Harrison himself would probably have reconsidered, had he lived; it seemed to Ralph ridiculous that his temper tantrum be respected as a last wish, while so much of what the man really cared about would no doubt be dismantled. Every psychologist Ralph had ever met seemed to have a different idea of how to help patients, what the clinic could hope to accomplish, and what was beyond their resources. So why was it necessary to lose the one resource that made life meaningful to him?

A frog splashed into the green water behind him.

He would have to speak to Marsha—hadn't he saved her behind on more than one occasion, when the electrical circuits in her lab lit up like a Christmas tree? Ralph thought he could persuade her, indirectly, to reconsider Helen's place at the clinic in light of her evident accomplishments there. Her interns would all rally to her cause. The real obstacle, he knew, would not be Marsha, but—as usual—Helen herself.

He had advised her to sit tight, to give up her rounds and other responsibilities for a while, if she liked, and kill a few days or even weeks as his guest in the cabin by the lake; to give Harrison's board time to decide who would be running the clinic, and to give that person some time to realize how important Helen Kaufman was to the soul of the place. But Helen had insisted, as she always did, about everything, that her way was the only way to respond. And her way now was to leave. So she was packing up her things at his cabin, even as he worked on the rusted lug nut, which was not turning, even with the full weight of his anger set against it. Ralph stopped struggling for a moment, withdrew his wrench from the stubborn lug nut, and contemplated the dark brown underside of the pier for a moment, listening to the water lap at the posts supporting its uneven boards. The light on the lake was beautiful now, winking as it shifted with the afternoon wind, drifting off from his hip boots toward the far shore. He allowed the wrench in his hand to drop for a moment, until it touched the surface of the lake, and then lifted it out—each drop of water on it reflected the greens of the lake lined by his home forest, the cloud-washed blue of the sky, the white-hot yellow of the sun straining through the dock overhead. His other wrench glistened in the sand at the foot of the dock.

He peered at the glint in the sand. One wrench? He had the second in his hand . . .

Where was his third? He remembered trying it first, finding it overlarge, and dropping it with a clink against the smallest one. That had been about twenty minutes before. Had anyone come by who might have lifted it? He couldn't remember seeing anyone, but he had been staring at the nut on the underside of the pier—then through the slats, as he tried to reach it—concentrating on something else entirely. He cursed himself silently for his inattention, focusing all the frustration he had been feeling on the loss of it. It was his largest wrench, and although it rarely fit any nut he had to turn, the mere possession of it had given him a sense of control over the machinery of the clinic. Without it, Ralph felt himself at the mercy of any nut large enough to sneer at his attempts to loosen its grasp.

Even the stubborn nut on the underside of the pier seemed to laugh at him as the lake water leaped up at it—rusting it even further, making it that much less likely he would ever be able to pry it loose. He stepped backward, the rubber heel of his boot sliding into a nook between rocks on the lake bottom that might give him more support for a final assault on the nut—

When the rock behind his heel eased out of its spot in the mud, his foot slipped into the place vacated by the rock, and his legs spread wider to accommodate his new footing—

And he landed on his ass in the lake.

His shorts drenched through as he sat for a moment on the slippery moss-covered rock, trying to hold his wrench up to keep it out of the water. And then, with a distant rumble, a motorboat passed through the center of the lake, sending a series of waves toward the periphery

—where they overran Ralph as he sat chin-high in the lake, splashing the wrench in his hand. He stared at the offended wrench, which seemed to have started to rust at once—or it might have been the gleam of the sun starting to set. He could have thrown it into the center of the lake in frustration, had he not at that moment heard a shriek that did not spring from the loons along the far shore but was inescapably identifiable as the scream of a human female.

Helen? No, he knew her scream. This was deeper in pitch, fuller throated, like the wail of a robin in the talons of a hawk. It was coming from his left, beyond the line of trees . . . from the direction of the pigeon house, he thought. This guess was confirmed a moment later by another cry that modulated into recognizable words.

"Help! Somebody help me . . ."

He ran down the dock in three thumping strides, crashed through the Queen Anne's lace, and came upon Marsha Mullens, stumbling down the three steps from the porch of the white pigeon coop. She held her arm in front of her, shielding her eyes from him, he thought— then realized she was still protecting herself from something she had seen inside.

"I'm all right," she insisted, trying to take control of her breathing, which was coming in heaves. She gestured behind her and made a terrible face. "In there—"

"I'll check it out."

She sank her fingernails into his arm. "Don't!" She stared into his face, seemed to recognize him, and then released her grip. "Be careful. It's awful—"

Ralph didn't know what to expect. Maddened pigeons? The trail of a hungry cat? He set his foot in something slippery, picked up his boot, and saw the glistening fluid stuck to the edge of his sole. Blood. There was no sound of moving birds, although he saw loose feathers in the straw now, and the shapes of pigeons on their nests . . . cowering? Ralph moved deeper into the coop, where the thin light through the windows fell across a nest, and saw the pigeon there lying quite still, on her side, bleeding profusely from a jagged gash in her head. He turned and checked one nest after the other, and saw the same evidence of violence in all of them— dead birds, scattered straw, and bloody feathers. From behind a wooden crate on the floor he heard a scratching, the sound of clawed feet on the wooden floorboards. Ralph peered between the crate and another next to it, and found three shaken birds bobbing there, staring through the widest eyes he had ever seen on a pigeon. They were cooing, loud and fast, moving erratically. The wing of one was broken, and the other two pecked at him, crowding behind him in an effort to get away from some object which lay halfway between them and Ralph's eyes. It looked like some sort of mechanical claw. One end of it was muddy, obscure in the poor light. The other end was shining.

Ralph moved his head away and reached in with his arm, past the wet elbow . . . and knew it as soon as his fingers touched the cold bumps along its flat, narrow midshank.

Raised letters.

He had found his missing wrench.

18

MARSHA MULLENS WAS SITTING ALL ALONE IN THE WHITE GAZE-
bo at the crest of the hill when Shelly and Homer trooped
up to talk with her. She did not look like an administrator in charge of a clinic whose director had been murdered, whose statistician had been run over by a delivery
truck, and whose interns had been reduced by one
attempted suicide. She did not even look like a doctor, at
the moment, having changed from her professional suit
into an unstructured shift of white linen, which fell from
her bony shoulders to her bare legs without regrouping at
her waist or narrow hips. Together with the leather
sandals laced around her calves, it made her look slender
as a goddess, or at least a priestess of the Delphic oracle,
the gray streak in her black hair lending authority and
dignity to her divinations of heavenly will. When they
came up behind her, she stood near one of the white
marble pillars, one palm on its smooth curve as she
stared out over the traffic inching along the highway far
below.

"Dr. Mullens?" asked Shelly quietly.

"Yes?"

She did not turn to look at them, and signaled for
Homer to stay where they were, while he circled around
to greet her from the front.

"We were hoping for a chance to talk to you."

"About the birds?"

"Among other things."

She waited until he brought himself into her field of view before replying. "It was a goddamn bloody mess."

"Yes, it was."

"You went to see the pigeon coop?"

"Part of our job."

"My job has parts like that, too," she said. "I've injected my share of poisons into the necks of animals, you know. Henry used to stick electrodes into their heads."

"How nice for them."

"Not really. But he learned something from it, I suppose. Maybe not a whole hell of a lot, but you never know where the big breakthroughs are going to come until you make them, do you?"

"That's not what happened at the coop."

"No, you don't go after a houseful of birds with a wrench to do research, that's true. What I can't seem to figure out is, what sort of person does something like that? You'd think if we had someone on the grounds with that sort of pathology, one or another of the bright young minds around here would've picked it up already, wouldn't you?"

"I was going to ask you about that."

She shook her head. "Nobody's willing to think it might've been one of *their* patients."

Shelly could understand that. "Wouldn't reflect especially well on the therapist, would it?"

"That's not the way therapy is supposed to work," she fairly spit back at him. "We are not in this to protect our own egos from the vicissitudes of our patients' fortunes. We are supposed to help them discover the truth."

Shelly liked the sound of that enormously. "Sounds sort of like my job."

"Therapy is sort of like your job," she said, "when it's done well. Patient and therapist collaborate to unravel a story that accounts for unexplained behavior. When we sort it all out, the problem is supposed to go away."

"Sounds right."

"Only sometimes it doesn't work that way." She sighed. "So we try other treatment modalities. Chemicals. Electric shock. Whatever diminishes the pain."

She closed her eyes, apparently in some distress herself, and Shelly wondered if they weren't having a more personal conversation than her words suggested. He remembered what Helen Kaufman had told him about Harrison's relationship with Marsha, and decided to risk a question.

"Was that Henry's policy? Whatever worked?"

She opened her eyes and nearly laughed. "Henry never liked to bother with talk first."

"As a treatment for the patients here?"

"For himself." She turned her thoughtful brown eyes on him and bit her lip.

Shelly gave her a few minutes to find her way out of the mood into which she had lapsed; but when she matched him silence for silence, he said, "Everyone I meet tells me he was an awful bastard, you know."

"I'm sure." She nodded. A pause. "But he wasn't, always."

"Nobody is," said Shelly.

"He could cook—elaborate meals, with sauces that made your mouth water just passing through the kitchen. He was as graceful with a tennis racket as any man ever. A wonderful neighbor at dinner parties, full of sly comments about the matrons across the table. He could dance, when he had to. Loved concerts, museums, and archaeology, collected prehistorical artifacts—"

"It's just people he didn't like, then."

Marsha Mullens turned from him to Homer, still standing at the far side of the gazebo, on the steps. She felt the gazes of the two men on her and readjusted her shift, balancing it between her shoulders. "Sit down."

It was half an invitation, half a command, and Homer obeyed readily, slipping into one of the chairs at Harrison's table, sliding his long legs under it. He leaned forward on the cool marble top, folding his hands palms-down on it. She looked away, striking a pose between the marble pillars, gazing out over the rush-hour traffic. Shelly waited until Homer had resettled himself in undistracting silence, before observing, "Nice spot, isn't it?"

She glanced back at him over her shoulder. "It was Henry's favorite place to be alone."

Though not always alone. Shelly furrowed his brow and asked as if to clarify an uncertainty, "Isn't this where he had lunch with Neela Zapotnik on Wednesday?"

She shivered slightly and dropped her hand from the column. "Did he?"

"Didn't he tell you about that lunch?"

"No. Why should he?"

"Just to help him reexamine what had happened between them. She went straight from here to the lake."

"Henry did not suffer from misdirected guilt."

"I was thinking along the lines of properly directed guilt."

She seemed genuinely surprised. "Do you know something I don't, Mr. Lowenkopf?"

"Depends what you mean by *know,*" Shelly said. "I'm starting to get a picture."

"What sort of picture?"

"He's reported to have said some pretty painful things to her, here. About her career."

"Reported by Helen Kaufman?"

"Is it true?"

"I have no idea," she told him truthfully. "Henry was not the sort of man to suffer fools gladly. Or to hold his tongue to protect the feelings of an incompetent subordinate. If he felt the Zapotnik girl lacked the potential to be a psychologist, I'll bet he gave her his honest opinion."

"Whether or not she had asked for it?"

She hesitated. "Probably."

"Do you think his honest opinion of Neela Zapotnik was well-founded?"

"I wasn't her supervisor."

"Helen Kaufman was—and she says Neela could've made a first-class therapist."

"There's more to psychology than therapy," Mullens replied.

"Like research?"

"Exactly."

"Do you think Henry's assessment of Zapotnik's research was well-founded?"

"I couldn't say."

"No one seems able to," Shelly muttered, shaking his head in frustration. "But weren't you people supposed to be teaching her how to do it?"

She was silent for a long time, trying to resist his obvious baiting but unwilling to let the question go without an answer. Finally she shrugged. "I would say your criticism of our program is probably justified in that respect, Mr. Lowenkopf. It does seem as if we have not been supervising the research of our young people as carefully as we should, perhaps. Henry had assigned himself as Miss Zapotnik's research supervisor, very sensibly, if you ask me, since she was trying to replicate one of his early projects. It appears . . . he might not have given her the attention she needed."

"Appears from what I've said?"

"And other things."

"What other things, Doctor?"

"From his files."

"You mean he left a note in his files criticizing himself for his lack of adequate supervision?"

She shook her head. "Henry never criticized himself for anything, Mr. Lowenkopf! I'm surprised you haven't realized that yet, from all you've pieced together."

"I was rather hoping to hear it from you."

"Well, now you have."

"Thank you. But he was never unwilling to criticize others, was he?"

"No. He was never reluctant to do that."

"Including you?"

"When I deserved to be criticized."

"And when you didn't?"

"That's always a matter of judgment, isn't it? Henry made his opinions about everything very clear."

"And none too gently, either."

"He felt strongly about what he saw," she retorted, trying to maintain her professional demeanor. "If he felt frustrated about something, the level of stridency in his voice might go up, and even at times the volume."

"What was he frustrated about?"

"All sorts of things."

"At the clinic? Professional issues?"

She scowled. "Yes."

He picked up on her hesitation. "Personal problems?"

"Those, too."

"What sorts of personal problems," he said, "left him frustrated, Doctor?"

Her teeth clenched and she glared at him. "I'm not sure—as his doctor—I should answer that question."

"You were his . . . *personal* physician?"

"Yes."

The question *How personal?* hung in the air between them, and Shelly chose not to relieve the tension by asking it out loud. Instead, he pursed his lips and thought it over while she waited for his next question.

"Is there something wrong with that?" she demanded.

He looked her straight in the eye.

Her anger was evident now, though restrained by her will, and Shelly began to wonder if he hadn't pushed her too far. The sight of the pigeon coop had unnerved her, and the loss of her lover must have made her ache—particularly when she was not free to acknowledge her loss publicly. Shelly had assumed their affair had been kept secret to avoid the appearance of impropriety, but a new thought crossed his mind, and he dropped the belligerency of his tone several notches to ask it.

"Is there a Mr. Mullens out there somewhere, Doctor?"

She almost snapped at him but fought for control and managed to reply with admirable self-possession, "I am married, if it's any business of yours."

"I'm afraid it is," he said matter-of-factly, "if you were in love with Henry Harrison."

"In *love* with him?"

"I know—he didn't believe in it. But most people do. And that includes you, doesn't it?"

She stared at him coldly, the corners of her mouth tugging down, struggling to preserve her professional detachment. And yet she wanted to talk about it, to express her feelings of loss to someone. "This goes no further."

He nodded. "Unless you actually murdered him."

"I didn't."

"I didn't think you had."

"Then why are you pushing me on this?"

"Somebody has to."

She studied him, her lip twisting, as if he were a specimen on the dissecting table. "You're merciless, Mr. Lowenkopf. You could have been a therapist."

"Tell me about Henry Harrison."

"What do you want to know?"

"Something only you can teach me about him."

"You've guessed already, haven't you?"

"He was impotent?"

"Let's say I was uninspiring."

"That couldn't've been the case," said Shelly, looking her straight in the eye.

She blinked. "Thank you. But he . . . couldn't perform, half the time. As for the other half—he was never an especially generous lover. He was still a boy in many ways. Isn't that how it's usually described?"

"Describe it for me in your own words."

"As a doctor? Or a woman?"

"As a woman doctor."

She took a deep breath. "Henry Harrison was a brilliant man of science. His mind was quick and painfully sharp, a finely honed instrument. You should understand how deeply I respected him. And still do."

"I understand," Shelly assured her.

"Unfortunately, his emotional development . . . was arrested, in comparison."

"He never grew up."

"He never grew *in,* I would say, rather," she insisted. "He kept getting taller, and more sophisticated in his

190

functioning. But he never became really comfortable with his own psychodynamic processes. I'll bet he was like that from the start. But the death of his first wife, Susan—"

"I didn't realize he married again."

She blushed deeply. "He never did. He would talk about it, with me."

"I see."

She fell silent for a moment, and Shelly kicked himself for interjecting. She said, "He never got over that, I think. It was an iron door closing him off forever from whatever lay locked inside him up to that point in his life. After Susan's suicide, Henry turned a cold eye to any sort of clinical approach. It was just too painful for him."

"Is that the sort of approach Neela Zapotnik was using?"

"No! She was simply trying to replicate his own work with pigeons, in the first chapter of his book."

"The book about Joseph?"

"Yes. It begins with a general discussion of conditioning and training, and scores a few preliminary points by describing a series of tests he ran with pigeons beforehand. That laid out all the theoretical groundwork underlying his approach to the chimpanzee."

"But she had a few problems?"

"No one seems to have looked over her research design very carefully," Mullens explained, "and her results unfortunately reflected that."

"And that's what he used to tear her to pieces?"

"That was the basis of his criticism, yes."

"How do you know?"

"From his files. I've inherited most of his files, as the new clinic director. Mostly administrative, but some include personal issues. I found a note in one of them."

"In his handwriting?"

She shook her head. "The note was typed—by Neela Zapotnik. Asking for his help."

"Why?"

"She was not getting the outcomes she should have been from the data."

"You mean, when she ran his old experiments again."

"Her pigeons didn't act like Henry's. That's why I went to the coop today—to look them over." At the thought of what she had seen there, her jaw tightened. She turned away. And then a new thought occurred to her, and she put a cool hand, backwards, on her forehead.

"You don't think . . . could that be why they were massacred?"

19

NEELA ZAPOTNIK WAS NO LONGER INTERESTED IN PIGEONS. SHE was no longer interested in problems with her research design, the concerns of the Care Clinic, or the discipline of psychology as a whole. She sat in a white nightdress under a white sheet and flowered comforter, with a neat stack of unread textbooks at the foot of her bed. The floor to either side and the bed itself were covered with classified sections from the local newspaper, all folded to the same corner square in which the daily crossword puzzle appeared. All of the crossword puzzles had been started, in blue or black ink, though none of them had been completed—Neela did not believe in finishing one day's puzzle with answers printed in the following day's paper. So she held on to them all, attacking the newest puzzle first, abandoning it in frustration only to resume contemplation of the clues she had been unable to solve on one of the older puzzles, which smeared newsprint on her fingers, and the sheets, and the photocopy of her note to Henry Harrison, which Shelly Lowenkopf handed to her when he and Homer Greeley came to visit.

She glanced at it quickly, seemed to recognize it, but said only, "Cockeyed lions snooped?"

Shelly wasn't sure exactly how to respond. "We don't

mean to intrude, Miss Zapotnik. But if you'll tell us whether you wrote that note—"

"An *'r'* in the second place," she insisted.

"Pried," said Homer.

She wrote it down and Shelly made a face at his partner.

"Lions with the *s* mean a group, which is a *pride.* The word *cockeyed* suggests we're going to have to rearrange the letters. *Snooped,* of course, is what the missing word means, so with some fast shuffling, we get—"

"The answer to a crossword clue," Shelly said, hoping that Homer's clue might have allowed the poor girl to talk to them. She seemed lost in her pillow, her square-cut black hair framing a face that was paler than any twenty-year-old face ought to be. Neela Zapotnik had been pulled from a lake, resuscitated at the last possible moment, and rushed to a hospital, where her stomach had been forced to yield its contents. Her deliberate death had been thwarted, and her clenched jaw showed her resentment; but it trembled now and then, shivering at a memory of the underside of the lake, and the hand that held her ballpoint pen shook when it wasn't pressed against the page.

"P-R-I-E-D," Neela admired out loud, reciting the letters she had scrawled into the boxes. Then her nose screwed up as if she'd smelled a fish. "That gives me *T-D-something-something-M,* going down through the last letter. That can't be right, then, can it?"

"Miss Zapotnik," said Shelly. "If you could give us just a minute—"

Her glance cut through him like a shard of ice through a dangling fishing line.

"What's the clue?" asked Homer.

"'Tis in it, a fool's way of talking."

He checked over her shoulder. "That's not a *T*—it's an *I* you've written there."

"Oh, all right. *I-D-something-something-M.*"

"Idiom."

"Huh? Oh, I get it—an idiom is a way of talking. With *'tis* in it, you get a fool's way. *Idio*tism."

"Right."

"You're pretty good at this stuff, aren't you?"

Homer shrugged. "I pay attention to lots of little things. Details."

"It's the details of this, we want to ask you about," Shelly said, tapping the Xerox of her note. "You wrote this to Dr. Harrison, didn't you?"

Neela met his gaze and the blood seemed to run out of her face again; her limbs grew visibly heavier, as if she were changing back into ice. Shelly could have sworn her lips were actually turning blue when she said, "I don't want to talk about that now."

Shelly was about to press the point, just a little more, when Homer picked up one of the half-finished crossword puzzles lying on the bed.

"Why don't you give us a chance here?" he suggested.

Leave Homer to do the interviewing? This was a new idea, a new arrangement. But he had developed a rapport with this girl, hadn't he? Shelly shrugged and—with a backward glance at his partner, sitting nonchalantly on the edge of the bed—trooped off downstairs.

"Let's try this one," he heard Homer say as the door to Neela's room closed behind him.

"What's the clue?" she mumbled.

"Cooperation," Homer replied, and a long silence followed that was cut off only by the click.

Shelly stood in the dark staircase, examining his silhouette in the glass panes framing portraits of the Zapotnik family—mostly Neela at every stage of her academic career from the early fuzzy shots of a chubby kindergartener to the happy shot of a chubby high-school senior on graduation day. There were a couple of pictures also of an older boy, in a mechanic's blue overalls and then in a corporal's dress uniform. That was the latest shot of him, and didn't seem very recent—Shelly wondered if he had survived his stint in the service. There was even a shot of the whole gang together: Neela, her brother, the man who had let them into the house who had to be George Zapotnik, and a square-faced woman with a blunt nose who looked somehow familiar to

Shelly. He heard the sudden silence that made him aware that a lawnmower had stopped, and a dry voice called up, "Nee-lah!"

No answer from above; of course, the door was closed. But the man outside didn't know that. "Hey, Neela!"

Shelly didn't want to risk any interruption of Homer's talk with the girl, so he answered the call himself, following it to a small yard outside the living-room door, where George Zapotnik was waiting in the morning sun with a portable CD player held in his hands like a torpedo set to detonate on a timer. The disk inside twanged painfully, and George kept hitting the *stop* button to make the machine silent, but it insisted on returning to the same song, over and over again.

"I didn't know you fellahs were still here," he said when he saw Shelly.

"Sorry to keep her," Shelly replied, glancing back toward Neela. The other man followed his gaze so helplessly that Shelly felt obliged to offer, "Is there anything I can do?"

"I doubt it." George shook his head and looked suspiciously at the CD player booming in his grip. "This damned thing keeps playing the same song."

The music started with a crash of cymbals and a throbbing bass drum, followed by a *twa-a-a-ang* from a high-pitched electric guitar and a whoop from the lead singer—just the thing to drive George utterly bonkers.

Shelly looked at the black boom box and thought he might be able to figure it out, if George had held on to the manual; but before he took a stab at the digital dials, a seven-year-old boy marched out of the house, allowing the screen door to bang shut behind him. George gave him a look of disgust, but there was an element of pleading in it, too. The reason soon became clear, when the boy spied the boom box in his uncle's grip and reached out his hand to claim it.

"She program that again?"

"The sixth one, this time," George said, as he might have complained about vertebrae to his chiropractor.

Twa-a-a-a-a-ang-ang-ang!

The seven-year-old touched a series of controls quickly, and the digital readout in the center on top reverted to an innocent *00*. The drum, guitar, and lead whooper lapsed into silence, and George's shoulders collapsed in grudging gratitude. The boy handed the CD player back to his uncle, and stepped over a lawnmower lying idle in the grass on his way to a chaise longue of green and white mesh, where he stretched out full length and crossed his hands behind his head, eyes protected by coal-black wraparound Ray-Bans.

"My nephew," George explained. "My wife Stella offers to watch him whenever her sister wants, but she's working and I'm not that much, lately. So who do you think gets to sit around and enjoy his company?"

The lawnmower clacked. "Any chance you could get him to tackle the rest of this crabgrass?"

"What do you think?"

The boy starting humming something, perhaps to drown out the sound of their voices buzzing in his ears. It was a familiar melody which Shelly could not place, until the boy gripped the doubled aluminum tubes that served the chaise longue as arms and sang out the lyrics, *"Whistle while you work. Hitler was a jerk. Mussolini wore a bikini, and Himmler wore a skirt . . ."*

A ditty from Shelly's childhood—one of those songs passed from child to child, which must have been written by somebody, although none of its singers knew whom. During the Second World War, no doubt, to stir public antagonism against the enemy, and surviving among children because of the silliness of the lyrics and the catchiness of the tune . . .

Then the screen door opened behind him, and Homer stepped out. He had a look of satisfaction on his face, which turned out to be misleading when he shook his head and murmured to Shelly, "She won't say a word."

George heard that, and grunted—with pleasure, it seemed to Shelly. It must have been vindicating, he supposed, that they hadn't been able to elicit more from his daughter than George had been able to discover for himself.

"That what she told you?" Shelly asked.

George grunted in the affirmative. He picked up a rake and poked at a perfect pile of leaves.

"Did she ever try . . . anything like this before?"

"Like what?"

Shelly sighed. So much for protecting the man's feelings. "Like trying to kill herself."

George shook his head. "Nobody around here ever did." That's what you get, his face suggested, when you send a girl off to college.

"Did she say anything? In the hospital?"

"She said they'd never let her be a therapist now."

"Did that upset her?"

"No—she said it like it was an accomplishment, like she'd done something to be proud of. They weren't gonna let her be a therapist now—she'd seen to that."

"Did she ever tell you . . . or let on . . . that she wanted out of the program?"

"Nope. I wanted her out of it—I thought it wouldn't do her no good to be messing around in people's minds and all. But she was determined, Neela was, as she always is, about everything. She was gonna make herself a psychologist, the first college grad in the family. Only she shot too high."

"Didn't you want her to become a therapist?"

"I told her to be a teacher! If she had done that, she'd be working now, at a profession that really pleased her. Instead, she's upstairs, locked in her room . . . you saw her!"

Shelly nodded. What could he say?

"Look," said George, "I worked on the line in the Putnam plant in Trenton for over fifteen years. I've been out for eleven months now, and my hands still aren't clean. Did I want something better for Neela? You bet I did! They laid me off just like that." He snapped his fingers. "But a Ph.D.? That's skipping a generation, isn't it?"

"What do you mean?"

"A teacher once explained it to me—first, a family graduates a bachelor's degree—like in teaching, for instance. Then that person's son goes for a professional degree, a master's in law, maybe, or engineering. Then, a generation or two later, there's a chance for somebody to hang out in school long enough to earn a doctorate degree—which doesn't really guarantee a job, they say. Talk about a luxury education! And we could've gotten there, as a family, step by step. But Neela, she wanted the whole hog, herself."

"Why shouldn't she? If she was capable of it?"

"Look what it done to her!" He glanced at the screen door, and the stairs to the second floor behind it. Then he spat bitterly into the dirt at the edge of his lawn.

"You think she couldn't handle the pressure?"

"Looks that way, doesn't it? I'd say she bit off more than she could chew."

That was not the impression Shelly had received from Helen Kaufman about Neela—that she had succumbed to the pressure of graduate school. True, she had been having some trouble with her research data, but there were warning signals, weren't there, before a graduate student blew her cork? Helen had thought Neela was doing well, far better, in fact, than Harrison's evaluation of her. So which of them were on the money—Kaufman or Harrison? There was no way to know for certain with these things, that much he understood already. Harrison's blistering attack on the girl over lunch must have hit her hard. But had she been cracking already under the strain of examinations and research projects, a life of loan-supported poverty and no time for herself, not to mention the demands of superiors whose vanity had to be assuaged at the cost of her own sanity—or hadn't she?

"Did you ever get the feeling it was . . . getting to her? All the strain?"

"Me? I knew it from the start. From before the start,

when she first got the idea to begin this thing. I knew she'd never make it through."

Shelly was sure that had helped her. "But no gradual signs of falling behind?"

"She never gave up, once she started something. And never, never let it show."

"In the hospital—after she said they'd never let her become a therapist—did she say anything else?"

He shook his head.

"Nothing?"

Another shake. "Not about the school."

"About what?"

"She told her mother how awful she felt, about letting her down and all. She said she knew she couldn't show her face around the clinic anymore, but that Neela would make it up to her someday, some other place. Stella kept trying not to cry. She leaned over the bar on the bed and hugged the girl, kept telling her it was okay, not to worry about *her,* but Neela kept crying and Stella kept trying not to, and the nurses themselves were ready to burst into tears. I got out of there soon as I could, you can bet, and didn't hear any more of it."

He made a face that looked like he was chewing something that had come up his throat, but whether it was an emotional memory or just gas, Shelly couldn't determine.

"So she was sorry for what she did. But a little while ago you said she had sounded proud about it."

"Isn't that the trouble with psychology, now? People saying one thing, and feeling another, asking you to help when they're spending all their energy trying to stop you. That's what I told Neela in the beginning, and that's what I'm saying now!"

"Which is . . . ?"

"How's she supposed to help anybody else deal with their troubles, when she goes and throws herself into the lake over her own? And don't think she's any different from the rest of them, 'cause she isn't. They're all like that, them therapists—all of them seeing shrinks themselves. Neela told me herself! And the ones who aren't are worse."

Shelly could understand how a man whose daughter jumped into a lake at a therapeutic clinic might feel that way about the profession. He had seen Neela himself, upstairs, and murmured a silent prayer that his own son Thom might choose a less stressful profession when the time came. But something about the man's statement had set off a buzzer in his head, and Shelly reached for it among the notes and questions that always appeared when somebody spoke from the heart.

"Do you think she'll ever go back?"

"Neela? Or Stella?"

Strange question—Shelly had meant Neela, of course. Was there some reason the girl's mother might not go . . . back? Back to where? He felt that creeping feeling on the top of his scalp that told him he was about to discover a piece of the puzzle he hadn't known was missing.

"Stella."

"That's the easy one," George said. "Where do you think she is right now?"

"Why don't you tell us," Shelly said quietly. Homer reacted to his tone, leaning forward.

George noticed but didn't understand it. "Working."

"Where?"

"At that damned clinic, of course! Where do you think she works?"

"Stella?" asked Homer.

George scowled at the pair in disbelief. "Don't you fellahs even know my wife works at the clinic? I thought you said you were detectives."

"We are," Homer began, preparing to explain the difference between private and public service. But Shelly interrupted before he could launch into it.

"What exactly does she do . . . working at the clinic? Your wife, I mean. Stella."

George studied them both doubtfully. "I'm sure you've seen her plenty of times, if you've really been

up there, as you say. She's a black-haired woman—
Neela's color—who tends the main desk at the ranch
house."

"You mean . . . the receptionist at the foot of the stairs
to Henry Harrison's office?"

George grinned sheepishly. "That's my Stella."

20

THE NEWS WAS EVEN WORSE WHEN THEY RUSHED BACK TO THE clinic: Stella Zapotnik was not at her post at the reception desk in the lobby of the ranch house. It was staffed instead by the blonde with the ponytail Shelly had met at Helen Kaufman's office and again in Marsha Mullens's —Liza Gunnarson. She was wearing a white pocket T-shirt, above-the-knee canvas shorts, and her usual attitude of patient, wry cheer. She was hand-lettering names on strips of white adhesive tape, replacing the yellowed names under the mailboxes behind the counter. When she came to Harrison's name, she rolled the old name-strip into a ball of sticky paper and tossed it into the trashcan. The opening allowed her to move Mullens's name to the top box, which she did with feminist pride. And then she realized her problem—she had Ray Singh's name and Helen Kaufman's and Neela Zapotnik's . . . and where was she supposed to get names to put under all those empty boxes?

So it was with some relief that she put down her calligraphy pen and turned to greet Lowenkopf and Greeley.

"Hello," she said brightly. "Checking in again?"

She offered them a pen on a chain, which Shelly set

down on the check-in book, gripping his head in both hands.

"No, thanks. My head's had all the shrinking it needs for a while. But you do get around this place, don't you?"

"A regular jane-of-all-trades."

"Like Howard Davenport."

"How do you mean?"

"He did a little bit of everything, too. Washing test tubes in the lab. Watching the desk for Harrison's secretary. You ever get drafted into that?"

"Covering for Doris?" She laughed. "I think even Joseph's done a stint up there."

"He gets around, too, doesn't he? Carrying my bags—"

"We're all pretty flexible, I guess."

"Including Stella?"

Liza's sensors went up. "What about her?"

"Where is she, now? Trawling the lake, or performing brain surgery?"

"She's on a break."

Shelly glanced at a coffee machine behind the counter. "Not for coffee," Liza insisted.

He waited, closing his eyes and slowly opening them.

"It's personal," she said.

Shelly gave her a moment to explain further, and when she didn't, said, "Lots of secrets in this place, aren't there?"

Liza shook her head. "It's not like that—like with Helen. This is a psychological clinic, don't forget. We're all very understanding about the need for certain kinds of personal time. Since we all need it." She shrugged. "I mean, who doesn't? Everybody needs it."

That could only be one thing, here. "Therapy?"

"It's kind of a perk of the job."

"Is that where Stella is now? At her therapy appointment?"

"You can wait for her here, if you like."

"Who does she see?"

"Pardon?"

"Who's her therapist?"

"I don't know if I should tell you."

"Liza," he said, "Do you really think her therapist is going to reveal anything confidential? I've been around this clinic for two days, and everyone looks at me funny if I ask the time of day. Who's she seeing?"

"Why?"

Shelly sighed. "It's about her daughter."

"Neela?"

"You knew her, didn't you?"

"Still do."

A mistake, Shelly realized, his use of the past tense. But he felt he had to cover the base anyway. "Have you seen her since the . . . incident?"

Liza frowned. "Now you're talking like one of them. It was a suicide attempt."

"Have you seen her?"

"Not yet. I was planning to drive out there Tuesday, when I'm off."

"Has Stella seemed to you . . . edgy?"

"Who wouldn't be?"

"Then she has?"

Liza hesitated. "I wouldn't call it *edgy*, exactly."

"What would you call it?"

"*Upset.* I mean, after what happened to her daughter? She kept slamming her fist on the countertop here. Like this." She demonstrated, and the desk rocked under the impact. "Maybe even *angry*."

"Is it possible that Stella blamed somebody here for what happened to her daughter?"

"Like Harrison, maybe? Oh, sure. Or Kaufman."

"Why Kaufman?"

"It was her job to look out for them, wasn't it?" Shelly had nothing to say to that, taken by surprise. But Liza wouldn't have given him a chance anyway, because at that moment, her hand went to her mouth, covering it. "Oh, gosh."

"What is it?"

"That's where she is right now."

"Stella?"

"She's with Helen. Alone in that private office."

"Where we met yesterday?"

Liza nodded, her eyes wide. She was thinking of what might be happening there.

"Helen Kaufman's her therapist?" asked Homer.

Shelly led the way to Helen's office, taking the steps of the ranch-house porch two at a time, bounding down the lawn, and springing into the bungalow that had once been shared by Mullens and Kaufman, two offices and a waiting room. The waiting room looked just as it had the day before, the same couch and pair of armchairs and tables with one magazine, the same desk with its open log and the neat lettered sign. But when they burst through the door, the room that had been Kaufman's office was nearly bare of furniture—just two chairs in an empty room, straight-backed wooden uprights without cushions on the seats. In one chair sat Stella Zapotnik, her blunt black hair to the door; and in the other sat Helen Kaufman, who stood in anger as the two detectives entered uninvited.

"You're interrupting, gentlemen. This is a therapy session in progress."

"Are you all right?"

"Of course I'm all right. Please wait outside."

Stella Zapotnik turned around and they saw that she had been crying. She did not look very threatening, wiping her nose on a Kleenex, but it was possible that her tears expressed remorse for a heinous offense, wasn't it? And who was to say her guilt and fury wouldn't drive her to commit one more?

"We need to talk."

"When we're finished here."

Shelly shook his head. "Better not."

Helen noticed how he looked at her client and interposed herself between them. She was halfway to the door, and he waved her on. Helen hesitated, but decided it was best to get rid of them, and if the only way of doing that quickly was to join them for a moment in the anteroom—

"Excuse me," Helen told Stella, holding up her index finger. "I'll be back in one minute."

Stella sniffled and the door closed between them with a discreet metallic click. Whereupon Helen turned a fierce face on Shelly and Homer.

"What do you want here?"

"We thought you might be in danger."

"From Stella?"

"Did you know she's Neela's mother?"

"Of course."

"Who might be holding a grudge against Harrison, for what he did to her daughter? And against you?"

"We've been working through the material on Henry just now. Yes, she does hold him responsible for his cruelty to Neela. And I can't say that I blame her." Her indignation faltered. "But why do you say . . . against me?"

"You were director of internships, weren't you?"

"I was."

"Whose job it was to protect her daughter from the stresses of your line of work?"

"That's not entirely fair . . ." she began, and then lapsed into silence.

Shelly had known a lot of therapists, who are usually pretty good at ducking guilt that doesn't belong to them—they have to be, considering all the blame thrown their way. But when you hit on something that they feel themselves responsible for . . . Shelly felt it when the arrow struck.

"It isn't fair," he said. "But sometimes people carry ideas in their heads that aren't fair at all. Sometimes they even act on them."

Helen thought for a moment about her own culpability. And then shook her head. "Not Stella. She wouldn't."

"Wouldn't hurt you? Or Harrison?"

"She wouldn't harm me," Helen said with an impressive degree of certainty. "Or him, either . . . I don't think."

"But she could have?"

"Anybody could really do anything, couldn't they? But if you're asking me for a probability, based on my clinical judgment of her, I'd say Stella Zapotnik would be

207

very unlikely to injure me, and nearly as unlikely to kill Henry."

"Would you bet your life on it?"

Dr. Kaufman thought about that for a moment—and knocked on the closed door and called softly, "Stella . . ."

At the sound of her name, the woman in question opened the door and stuck her head in the waiting room. "Dr. Kaufman?"

"Stella," said Helen, opening it wider. But she didn't pass through into the office.

"Are you coming back?"

"These gentlemen have some questions," Helen explained, "which they've been asking of me, although they should properly be asking them of you."

Stella appeared before the two detectives. "Go on."

"About your daughter," said Shelly. "Do you have any idea why she did what she did?"

Stella's eyes reddened, but no tears slipped out. "She was unhappy, I guess."

"Because of Harrison? Because of the things he told her?"

She glanced at Kaufman and nodded.

"Did she say anything about it? What he told her?"

"Only what we talked about," Stella said to Helen, who gave her the slightest nod of encouragement. "How they'd never let her be a therapist now . . ."

"Did she tell you what he said to her?"

She shook her head. "Not exactly. Just the general idea. How she didn't have the stuff to make it in his field. That she ought to just throw in the towel now . . ."

Shelly nodded. "Making the most of the problems with her research data—"

Stella looked at him for the first time blankly. She turned to Helen, who wore the same expression on her professional face. The two women carried on a silent conversation before Helen said, "What problems with her research data?"

Shelly's scalp buzzed. "She didn't tell you about them?"

Both women shook their heads.

"Who would she have told?" Shelly asked carefully. "About a problem that really got to her? Someone she trusted, and could talk to like an equal around here?"

Helen shook her head.

"Was there anyone she talked about? A friend?"

The last word made his question intelligible to Stella, who shrugged and said, "The only friend she had around here, not counting family or teachers—"

He shook his head. A *friend*.

"Was that girl in the next room," Stella Zapotnik said. "Right next door to Neela. What was her name? The strange one." She made a cuckoo sign at her temple.

Helen wrinkled her brow.

"You know," said Stella, "with the records—"

Homer turned and walked to the door, where he waited for Shelly to follow. The others looked at him.

"Adrienne Paglia," he said.

21

THEY FOUND ADRIENNE PAGLIA WHERE LIZA GUNNARSON told them she'd be: in the ranch-house kitchen packing a picnic basket for her usual Monday lunch for two. She had wrapped two cheese-and-lettuce sandwiches in white paper and was trying to secure them among two goblets and a bottle of Chianti she had already packed in the basket. On the table beside her were scattered almonds and shelled walnuts, red-and-white peppermint candies, a new box of chocolates still wrapped in plastic, and two whole bunches of overripe bananas. It was the sort of basket one carries over the forearm, so squeezing all of the food on the countertop into it was going to prove a challenge. She took out one of the goblets, turned it around, and placed it back in again.

It was a large kitchen with aluminum working tables and a big eight-burner stove. Preparations for the clinic's lunch had not yet begun, so Adrienne had the place pretty much to herself. She was wearing a sleeveless pink shirtdress that showed off her white shoulders but concealed her legs to her ankles, and a floppy straw hat with a purple band and a brim that fell over her eyes. Homer watched her with envy as she packed the feast for two, while Helen tried to hold her tongue and Shelly struggled to engage her in helpful conversation.

"Please, Miss Paglia, try to remember—did Neela tell you anything about her data?"

"Dates, yes," she said, taking out the other goblet now, turning it over so that it matched the first one, and stuffing it back in again. "Data, no."

Helen couldn't restrain herself. "She never complained about her research results? Bitched about the trouble they were giving her?"

"She never *bitched* at all," Adrienne said, reaching under the counter for a jar of Spanish olives, popping off the lid with dexterity.

Shelly glanced at Helen with reproof, thanking her for her contribution, which had succeeded only in stirring Adrienne's resentment. He recovered the interrogatory lead by grumbling in the back of his throat, a sound which eventually formed itself into a question.

"Did she ever talk about them?"

"Who?"

"Her research subjects. The birds."

"Pigeons," she corrected him, and then bit her lip, unable now to deny it.

"Yes," Shelly agreed, picking up on it. "Pigeons."

"Now and then."

Homer looked relieved at even this grudging cooperation, but Shelly wasn't so sure. She could hardly deny having heard about the birds now, could she?

"What did she say? When she talked about them?"

She reached a finger into the jar, fished out a green olive, and sucked out the red pimento. Then, chewing the olive, she resealed the jar and packed it between the sandwiches, stuffing them more securely between the goblets.

"I don't recall."

"We know she had some trouble replicating Harrison's data," Helen said.

"That wasn't *her* fault," Adrienne retorted, spitting the chewed olive gracefully into a trash bin under the table.

Helen scowled. "Adrienne—"

211

"What do you mean?" Shelly asked firmly. "Whose fault do you think it was?"

"I don't think I should be saying anything else," Adrienne replied with a sidelong glance at Homer.

"It'll only help Neela," Homer tried to reassure her.

She hesitated, and Shelly saw the way to bring her around. He shrugged. "Marsha Mullens told us she found a letter from Neela in Harrison's files, reporting her results. He used those numbers to underscore his assessment that she would never be a good psychologist."

"That *asshole*," said Helen.

Adrienne looked a little startled to hear her use that word but coughed to hide her smile.

Shelly mused, "If there's anything you know that contradicts his evaluation . . ."

Adrienne grinned at his ploy; she saw through it but didn't seem to mind. "So, it's up to me, then? Either I talk or Neela's an awful therapist?"

"We have to go on what we know."

She shook her head ruefully. "All right, already! You've convinced me—you're friends of Neela's . . . and mine." Another sly glance at Homer. "Aren't you?"

He reddened, and Shelly said, "Sure we are! All friends of Neela's here."

"Helping us is helping her," Helen said earnestly.

Adrienne nodded, imitating her sincerity. "That's good to know—comforting." Her eyes glinted, although it might have been the morning sun through the windows. "I'm sure Neela would tell you herself, if she could."

Shelly thought of the girl sequestered in her room at the top of the stairs, lost in a sea of crosswords; he had to swallow the stone in his throat before agreeing, "I'll bet she would, too, if she could."

"She was very dedicated—very capable," Adrienne informed them, letting the statement hang while she looped the first bunch of bananas under the feet of the goblets. Her statement was a trial balloon, testing the response from Helen Kaufman, although Adrienne never looked at the woman, ostensibly focusing her gaze on the bananas in the basket, on Shelly watching her pack, and finally on Homer.

The psychologist nodded. "She certainly was."

And that was apparently the code Adrienne needed to reveal what she knew, because once she heard Helen utter those words, confirming her own estimation, Adrienne looked at Shelly with an entirely new expression on her face. She wrapped up some nuts in cellophane, stuffed them into a corner of her basket, and did the same for the peppermint candy.

"So you want to know what she was up to?"

Shelly nodded, blinking, looking attentive but not too anxious to hear. "Uh-huh."

Adrienne sighed. "Have you read it? Has anybody read it, I wonder? The first chapter of Harrison's book on how he says he trained Joseph?"

"'Affective Response in Avians,'" said Kaufman promptly.

"That's the one. Neela used to talk about it all the time. All about training pigeons to show affection without showing them any yourself—using those white food pellets and electric shocks. Henry's usual stock in trade."

"Like the treatment sessions they give here," said Shelly.

"Exactly," Adrienne said.

Helen Kaufman pursed her lips in equivocation. "That's part of what he discusses there."

Adrienne shrugged off the rest. "That's the part Neela was interested in reduplicating."

"Replicating," corrected Helen.

For an instant Adrienne smiled at her, the habitual mother. "Neela's project was supposed to *replicate* the experiments in which Harrison claimed he made his birds love him."

"I thought he didn't believe in love," Shelly said, more or less to Helen.

"He didn't believe what most people do about it," she told him. "He couldn't deny its existence as a set of observable behaviors we consider linked. His experiments were designed to prove that pigeons could be trained by operant conditioning to perk up when they saw him, to eat from his hands, and to nestle in them— demonstrating three distinct behaviors we associate with 'affection.' Henry carefully avoided any behavior on his part that might suggest to the birds any particular sympathy for them: He never stroked them, or spoke to them by name, or gave any of them an extra morsel of food on occasion. Yet his results tables show marked increases in pigeon-prompted physical contact—the best measure of 'affection' anyone has offered, with a great deal of intuitive appeal. If a living thing wants to touch you a lot, it's got to trust you a little."

"And Harrison's pigeons wanted to touch him?"

"According to his data—and a couple of photographs included in the book."

"But Neela couldn't dupe—I mean, she couldn't replicate his results?"

Helen shrugged. "Apparently not."

"Well," Adrienne said demurely, "That's not entirely true. The numbers on his tables she couldn't approach— she used to joke that her pigeons hadn't read the study. She gave them the same regimen of electric shocks and pellet things as Harrison wrote he had given his, but her birds refused to come when she held out her hand to them. Instead of nestling in her palm, they sent up a squawk that woke up the lake every morning!"

"That's just what we mean, dear," Helen explained, "when we say she couldn't replicate—"

Adrienne held up the second bunch of bananas, in search of a spot to stuff it. "But she could, and she did—some of it. She replicated his photographs."

Helen smiled sympathetically, indulgent of the layperson. "Henry never offered them as documentation. They're hardly clinical proof."

"But they are the part we believe," Adrienne said, just as sweetly. "The tables rack up the numbers, with the little n's and probabilities. But how do we know those numbers are the ones he actually observed? We can't, of course—but the pictures of the pigeons in his hand chase all those doubts away."

"Are you saying," Shelly asked, "Harrison faked his results in the book?"

Adrienne shrugged. *Why not?*

"Couldn't have," said Helen, shaking her head. "Much as I'd like to believe it about Henry. His first chapter, about the pigeons, just laid out the principles he put into practice in his last chapter—the one on Joseph. They certainly worked well in training the chimp. Why shouldn't they have worked equally well on the pigeons? It's difficult to believe he would have risked his real accomplishment with Joseph by inventing results with the birds."

"That's just what stumped Neela," said Adrienne.

"It should have," agreed Helen.

"For a while," Adrienne went on. "Until the idea was placed in her head that Joseph was faked, too."

Helen was dumbstruck. "Joseph . . . *couldn't've* been faked," she sputtered. "We've all seen him in action around the clinic! How could she have doubted his abilities? One doesn't have to be much of a research psychologist to recognize—"

She stopped in midsentence but her meaning continued, and Shelly watched her reevaluate her judgments in silence. Had the girl tried to question Henry about his work with Joseph? If so, his anger was understandable. You had to expect presumption on the part of graduate students, but this was downright rude . . . and so badly lacking in insight! Which raised a horrific possibility that Henry could have been *correct* in his assessment of Neela's true prospects in the field . . .

Adrienne did not like the direction in which their questioning of her was leading. She scowled at Helen and turned accusing eyes on Homer.

"Neela's friends, are we?"

Shelly intervened to rescue his partner, who was stuck for an answer to give her. "We haven't said we believe she was wrong, have we?"

"Dr. Kaufman just did."

"She was certainly wrong," insisted Helen. "If that's what she really thought."

Shelly did not want the strength of Kaufman's opinions to shut down Adrienne's willingness to express her own—even if Kaufman was right. "We don't have to settle that question right now, do we, Helen?" He lifted an eyebrow at her, and she shook her head, but let it drop. Which allowed him to return to the blonde, to follow up another line. "Adrienne—you said the idea that Joseph was faked . . . had been *placed* in her mind?"

She evidently hadn't intended to. She hesitated long enough to secure the box of chocolates at the top of her basket, stuff an orange and a paring knife along the side, and cover the whole thing with napkins and a folded blue-and-white checked tablecloth.

The others watched her, more or less patiently, waiting for a response.

"Did I?"

"You did. By whom?"

She made a sour face, hoping to steer clear of this sort of thing. Clearing Neela's professional reputation was one thing. But this . . .

"You want gossip? Or information?"

"Both," said Shelly pleasantly.

Adrienne sighed. "I hate this." But when no one spoke up to relieve her from replying, she said, "You know that phony Reverend who drives up every Tuesday to check on his flock in the cabins by the lake?"

"Illuminati?" asked Homer.

"Eleazer," she said. "That's what he asked her to call him. He was trying to get into her pants, of course—after I gave him the brush."

Helen stared at her. "The Reverend placed this . . . idea in Neela's mind?"

"What exactly did he say?" Shelly asked.

Adrienne looked at Homer, who nodded.

She shrugged. "That she shouldn't lose any sleep over not being able to 'duplicate'—his word, not mine—what Henry said he'd done with those filthy pigeons."

"Why not?"

"Because Henry'd never managed to do it, either. That's what the Reverend said. Neela told me he laughed

216

when he told it to her." Her look at Shelly implied, *You know how it is, when they're trying to seduce you* . . .

Shelly nodded.

Adrienne pursed her ruby lips and cast a thoughtful glance toward Homer.

Helen frowned deeply. "He laughed?"

Adrienne nodded, dimpling.

Homer said, "I can see him doing that."

Adrienne swung her basket over her arm, like a pink-and-blue older sister of Little Red Riding Hood. She gave Homer a soft, fetching smile, and headed for the door, when Helen took the girl by her white upper arm.

"And to what source of misinformation did he attribute this nugget of slander?"

Adrienne pulled her elbow free.

"To the only one Neela herself might possibly have believed. She asked him where he had heard such a thing, and he told her, 'In the confessional.'"

22

THE REVEREND ELEAZER ILLUMINATI WAS NOT IN HIS TELEVI-
sion showroom, but with information from the kid
named Fred behind the cash register, Shelly and Homer
managed to track him down to a tiny coffee shop in the
mall. The shop sold nothing but whole beans, which they
would grind for a price, and samples served in mugs with
their name—*Cafe Ole!*—colorfully etched on the side.
The shop's designer, proprietor, and sole salesperson was
a slender, twenty-six-year-old Korean-American named
Eddie Kim, whose worried attention kept a shine on the
big brass espresso machine behind the counter bright
enough to illuminate the place by its dazzling reflection
of the ambient light from the mall hallway alone.

If the success of Eddie's venture could have been
assured by the cleanliness of its venue, his constant
wiping and waxing of every surface would have guaranteed a bonanza; but the purity of his conception was no
less spotless, and this, alas, presented a problem when
the actual dollars and cents were tabulated at the end of
Eddie's long day. Eddie's plan had been to sell coffee and
nothing but coffee, a business model seeking to emulate
the success of the new specialized stores devoted to
nothing but light bulbs, or chairs, or packing crates. The

expectations of the coffee-drinking public, however, were quite specific in their own ways. Eddie's customers kept asking for a little something to eat with their coffee, and this unrelenting demand forced Eddie to stock a single tray of Danish pastries on his otherwise spotless counter, which, though it spoiled the purity of his original conception, provided a significant boost to his revenues. And so the coffee-only store now sported a sign in its window, which advertised the imminent arrival of croissants—which might reduce the place, Eddie feared, to just another coffee shop. What was there left to distinguish it? The decor was nothing remarkable: a long white counter with a register at the end, round white tables of hard plastic, matching white chairs of softer plastic, and pictures of the coffee-growing mountains of Colombia sketched on the southern wall. In one of those chairs, Shelly and Homer found Eleazer Illuminati—lingering over a mug of decaffeinated espresso while he watched the girls in short summer skirts moving across the big plate-glass window—humming under his breath, as Eddie buffed the glass to a blinding brilliance.

Homer tilted his head toward the Reverend from outside, but there was no real need for that: *Cafe Ole!* was empty of any other customers, and Illuminati looked just as Shelly had expected him to—a television salesman with imposing stature and a flair for the dramatic. He was wearing a blue wool blazer and gray slacks, though the buttons on his jacket were silver stars that picked up the saturnine motif of his necktie. His white hair was slicked straight back, showing the lines of the brush, and he wore a pair of octagonal glasses low on the bridge of his nose. In a single gesture, his hand shoved the spectacles farther up his nose and continued on through his white mane, smoothing down the left side for an instant before it stood up stiffly again.

When the tin bell clunked over the door, Illuminati looked up and squinted, perhaps in recognition of Homer. He blinked when the two detectives shook their heads at Eddie as if they were joining a friend, and came right over to his tiny table, looking above him for a moment before Shelly asked, "Reverend? Could you spare a minute for a word for us?"

Their manner was pure policemen, and Illuminati screwed up one eye at Homer.

"Detectives, eh? I knew you weren't really interested in a TV set, the other day."

"I was asking about the Church."

"That either."

"But we are," said Shelly. "Or at least, your role as a man of the cloth."

"This a bust?" asked the Reverend, gripping the arms of his chair as if to hang on.

"We're not cops, at the moment," Shelly explained sternly, "though we still have a few friends on the force. For the moment we're here on a private matter."

He let Illuminati work that through and find the threat in it, which didn't take him more than a minute. "In other words," said the Reverend, "you're private dicks. So I'm not in trouble, yet."

"Do you mind if we sit?"

Illuminati waved his arm expansively, as Moses might have done before the gathering of the tribes. "Any chair you like is fine by me."

Homer pulled two of them over, lifting them so their soft plastic feet wouldn't scrape on the floor. He set one on either side of the Reverend, and shook his head at the ever-hopeful Eddie, who tried to approach with an order pad. Eddie put the pad back in its spot under the counter and picked up a sponge from the sink.

Shelly sat and edged his chair in close. "Okay," he said, nodding his head in encouragement. "Tell us about the sanctity of the confessional."

This was not what the Reverend had been hoping to discuss. "What about it?"

"How much does it trouble you to betray it?"

His answer came quickly. "Depends on what I'm asked to betray. And what I'm offered in compensation for the sleepless nights of doubt that always follow."

"How much?"

"What do you want to know?"

"Something very personal about Henry Harrison."

Illuminati shook his head. "Forget it. I'd love to help you out. But Harrison was not what you'd call a spiritual man—he never sought the comfort of confession with me."

"Never?"

"He's dead now, isn't he? If I had something to sell you guys, what harm would it do him now? But I'm not going to invent a whole bill of goods just to pocket a few extra dollars. I've got my principles, you know."

"You don't want any trouble from us."

"Exactly."

"Then just tell us the truth: You lied to Neela Zapotnik, didn't you?"

"To Neela? About what?"

"When you told her that Harrison confessed to you he never did the stuff he wrote about the pigeons."

"I never told her that."

"Neela said you did. She told her next-door neighbor. And that you suggested he might have faked his chapter on Joseph, too."

"Joseph?"

"The chimp at the clinic."

"The monkey? No, that wasn't Harrison—" The light dawned for Illuminati; he paused, nestling back in his chair, making himself a lot more comfortable. "Y'know, I might have something to sell you fellahs, after all."

The silence with which they greeted this was like a positive boom in the room. Eddie Kim looked over to see if he had been called. Homer shot him a glance and Eddie went back to scrubbing the counter. He started to whistle—just to let them know he wasn't listening.

Shelly said, "What've you got?"

The Reverend picked up his espresso, drained it, and set the miniature mug down with a beatific grin. "I think I know what you're after."

Shelly knew what Illuminati was after, too. They had missed something, he realized, but he couldn't figure out what it was. He reached into his pants pocket, peeled two bills off the top of the roll, and slapped them onto the plastic table—both twenties. Next time he'd look first.

"That's our final offer. Take it, or we'll have some pals on the local police force do our interrogating for us— and who knows how much of your Church financing they'll feel the need to investigate?"

The Reverend glanced at the twenties and passed his hand over the table, clearing the donation like a stage magician. "There's no need for threats, Mr.—"

"Lowenkopf."

"The Church is above reproach—or legal action, anyway. And I'm always anxious to assist the police—or their friends and colleagues—in any way I can."

"An exemplary citizen," Shelly replied. "So tell us whose conscience was guilty."

"Pardon?"

"What did Harrison confess?"

Illuminati shook his head. "It wasn't Harrison—that's what threw me when you asked, at first. He never told me anything. It was Ray Singh I heard—who didn't come for absolution, either. Just a little spiritual advice."

"About what?"

"About the chimp," the Reverend said. "Aren't you following your own line of questioning?"

Shelly was trying to follow the answers. "Ray Singh? The statistician?"

"The one who was hit by the truck."

"You mean . . . Singh had something on his mind? Something about Joseph?"

Illuminati nodded, gratified to know something they didn't. "Who do you think actually trained him?"

Homer said, "Ray?"

"Not Ray—nobody had to train *him!* I'm talking about the monkey!"

At the sound of raised voices, Eddie stopped whistling. Shelly shook his head at the unfortunate proprietor and leaned closer toward Illuminati.

"Are you trying to tell us that Ray Singh claimed to have trained Joseph himself?"

The Reverend shook his head, irritated with their doubts. "Not *claimed*. Did."

"What makes you so sure?" asked Homer.

Illuminati looked at Shelly—did he have to answer questions about his own judgments? When Shelly said nothing to interrupt, the Reverend shifted in his seat, turning to face Homer.

"A clergyman gets a feel for these things. If Singh were bragging, or wondering whether to expose Harrison, or threatening to expose him—that would be one thing."

"Extortion," said Homer.

Illuminati raised his nose in the air. "I don't condone that sort of thing. If I did, I could've hit on the Doctor myself, couldn't I?"

He waited for them to acknowledge the moral courage he had demonstrated in deciding not to blackmail Henry Harrison. Shelly gave him a brief nod, which, when he saw it was all he would get, he accepted as a sign of respect, closing his eyes momentarily to commune with a higher power.

"That wasn't what Singh wanted advice about?"

He opened his eyes at the question, disgusted by Shelly's rudeness in the presence of spiritual grace.

"No. Singh's doubts were all about Joseph himself, the chimpanzee's personal welfare. He had trained him, Ray told me, by treating him like a child—showing him plenty of affection and genuine love. And the chimp reciprocated, love for love, like anybody else. Ray swore when he blinked at you, you could see it in his eyes."

Shelly had seen the chimp together with Singh when he first checked into the clinic, and thought he knew the look Ray meant in Joseph's big brown eyes.

"But why would he allow Harrison to claim him?"

"I'll tell you," the Reverend said, "if you give me a chance to relate the whole story properly."

"Go ahead."

"Thank you." He took a breath. "Singh allowed Harrison to claim he had trained Joseph, because he cared more for that monkey than he did for his own reputation.

Harrison owned the chimp, you see—when Singh first came to the clinic, he asked for a research animal, which Harrison bought in the name of the clinic. Ray was planning to plant an electrode in his head, but when he got to know Joseph, and saw the goodness in the beast, Ray just couldn't do it. He scrapped his research project, and made the chimp his pet—his friend, really, from the way he described it to me.

"When Harrison learned what had happened, his first response was anger—that Singh had made him buy the chimp, and hadn't carried through with his research. Ray tried to demonstrate why he had scrapped it by introducing Joseph to Harrison, who had one session with the trained chimp and read his fortune there. He told Ray he planned to go ahead with the project himself and plug an electrode into Joseph's brain—unless Ray agreed to a bargain."

"A deal?"

"He said they both believed in behaviorism, didn't they? And whatever helped the general public—and the scholarly community—accept the tenets of their faith would be good for all of them, wouldn't it? Even more, it would be good for *science,* Harrison argued, dismissing what he called 'vanity squabbles over who had done what, when.'"

"As in who got the credit for Joseph."

"Ray was no fool—he knew what Harrison was stealing from him. But the choice presented to him was clear: he could allow Harrison to write his book about Joseph, describing the chimp's training with a total invention; or Harrison would stick a rod in Joseph's head, take a few measurements, and then kill the chimp so that his brain could be sliced up and analyzed."

"Extortion."

"Of the monkey variety. Ray felt he had no choice and agreed not to challenge Harrison's fraudulent account. Part of the deal was that Ray could see Joseph for an hour or two a week, but Harrison would take charge of his further training. That, you see, was the problem which brought Ray to me. It seemed to him that Joseph was becoming more and more unhappy—more nervous, he thought, clutching at him as if Joseph were under some awful strain. He couldn't decide whether what he perceived were the chimp's feelings or a projection of his own, and couldn't decide what to do about it, either way."

"What did you tell him?"

"I suggested he place Joseph under video supervision, and to trust in the wisdom of the television monitor. If there was a change taking place, the camera would pick it up, and the TV set would reveal it to us. He said he would have to think it over. He had to think of the chimp's right to privacy. That was how we left it in our last conversation. The day before he was hit by that truck."

Shelly tried to make the connection; the Reverend nodded at him, sitting back in his white plastic chair. He signaled for Eddie Kim, who came over, picked up the empty espresso cup on the table in front of Illuminati, and returned a moment later with a refill. He turned to Shelly, who stared at him blankly, and then to Homer, who broke down and ordered a cup of regular American coffee. Eddie delivered Homer's mug and watched Shelly, who was still lost in thought. Eddie shrugged, retreated to a corner and started to sweep the floor.

Whistling again, tunelessly—no, the closest thing. It was the most banal and innocuous whistling tune ever, from *Snow White* or one of those animated movies with a chorus line of dwarves. "Whistle While You Work."

Shelly tried to focus on what the Reverend had said. Had Ray Singh threatened Henry Harrison? That might explain why Ray had been hit—but not what happened to Harrison, since Ray was incapacitated by the time someone chopped Henry to pieces. There was no way Harrison and Singh could have both done in the other; and if that was true, what did this new piece of clerical hearsay mean for the larger puzzle? Shelly tried to sort out the images floating through his consciousness—of Neela Zapotnik afloat, the pigeons battered by a stolen wrench, the feathers in Harrison's office . . . but his mind kept returning to the catchy tune Eddie Kim whistled while he worked.

The same tune the Reverend had been humming when they first entered the shop.

Shelly's scalp began to tingle in the back.

Homer sipped his coffee, glanced over, and noticed a change in his partner. "Shelly?"

Shelly stood up, kicking back his chair, scraping its white plastic back against the polished wooden floor. Eddie Kim stooped to pick it up, and Lowenkopf gripped his arm.

"Do you have a telephone in here?"

Kim's eyes widened; he shook his head. "No public phone," he said.

"We've got to use *your* phone—you understand? In the back." He pointed a finger at the Reverend. "He'll call."

"Me?"

"Homer and I have to hit the road, fast. To prevent another horrible murder."

23

"YOU WANT TO EXPLAIN THE BIG HURRY?" HOMER ASKED, AS
Shelly squealed the squareback Volkswagen up on two
wheels, rounding the curve out of the mall parking lot.
There was a green light at the corner, which they
managed to make by the streak of burned rubber they left
behind on the asphalt, cutting off a block-long Caddy-
cruiser as they roared into the fast lane. The Cadillac
pulled up short and the Metro behind him squeaked to a
stop scant inches behind a gleaming chrome bumper that
would have crushed him like a cigarette butt. Both
drivers stuck their heads outside their windows, but
Shelly didn't have time to see the gestures they made
before they disappeared in the Volkswagen's *putt-putt-
putt* exhaust.

"You hear that song he was humming?"

"The Reverend?"

"The coffee-shop guy."

Homer thought back. "What was it? 'Heigh-Ho,
Heigh-Ho'?"

"Right film, wrong tune. 'Whistle While You Work.'"

"That's the one I meant."

"It was the same one Illuminati was whistling when we
first walked in."

"So what? It's a catchy number. Somebody whistles it,

and somebody else picks it up, and soon everybody's got it on the tip of their tongue . . ."

"I heard Ray Singh whistling the same tune, in the driveway. The day he was hit by a truck."

"Somebody must've been whistling it by the lake."

"Who, Homer?"

The blond detective shrugged. "Who do you have in mind?"

"Well," said Shelly, "Adrienne Paglia has a whole collection of those Disney musicals, doesn't she? And she plays them all the time. She could've been playing a *Snow White* record on that portable phonograph of hers."

Homer shook his head. "She wasn't down at the lake when Ray Singh was killed."

"You checked?"

Homer slunk down low in his seat. "She was in a bathtub. Aquatherapy."

Shelly looked at his partner curiously, and said quietly, "All right. But she *does* play those records all the time. Imagine what it would be like, having the room next to hers, listening to those tunes all day long through the paper-thin walls . . ." He let the thought settle for a moment. "One of them might get stuck in your head."

Homer sat up immediately. "And if you happened to have . . . say, a pigeon coop . . . down by the lake that you had to take care of each morning—"

"Somebody might overhear you whistling while you scooped out the pigeon shit."

Homer looked at Shelly, hopeful, but afraid to trust in it. "It's a lot of *if*s."

"I dunno," Shelly said. "Guess what song Neela's cousin was singing in the backyard when we went to see her?"

" 'Whistle While You Work'?"

"Close enough."

Homer leaned forward, resting his elbows on the dashboard, thinking hard. "All right. So let's assume Neela Zapotnik used to whistle that tune—and Ray Singh picked it up from her, on his morning constitutional around the lake. What does that give us we didn't have before?"

"I'm not sure," said Shelly, coming to the end of his line. "But it's a thread, isn't it? Connecting some of the pieces? Ray to Neela—"

"But not to Harrison. It's hard to imagine Henry Harrison whistling anything."

"He had a whistle on his key chain."

"Yeah," said Homer carefully, "but that only proves the point: a man who can whistle with his own lips doesn't need to carry one."

"So let's say he couldn't whistle. There are other ways to play a tune, aren't there?"

"You see him with a flute?"

Shelly shook his head. "Didn't we see a reel-to-reel tape recorder in that office of his?"

"You listen to it?"

"No, but that would tie them all together, wouldn't it? All three with the same music?"

"Not only them, remember. Neela's cousin was singing that tune, and Adrienne's records . . ."

"The cousin's not in danger—he must've picked it up from Neela, around the house. But Adrienne's still at the clinic, where whatever was going on, still is. So we'd better make sure she's not in danger, shouldn't we?"

Homer frowned, mostly to reassure himself. "You can't kill somebody with a melody, Shell."

"Maybe you can."

They went straight to Marsha Mullens's office on the third floor of the ranch house when they reached the clinic. Doris was sitting outside, and stood up to stop them as they entered, but Shelly wasn't about to stop for her, and Homer blocked her route to the inner-office door.

"You can't go in there," she insisted ineffectually from a distance.

"Oh yes we can," Shelly said, opening the door.

Dr. Mullens was inside, using the depth of Harrison's mighty desk to keep Ralph Kotlowicz at bay. He was setting his weight against the near side, straining over it.

"That's your choice—either both or neither," the handyman was saying.

"I had no idea you felt so strongly about her role at the clinic," Mullens replied coolly.

"I feel strongly about Helen, yes. And she feels strongly about me."

"Does she?"

"Do you have a problem with that?"

"Me?" asked Mullens. "Not at all. I thought Helen had a problem with it."

"She thought you were her problem."

"Not at all."

Their conversation was interrupted by the arrival of Shelly and Homer, who approached the desk from behind Ralph, moving around him and Mullens to the shelf behind her seat.

"Is there something I can do for you?" she asked Shelly, twisting around to face him.

"Don't mind us," he said, reaching for the reel-to-reel tape recorder on her wall.

"That may contain private information," she objected.

"We won't tell," Shelly said, pushing a button on the bottom that started the reels turning.

Ralph stood and gave Mullens a look that asked, *You want me to do something about this?* Mullens looked at Greeley, smiling between Ralph and Shelly, and shook her head. She turned back to Shelly, who was watching the reels expectantly.

"What exactly are we listening for?"

The first cheerful notes of the Disney song came whistling out of the speaker, and Shelly and Homer exchanged significant glances. Shelly hit the button to cut it off.

"That was it," he said.

Homer shook his head. "You didn't rewind it."

Shelly looked at the reel, which was indeed still at the very beginning of the tape.

"Maybe the locals did."

Homer shook his head the same way again. "Even

Stohler and Foley wouldn't do that. And then leave it here?"

"They wouldn't've known about the tune."

"Then why play it?"

"To hear if there was a patient on it, maybe."

"And then, when they heard this? Why would they rewind it?"

They wouldn't. Shelly frowned.

"And besides," went on Homer, "Davenport didn't hear music through the wall—remember? He said he'd heard some in the past, but this time—"

"Do you mind telling the rest of us what you're talking about?" Mullens said.

Shelly looked at her, and at Ralph, who was no less annoyed at their intrusion. Shelly said, "The song on the tape—it makes some sort of connection between Harrison, Singh, and Zapotnik . . . we don't know how, exactly. But it's the first thing we've got to go on."

"You think it's a clue?"

"Maybe. But the tape didn't need to be rewound just now—it was still at the beginning of the reel. Which means it couldn't have been played when Harrison died."

Mullens scowled at them. "What makes you think that silly little song—?"

But Ralph wore a different expression, of personal concern, before he said gruffly, "Count me in, too."

"In what?" asked Mullens.

"I was whistling that song . . . I think . . . while I was working on the dock."

"When someone took your wrench, and—"

"Butchered the pigeons." Ralph nodded solemnly.

"Where'd you get it?" Shelly asked.

"The tune? I used to hear it in the morning all the time. On my way in from the cabin."

"When you passed the pigeon coop?"

"Yeah," said Ralph, remembering. "How'd you know?"

"I had a hunch," explained Shelly, "that Neela

might've sung it to the birds—" And he stopped there, midsentence, as a new thought occurred to him, from the way he had phrased it. Had she sung, or hummed, or whistled the song to herself . . . or the birds? It was possible she used it to keep herself cheery as she scooped out the pigeon dung; but it was also possible she had sung it *to* them, for another reason entirely.

Ralph nodded seriously. "I'm sure now. She did."

Marsha Mullens stared at the three of them, looked in their faces, and said, "This is ridiculous. What sort of connection do you imagine links these three incidents?"

"Four," Ralph insisted.

"Four, then?"

"I was hoping you might help us figure that one out," Shelly said distractedly.

"I don't see how I could. I'm not an analyst."

"It's not a shrink we need."

She pursed her lips. "You don't think *I* had anything to do with—"

"We don't think anything, yet," he assured her, "but we're starting to think all sorts of things. You want to help us think straight? Or do we do our best without you?"

She sighed. "All right. Let's discuss whatever's going on in that mind of yours. I'll give you fifteen minutes."

"I thought the usual period is fifty."

"You said it wasn't therapy you needed from me."

"It isn't. I was hoping you could tell us something about working with animals. In research."

She blinked, unable to follow his wandering line of thought. He nodded. She took a deep breath.

"Listen to me—I'm a researcher. I do my work with animals, in a laboratory. People tire me quickly. That's the reason I think I'm no good for this job of Henry's— but that's a different issue. I'm just warning you, my cooperative spirit runs out in no time at all."

"You ever work with pigeons?" Shelly asked.

She shook her head. "Historically, they've been used in tests of operant conditioning. I'm into drugs, myself. Plenty of rats and gerbils."

"What about monkeys?"

"Most serious researchers have to, sooner or later. They're the closest we can come to human beings. You can try whatever you feel like on a rat or a bird, but there's no way to know how it'll affect larger animals without testing it on them."

"You mean people?"

She shrugged. "It's far more difficult to obtain permission to test a drug on a human being than it is to test the same drug on a chimpanzee."

"Like Joseph?"

"No drugs were ever used on Joseph. Henry would never have permitted it."

"That's not what Ray Singh said."

Mullens hesitated. "To whom?"

Shelly shook his head. "An unreliable source. But one with no reason to lie about this."

Mullens made a face. "Ray Singh was a statistician. Never a serious researcher."

"But he knew how to train a monkey."

"Did he?"

"You mean Henry never told you? His colleague on so many experiments?"

"We never discussed his work with Joseph. That was before we began to collaborate."

"And you never had suspicions of your own?"

She sighed deeply before answering. "I never allowed myself to dwell on it. There were . . . questions which occurred to me, when our research together produced results that might have been at odds with Henry's data in his book on Joseph. It would make him very angry and upset. He would take those results and worry over them, figuring and refiguring them overnight, in the next room, while I slept. And in the morning, they were sometimes a little different than I thought I remembered them. Henry watched me very carefully when I read them over—his reputation was on the line. There was no purpose, really, in challenging him over some numbers I hardly remembered. So I didn't."

"Did you know about Singh?"

"I . . . knew that Ray took an interest in Joseph. If that's what you mean."

"Didn't you know he trained him?"

"No."

"But you don't challenge that assertion now? You're not aghast to hear it?"

She looked down at her fingers, splayed on the giant desk, and murmured, "I'm not unnerved to learn it, no."

"Why not?"

"I've worked with some chimps," she said quietly. "They are capable of relationships which include a great deal of genuine affection. I saw Henry with Joseph on many occasions, and never felt any real affection between them."

"Didn't that make you wonder?"

"I told you. There was no purpose served by wondering. It was possible, I believed at first, that Henry was simply the kind of man who felt affection but concealed it in public."

"And later?"

"I realized . . . he didn't feel what he wasn't showing. But it was too late by then."

By the way she said it, Shelly understood she was no longer talking about Joseph. He sat down on the edge of the desk, far enough from Mullens so she wouldn't feel crowded but close enough to make her feel his proximity.

"Henry did work with Joseph, though, didn't he?"

"Apparently."

"Do you know what they were doing . . . with a pigeon?"

"No."

"He never told you?"

"He never told me anything he didn't want to tell me. And I was his closest confidante."

"What could they have been doing?"

She shrugged. "Anything. Chimps are very intelligent, and very trusting, once a solid foundation is laid. You can teach them to do all sorts of things—even language, apparently, using hand signals. Joseph is a very capable animal, who could learn a wide range of sophisticated behaviors."

"But Henry wasn't a teacher."

"No—behaviorists think in terms of inculcating responses to particular stimuli. Conditioning animals to react to specified signals in predictable ways."

"Like training a pigeon to push a button when it hears a certain bell?"

"Precisely."

"Could a song be used as a signal?"

"I don't see why not."

"So, then . . . Neela could've trained her pigeons to react to a whistled tune?"

"She could have," Mullens agreed. "Even one as inanely repetitive as the one on Henry's tape. But I don't see how that helps you. Pigeons are very stupid. There's not much you can train a pigeon to do."

Shelly knew he was on to something; he just wasn't sure where it was leading him. "Well . . . what about Joseph? He's not stupid, is he?"

"What about him?" Mullens asked.

"I was thinking," he said, and her face began to register the first signs of horror before he had shared his thoughts. "Would it be possible for one of the psychologists on the staff here to have trained Joseph to respond to the stimulus of a certain song . . . with an act of violence?"

She stared at him. "Do you mean—"

"Could somebody have trained that monkey to murder Henry Harrison?"

24

THERE WAS A SPOT BY THE EDGE OF THE LAKE, PAST THE SWIM-ming area and the last cabins, where the tall yellow grass had been beaten down to make what looked like a resting place for animals, above a narrow bay of lily pads. The water here was still, and dragonflies buzzed, and an air of sleepiness pervaded the spot, though it was brighter than the surrounding trees. A path along the border of the lake connected it to the cabins and one could hear an occasional shout from there, a laugh or call to the lake, but it was far enough, too, for a private rendezvous, a trysting place or a picnic.

It was called "Faun's Bed."

It was Adrienne Paglia's favorite spot, and she reserved it at the reception desk at least once a week, stretching out on a blanket with a book, or bringing a special guest. She had taken Neela Zapotnik there once, when they first discovered each other next door, and that had started their relationship off with just the right ease of intimacy. But Neela was gone, they wouldn't say for how long, and Adrienne had reserved Faun's Bed today for her luncheon with her pal Joseph.

The chimp had toted the picnic basket around the edge of the lake, following Adrienne, who walked ahead in her straw hat and butterfly sunglasses, with a tablecloth over one arm and her phonograph grasped in the other. It was a blue-and-white checked cloth, which she spread out on the crisp yellow grass once they had selected the most level spot, a few feet back from the curve where the ground jutted out into the water. She weighed down one corner with her shoes, another with the phonograph, and a third with the basket from Joseph's arm. The fourth corner she secured with a large stone streaked in white, which she knew they would find there since it had served as a pillow for her head or a prop for her books so many times in the past.

Joseph strolled over to the edge of the lake, grunting at the ripples caused by insects on the water and the nipping of fish below the surface when an unwary insect landed. He did not like water, he wanted her to know, and wanted to make it very plain. But it was a lovely spot, and she saw no reason to deny herself its beauty just because Joseph occasionally became afraid of falling through its muddy green surface and drowning in the tangled weeds below.

A frog croaked and plopped in the water, croaking over his accomplishment. Joseph chattered this news to Adrienne, evidence confirming his fears.

"So stay away from it," Adrienne said, shaking her head at the chimp. "It's not going to reach out and grab you on the shore. Why don't you help me unpack the basket? Or crank up the phonograph, instead?"

Her tone was insulting; there were things that scared *her*, weren't there? Joseph swung over, peered into the picnic basket, and sat down on the rock in the corner, watching her unpack the cheese-and-lettuce sandwiches by herself. He sat with his back turned and his hands folded in his lap, but he couldn't stop himself from peeking, and then bobbing up and down and clapping when a bunch of bananas emerged from the basket. He ambled over to lend a helping hand, reaching out first to take those heavy bananas.

Adrienne glanced at him coolly and placed them on a

napkin on the cloth. "I'll have it all laid out in a few minutes—by myself. Why don't you choose a record for us? There's a stack inside the phonograph cover."

He grunted, clapped again as a *second* bunch of bananas were lifted from the basket, and then did as he was told, trundling over to the phonograph and lifting its heavy cover. Inside were several red and black disks with colorful labels. He lifted the first one, put his eye right up against the label, and shook his head, squealing at Adrienne, holding it up so she could see the one he'd rejected. He took a second disk and concealed it behind his back.

"All right," she said. "We've heard *Sleeping Beauty* plenty of times recently—I'll give you a break. But not *Pinocchio* again, either, then," shaking her head firmly at the one she knew was back there.

The chimp shrieked, bouncing up and down from his knees without lifting his feet from the ground.

"Pick another one," Adrienne insisted. She held a bunch of bananas aloft, tearing one off and peeling it. Joseph watched her, his eyes widening as the soft, fleshy center meat appeared, unwilling to trade off "When You Wish Upon A Star" but unwilling to give up the fruit either . . . until she looked as if she might actually eat it herself. He tossed *Pinocchio* onto the cloth by her knees and shuffled quickly through the disks until he located a neutral choice—*Snow White*. He offered it up as a compromise. When she nodded, he fitted it onto the phonograph, dropped the tone arm onto the groove, and received the banana as a reward for his diplomacy.

Adrienne sighed, watching him chomp the fruit in two or three big bites. Dealing with monkeys was a lot easier than dealing with men, who never told you exactly what they wanted, or what they were willing to do to get it. You could make a deal, plain as this one, and they would take your banana and eat it and never play you your music. At least with Joseph, you got what you bargained for.

"Aren't you going to crank it?" she asked.

She knew he wouldn't object to that—he liked to turn the handle on the back of the phonograph, like an organ grinder with a monkey of his own. Joseph thrust the end of his banana into his mouth and waddled over, bouncing up and down on his knees. He turned the crank as if he expected a jack-in-the-box to spring from the speaker. When he'd worked the turntable up to speed, they listened together for the first scratchy strains of music. When it began, with the overture, Adrienne tilted the speaker so it would face the center of the tablecloth and smoothed out a section for them to sit upon. She took two goblets out of her basket, standing them in the smooth section, and then a chilled bottle of Chardonnay, which she gripped between her knees, insulated by the fabric of her dress. She twisted a corkscrew into the cork, drew it out, and poured a quarter inch of wine into each of the two goblets. She offered one to the chimp and tasted the other one, swaying from her hips to the rhythm of the overture. Joseph accepted his goblet, sticking his nose into it before stretching out his lips and tongue to lap up the golden liquid. She gave him a minute to swig it around in his mouth before commenting, "It's very good, isn't it?"

He grinned and screeched a few times, spitting out the first mouthful only to chug-a-lug it again.

"I thought you would like it," she said, gazing out across the lake, where a man in the briefest of bathing trunks dived from the float near the swimming area. Beyond the float, a pair of awkward rowboats were bumping their way from the pier. The oars of the first were mishandled by an uneasy man in his fifties who kept jerking the left from its oarlock, while the second boat was rowed by his son, who kept yanking both oars through the air. The boy's mother sat in the back of his boat, from where she felt she had the perspective to holler instructions at her husband. The first boat rocked against the swimming float, and the second rocked into the first.

On the pier, some men appeared—that aging hippie, Ralph, waving his arm around the perimeter of the lake as he talked to a curly haired man, who stepped aside, allowing Adrienne to see the blond cop named by his mother for the blind poet—Homer. For a moment, she'd thought it would've been nice to have *him* lunching with her . . . but knew he would've turned her down if she'd asked. She thought about the Ring-Dings from the machine at the end of the hall, tucked into her picnic basket after she left the kitchen. At the thought of the dark chocolate, her stomach twisted in revulsion, but she thought about opening the package anyway. So much for her treatment sessions! They had wired her brain to a TV set and programmed her to be ashamed of her eating habits, and her bulimic vomiting afterward, but had done nothing to ease the emptiness she kept trying to fill with chocolates.

Joseph began to shriek, shaking his head.

Adrienne frowned and shook her own head in imitation of him. "Really, Joseph, what's got into you today?"

He pulled back his lips, baring his teeth, and held out his goblet for a refill.

"If you keep drinking with no food in your stomach, you'll get drunk, and then what kind of company will you be? Really, Joseph, you're becoming more like a human male every time we go out together."

The chimp grinned, and a salacious glimmer lit up his eyes, as the overture ended. It was followed by a moment of scratchy silence and the next cut. "Heigh-Ho."

"Why don't we start on those sandwiches?" she suggested, tearing at the paper wrappings. "We've got American cheese and lettuce today. I asked the busboy for a nice piece of beetle, but he looked at me like I was crazy. Well, what did he expect, taking a job in a place like this?"

It was a joke; she let him know by smiling herself, and he responded by imitating it.

She was gratified that he appreciated her humor. "You're my best friend, Joseph—my only real friend here, now that Neela's gone and thrown herself in the lake! After all the time talking to me whenever *I* thought about it . . ."

She shook her head, and Joseph shook his in return. She put her hand over her mouth.

"You don't think I gave her the idea, do you?"

Joseph kept shaking his head, more vigorously, and she took some comfort from his certainty.

"I mean . . . you don't think I suggested it to her, do you? Talking about suicide all the time?"

He kept shaking his head.

"I know I shouldn't feel guilty for it. I know it's not my fault. But if I knew how to feel only things that are true, I wouldn't have to live here anymore . . ."

Her eyes filled with tears, and she turned to him like a hurt little animal. Joseph had seen that expression on newborn chimps as well as people, and puckered his lips in worry. He hung his head on one side, and ambled over, taking her into his long, hairy arms.

"Oh, Joseph—"

Adrienne sobbed, leaning into him, as his free hand patted her back. She opened her eyes and saw the loons at the end of the lake take flight, suddenly, all together; she felt terribly sad that the only creature who understood her walked around on his knuckles. As they sat on the tablecloth like that, her face buried in his shoulder, "Heigh-Ho" ended on the phonograph and the needle scratched in the silence for a minute before picking up the next cut . . .

The airy beginning of "Whistle While You Work."

Joseph sat up and brushed at his ear as if a fly had been buzzing there. But it didn't seem to go away, and he stuck a long finger into his ear, wringing it out.

"What's the matter?" asked Adrienne, looking up.

Joseph shook his head once or twice, as if to get something out of it; he thrust his jaw forward, and cheeped a few times, as he usually did in pain. But Adrienne did not see anything that might be hurting him, and she leaned over, searching through the thick hair of his neck under his ear in case there was a parasite he couldn't reach there.

But he pushed her away from him.

"Are you all right, Joseph?" she asked seriously, holding him by his arms as she searched his animated face. "Is something wrong?"

He raised his arms above his head, flinging his hands around like a housewife who had washed too many dishes. He bared his teeth and made hissing noises through them, shrieked three times, and flapped his elbows for takeoff. Adrienne started becoming alarmed —was he trying to warn her about something? Was there an animal nearby that he smelled, or another sort of danger her human senses were too dull to notice? Adrienne reached out her hand toward the monkey, to settle him down, and he surprised both of them by drawing back his arm and taking a whack at her hand with his fist.

"Joseph!" she said sharply, withdrawing her stinging hand and rubbing it with her other.

He pulled back his lips to laugh at her soundlessly through his teeth.

"That wasn't at all funny," she complained, holding up her aching palm in front of him, which was still red from the impact of his fist.

He looked away—into the picnic basket. He found an orange, which he lifted out, like a baseball.

"We're not ready for dessert yet. We haven't even eaten our sandwiches! I'll cut that up when—"

But she never got to finish her sentence, because Joseph suddenly threw it at her, hard—catching her on the soft part of her shoulder, below the collarbone.

"Hey!" she said, as the orange bounced off, leaving a welt of juice on her shirtfront. She rubbed the spot, a triple injury—the cloth, the skin below it, and the heart below that. "You hurt me! That does not count as play, Joseph! We're going back now. Our picnic is over."

She stood and stepped into her shoes, brushing off her skirt with her still-stinging hand, which she stopped and examined to see if it would ever fade. Joseph crouched by the picnic basket, reaching his arm into it to the elbow. When he took it out, he held a long knife in his hand—the knife she had packed to use to pare their orange. The sunlight flashed off the blade; Adrienne looked up and noticed it in Joseph's long-fingered grip.

"What do you think you're doing with that?"

She reached over to take it, but he twisted his wrist around to keep it from her. The blade turned and glinted in the sun. The music on the phonograph was horrifyingly cheery as the woman playing Snow White sang the melody two keys higher than necessary and a chorus of dwarves whistled at her encouragingly.

"Give it to me—"

She reached for it and he leaned back, away from his place beside the basket. But she moved in closer and he released it, unexpectedly tossing it at her. The knife sailed through the air, blade over blade, and landed on the cloth between her knees, where it sliced through the blue-and-white check as if it were a film of French cheese and stuck point-first into the grass underneath. It would have cut through her thigh just as easily, had it fallen a few inches either way.

She stared at the knife, and at Joseph, who would not meet her eyes. He knew what he had done was wrong, all right, but he wouldn't be called to account for it—not yet, at least, while he still had work ahead. Like a jungle fighter, under orders, who couldn't afford to ask himself how well he liked what he had been commanded to do. Adrienne pulled the knife out of the ground, and moved toward the basket to wrap it up again; but she glanced at Joseph, thought better of it, and stuck the knife into the belt of her skirt. Joseph saw it there, and his eyes grew more worried; he retreated to the treeline, dragging his hands along the ground, until one struck a length of branch, about as thick and long as his arm. He picked it up by the smaller end, thumped the knot at the other end twice against the ground . . . and then screeched at her, baring his teeth.

"What are you doing? What are you doing?"

He waved the club at her.

"I'm not going to put up with this one more minute, Joseph. This is not my idea of a picnic."

Adrienne made a show of shrugging at him, turning her back to roll up the blanket, telling herself urgently to stay calm. Animals could sense fear, she knew— chimpanzees were not predators, but recent discoveries had suggested they might not be above bashing each other's brains out. Had they ever attacked a human? Adrienne didn't know; but she did know that Joseph would never attack her . . . unless something was seriously wrong. Which put her in the middle of nowhere, with a possibly sick animal. She felt him move behind her, not toward her, but sideways—toward the path that led back to the cabins and the clinic.

"Joseph!" she said without turning around. "We're packing up to go now."

He screamed at her and it sent a chill up her spine. When she glanced over, he was grimacing at her, sticking his chin out, challenging her—to do what? He swung his club over his head and smacked it into the spare trunk of a sapling pine, which rocked from the force of impact. Birds in nearby trees grew nervous and took to the air with a rustle of leaves and wings that suggested something was about to happen. Adrienne looked over her shoulder and saw him claiming the ground with his upraised club, blocking her escape, swinging it at the birds.

The record player was still whistling, and she focused her mind on its music, which made her feel they were not in the wild, after all. There were people almost within shouting distance; she considered screaming with all her might, but knew that might push Joseph into violence, too. She could have plunged into the lake, but the water looked cold and deep, and she was not a good swimmer. She would have to turn her back on him to dive into the water . . . that sometimes made an animal chase after you, didn't it? If he jumped on top of her while she was dog-paddling in the lake, she knew she'd never crawl out of there again—what difference would it make to her if he never did either?

The whistling picked up momentum.

Joseph wagged his head, trying to shake that bee from his ear . . . but whatever it was stuck to him. He gripped his club in both his hands and took a step toward her. His mouth turned down as if he were anticipating the blow himself, as if he were in pain. She saw him closing on her and knew a scowled reprimand wasn't going to stop him now.

"Get back Joseph. Now!"

What did she have, really, when it came right down to it, to protect herself from a beast in the woods? She gripped the haft of the knife in her belt, like Tarzan, or maybe Jane . . . but could she really bring herself to use it against him? Was she prepared to thrust it into his flesh hard enough to sink through hide and muscle and sinew, to stick it in to the haft in her pal, Joseph? Not that he looked likely to give her the chance, as he circled, raising his club to her eye-level, waiting for his opening. If she let him, would he actually lift it over his head and bring it down on her skull?

The music swelled—

And he just went wild. His jaw clenched and his head came down; his eyes grew bigger and he swung his club, beating the ground between them and the sky above, as the weight of the knotty club pulled him after it, this way and that. It was tiring him, but he didn't give up, driven by something that twisted his face into horrible grimaces but did not let go. He let the head fall to the ground and leaned on it, panting, until he caught his breath and came after her again.

"Joseph!" she yelled. "Joseph!"

But he didn't seem to hear her. His eyes looked clouded, filmed over. Adrienne took a step back, and then another, until she felt the lake behind her, lapping the shore where the grass gave out behind her heels. Joseph stopped advancing. He had her trapped on an arc of land jutting into the water. She saw him take a careful step toward her, baring his teeth in a grimace of threat that horrified him, too. But she had no room for further retreat. She heard the dragonflies buzzing behind her . . . felt the cooler air of the lake, and a draft in front of her as the club was raised through the air between them . . .

And started hollering at the top of her lungs.

"Help! Somebody help me! I'm at the Faun's Bed! Under attack by a monkey—"

Which did indeed push him to an act of immediate

violence, just as she had feared—he lunged forward and the gnarled knotty end of his club swung by her, scraping the skin on her bicep, leaving a thin line of blood. That did it—the sight of one's own blood can be a tremendous motivator, and Adrienne used the extra adrenaline it provided to duck down and lunge at him, catching him by the legs. Joseph went over backwards, kicking up at her. Adrienne had just enough room to dash to his left, as he reached around, snaring her ankle. She tumbled forward, facedown onto the tablecloth, Joseph still clinging to her. The whistling song on the phonograph was drawing to its end, but the force of her fall on the checkered cloth and the springy grass beneath it made the needle jump on the phonograph, leaping back to an earlier groove of the same cheerful song.

She couldn't get up. He was on top of her, and her ribs hurt where she had fallen on them. Adrienne tried to turn and fight off the chimpanzee, hand-to-hand, but he was compelled by a force that permitted him no quarter, and he gripped her shoulder, jumping up and down on her lower back. His right arm dragged behind him, still clutching the club, whose head she felt against her hip, as he tried to finagle the leverage he needed to hoist it over their heads.

"Ugh!" she groaned into the cloth. "Get off my back, you big ape!"

He landed again, and she felt the wind knocked out of her lungs. He looked down at her face—she would've sworn his own was as twisted in pain or pity.

He closed his eyes and shrieked.

She grabbed the knife from her belt, tore her dress as she hauled it out between her stomach and the ground, and strained against the monkey's weight, trying to bring it up and around to where she could wave the blade between them. Joseph had his club free, but had to use his first swing against her knife, catching her wrist with the knot, which released the knife as a sharp pain shot through her. Her fingers splayed and she didn't think she could close them again. And the knife went flying clear across the tablecloth to the other side of the phonograph.

She didn't think she could reach it there—his weight on her back hurt and wouldn't let her move. But what else did she have? She screamed again, unable to twist her head around to the lake where anybody might hear her, but determined at least to send up a howl that might travel over the trees. "Help me! Somebody! Help!" And ignoring him, she gripped the blue-and-white cloth in her fingers and clawed at it, trying to crawl to the far side of the phonograph, to her knife.

The record whistled encouragingly.

While Joseph, she knew without looking up, was raising his club again. She twisted around, putting up both arms in front of her face, trying to ward off the blow. His eyes were fiery red now, staring at her, and he tore back his lips to scream at her—he seemed in awful pain. She tried desperately to reach him, the chimp she knew inside—

"Joseph . . . please! It's Adrienne . . . Adrienne, your friend! Don't you remember? We care for each other—"

He looked down at her and struggled to keep his eyes focused on her, on the target below him. But a shiver of horror passed through his frame, and he shut his eyes, screeching to block out the sound of her voice in his ears, raising the club in both of his hands—until it tottered over his head. But he couldn't seem to bring it down again. Adrienne watched it wavering there, the head too heavy for him to keep aloft, wobbling in the air below the looming trees and sky . . .

When the song on the phonograph finally came to an end with a burst of scratchy silence.

Joseph's head snapped around at the phonograph, the resolve suddenly drained from him. The knotty head of his club toppled, but fell to the ground at his side. He looked down at her, still under him in the yellow grass at the water's edge, but the threat had dissolved from his face. He scooted off, and then sat back on his haunches and offered his hand, wiggling his fingers at her to encourage her to accept his friendship.

She sat up warily, edging around between him and the path. But Joseph made no effort now to keep her from escaping. He looked down at the ground, and covered his eyes with the fingers of his inhuman hand, and refused to look up at her face again. He was ashamed of himself, plainly, and wouldn't have blamed her if she never spoke to him again.

Adrienne sat up and rubbed the spot where the orange had struck her. "Why, Joseph?" she said finally, her anger and fear overwhelmed by a desire for comprehension. "What on earth came over you?"

Joseph didn't know how to explain it. He shook his head and screeched at a bird on the lake.

Adrienne said, "Well?"

There was a sound of crashing through the yellow grass, from the direction of the cabins. Someone was coming up the path, in a hurry—more than one pair of feet, too. Adrienne turned, not knowing whom to expect, not knowing what to say—about Joseph, and what had happened between them, about anything that had happened, in fact, since Neela dove into the lake. She felt her eyes flood with tears as first Ralph and then Homer and his friend Shelly burst from the path into the clearing. Joseph ran around to the far side of the basket, and hid his head behind the phonograph. But Shelly stepped right in front of him, looming ominously over the chimp.

"Adrienne?" asked Homer. "Are you all right?"

"I'm fine," she said, though the words came out through a choked voice. "Now."

Joseph buried his face in his hands.

Homer moved quickly to her side, and helped her to her feet. When she was standing, they were very close together, and he didn't move an inch away.

"We thought you might be in some danger—"

"I was," she said.

"It's over now," said Shelly, squatting down. She thought he was going to clasp a pair of handcuffs on Joseph, but he just turned off her phonograph. Joseph squinted up at him, fearing due retribution, but Lowenkopf just took the chimp gently by his wrist and lifted him, too, to his feet.

"Do you . . . know . . . what went on here?" Adrienne asked.

Shelly nodded.

"Could you explain it to me, then?" Her eyes filled with water again. She looked at Joseph—who stood next to Shelly with one arm wrapped around his head from behind—and forced herself to look away again.

"He *attacked* me!"

Homer gripped her around the shoulders. "It's all right, now . . ."

She wiped away her tears with her hand. "My *friend*—" And she gave Joseph a look of such deeply wounded trust, the chimp beat his forehead with his palm.

25

~~~

HELEN KAUFMAN WAITED FOR RALPH ABOUT AS LONG AS SHE planned to, staring at the walls of the cabin that had been her second home. She had taken her toothbrush out of the porcelain rack on the wall of his bathroom, which Ralph had hung up for her, and her clothing off the bar and out of the cubbies in his closet, which Ralph had built for her. She left the pictures they had bought together on the walls, even the print that showed an alchemist's pharmacy of medicinal plants and herbs, with the ailments each were used to treat. The embroidered homily from Emerson she did pack, figuring she would need it on her next walls, wherever they were, more than Ralph would need it on his.

It was strange, this separating without really breaking up their personal relationship. It would survive, of course, her transition to a new job—what sort of relationship couldn't? But there was no way to deny it would certainly have to change; they couldn't go on living like kids together, sneaking from her place to his, taking care that nobody espied them. As she listened to the pendulum swinging inside the miniature grandfather clock on his mantelpiece, she had to admit it was all fun, really, their secret love affair—secret! As if everybody in the clinic hadn't been on to them from the start.

She sighed, thinking about the silliness they had engaged in together—her silliness, she knew, Ralph going along with it for her sake, for her—thinking about Ralph Waldo Kotlowicz himself. How on earth had she found him? Big, mustachioed, heavy-lidded Ralph, sure of himself in every situation that relied on machines alone, but so uncertain whenever it came to customs, norms, and social hierarchies. He was just the sort of man her mother had tried to keep away from her, just the sort her father knew she would fall for someday. Well, he had found her, trooping into her life with his oversize workboots and sleeveless undershirts, even a red bandanna hanging out of the back pocket of his overalls— and a dog-eared copy of Emerson in the other! She didn't know—no one knew—what to do with him, and what to do with him, except, and it was a big exception, in the privacy of their own little world, his own spare cabin in the woods. She had known what to do with him there, all right—and he'd known what to do with her, too. She sighed again, checking the tiny grandfather clock, which kept its balance, swinging back and forth . . . so where was he? The lake glistened in its bed through the cabin's big plate-glass window, and Helen decided, rather than waiting, to slip into the suit she had left in his closet and go for one last swim.

Which was where she was, floating on her back in the water near his cabin, far from the roped-off swimming area, when one of the two teenage boys who alternated between pot-washing in the kitchen and life-guarding at the swimming area drew up a rowboat alongside her and said, "Dr. Kaufman? Dr. Mullens asked if you would stop by and see her before you go."

He was the older one, maybe twenty by now, his hair thinning already. How lucky she felt to have found Ralph when she did! Helen didn't feel she owed Marsha Mullens much, and the sun was spreading long blue shadows all over the lake. But she did want to go out as much a professional as she had come in.

"Tell her I'll be in her office in twenty minutes."

"Not in her office," the boy said. "She wants you to meet her in the Research Building. Room 404."

Helen frowned. That wasn't even Marsha's own research lab. She thought 404 had to be one of those observation rooms with the two-way mirrors that she used for supervising interns as they worked with patients. What was Mullens up to now? Helen broke a crooked smile, wondering what craftiness her former office mate had cooked up. She had to hand it to Marsha, who always kept you intrigued, wondering what she was going to spring on you next. Helen gave the boy with thinning hair a nod and said, "Tell her I'll be there in twenty minutes."

The boy sank his oars in the water and Helen brought up one arm, rolling over into crawling position with a single stroke. She was a good swimmer, and reached the cabin in about five minutes, drying herself off, hoping that Ralph would walk in and tell her something that explained the mysterious summons from Madame Mullens. He never did. So when ten more minutes had elapsed on the mantelpiece clock, she stepped into her blue heels, which matched her darkest blue silk suit, and began the clipped walk to the Research Building and her final interview with the ambitious new interim director of the Care Clinic.

She knew it—as soon as she saw the note taped to the door written on Marsha's prescription pad. It read, *Had to step out. Back soon. Have a seat and wait for me inside. MM,* and Helen felt her suspicions reconfirmed. But what was this all about? She could turn around and walk back to Ralph's cabin, to her car, even, climbing in behind the wheel and driving off forever. But that option would remain an hour later, too, and Helen had to admit her curiosity was piqued by the odd invitation and meeting place. What was it exactly that Marsha wanted her to observe? The only way to find out was to do as instructed: go inside, take a seat, and wait and see what happened.

Helen opened the door.

Inside the room was not dark, as she had expected—as

it had to be, if they were to observe something going on in the next room, on the other side of the mirror. The light in 404 was on, and it was not empty. A familiar-looking chimpanzee, wearing a collar with rounded corners and a string tie, sat at the table in the middle of the small room, watching a monitor mounted high on the far wall. The monitor was on, playing a tape from an unseen feed—Helen recognized it as the original Disney animated version of *Snow White*, who was busy putting the dwarves to bed, tucking in Bashful. Joseph was watching the tape, his hand resting on the oval table, in the middle of which a red fire ax, taken down from its clamps in the hallway, rested, within reach of both of the chairs.

Helen sat down in the free chair and waited, watching the door for Marsha to arrive, watching the tape, watching Joseph as he watched the tape. He didn't seem at all well—not bothering to salute her as she entered the room, for example, or to make small talk with her, chattering and grunting to fill the awkward silences. The sight of him made Helen even more curious about Marsha's intention in arranging this meeting. What sort of chat could the three of them have together?

There was a break in the tape, an old copy, presumably, and Snow White was now cleaning house after the little men marched off to work. She was singing as she mopped, to the birds flying around her, who seemed to be whistling back the chorus right on time. Was there some purpose to this tape, too, some connection to their business? She looked again at Joseph, who ignored her, and the fire ax on the table between them. She stood up and crossed to the mirror, shielding her eyes with her hand, staring directly into the glass.

"Hello? Anybody home? Somebody want to tell me what's going on here?"

On the other side of the two-way mirror, Ralph Kotlowicz frowned at the face of his lover and turned to Marsha Mullens for clemency. "I told you she didn't know anything about it," he said. "Can I go and get her now?"

Mullens looked at Lowenkopf, who nodded. She said, "You're very loyal, Ralph."

"I told you," he said, "I love her."

"I can see that," said Mullens, turning to the face of Helen Kaufman, still pressed against the glass in the next room. "I hope she appreciates how lucky she is."

Ralph didn't try to answer, but stepped out of the room, and the next moment through the glass they saw him enter into 404. The chimp at the table looked up at him for a moment and returned to his contemplation of the monitor overhead. Ralph took Helen by the hand and led her out of 404, and a moment later the two of them entered the adjacent room together, where a host of familiar faces were waiting.

Shelly and Homer were there, and so was Marsha Mullens, but the room was crowded also with Stella Zapotnik, who cradled Neela in her arms; Adrienne Paglia, who sat next to them, watching the Madonna-and-Child posture with tears in her eyes; and the pair of local police detectives, Stohler and Foley, who scowled at each other a lot but said nothing that might leave them behind, should anything come of Lowenkopf's little show-and-tell. Each of the guests had a folding chair, though Lowenkopf leaned on the table, scratching off names from a list he had printed in his notebook. As Ralph led Helen to a chair near the table, she saw Lowenkopf scratch the name *Kaufman* off his list, running a thick black line through it three times with his pencil. Helen sat, crossed her legs, and folded her hands in her lap, as Ralph pulled up another chair behind hers.

"You're in the clear, babe. On Harrison's murder. You've just proved yourself innocent."

"I did? How?"

"You didn't touch the ax on the table in there."

"Why would I do that?"

"She really doesn't know," Ralph said to Homer. "See?"

"Why should I?" asked Helen.

"You shouldn't," said Homer. "But you would, if you were the murderer."

Helen looked at Lowenkopf, writing. "This is your scheme, isn't it?"

"How do you know?" he asked.

"Feels like your sort of thinking. Your way of working things out."

"Want to tell me what I'm thinking, then?"

She didn't know, but tapped her upper lip with her fingers, ready to figure it out. She looked back through the two-way mirror, which was just plain glass from this side, with the light out overhead. On the other side of the glass, the chimpanzee watched his television screen.

"Something to do with Joseph, it seems."

He nodded. "Only that's not Joseph in there."

"It isn't? It looks like him. Dressed like him."

"That's what he's supposed to look like."

"You're giving me a hint, aren't you?"

He nodded again at her.

She stared at the monkey. "You think he saw who did it? Of course, he was locked in his cage in Henry's room when the murder took place."

"No, he wasn't."

"He wasn't in the room? He wasn't *locked in his cage?*" she asked, incredulous. "But he had to be—the door was padlocked, and the key was still in Henry's fist."

Shelly shook his head and smiled. "You don't need a key to get *into* a cage."

"You mean Henry let him out? So that Joseph only had to close the door behind him and snap shut the padlock when he shut himself back in?"

Shelly shrugged. "He could have."

She stared blankly. "But why? To get away from the killer? But the killer could have opened the cage easily enough."

"What killer?" asked Shelly.

"Whoever murdered Henry," she said.

"Nobody could've gotten past Howard Davenport," he said.

"Somebody did."

"I don't think so."

"But you don't know for certain?"

He shook his head. "That's why we're here. To find out. Dr. Mullens?"

Marsha scrawled a note on her prescription pad and handed it to Homer, who stepped out of the room and reappeared a moment later without it.

"He just stuck that on the door?" asked Helen. "Like the one left for me?"

Shelly nodded.

"Okay," said Helen, looking at Ralph, remembering what he had told her. "This is a test. In there. We're testing the people who pass through. All of the people in this room have already been tested?"

"Not me," said Ralph.

"Except him," Helen repeated. "Who's coming next?"

"A doubleheader," said Shelly, and didn't have to explain further, because the next moment, the door to 404 opened again and a young couple stepped inside: the blonde with the ponytail Shelly had met in Mullens's offices—Liza Gunnarson—who placed her hand gently on the shoulder of a resident in tortoise-shell glasses after he had occupied the only free chair.

"Arthur Jenkins," said Homer. "I saw him here my first day, during Harrison's Dependency Group."

"Henry treated him pretty roughly, then," said Helen.

Shelly recognized him, too. "Are they an item?"

"Looks like it," replied Homer.

Helen said, "Yes."

Jenkins glanced at the chimpanzee across the table and then at the tape overhead, which Gunnarson was watching already. He looked up at her, and ran his hand along the curved red handle of the fire ax.

Stohler leaned forward, toward the two-way glass. "Did he just reach for it?"

"It was a stroke," Shelly said, shaking his head at the cop. "A man with an ax—a macho thing. We're not even playing the right part of the movie yet."

"You think somebody's going to pick up that ax and start swinging it?" Helen asked Shelly. Her tone implied plainly, *Don't hold your breath.*

He shook his head. "I hope not. The only one who ought to is safely locked up tonight."

"You mean Howard Davenport?"

Shelly frowned at Stohler and Foley. "They're going to have to let him out, tomorrow."

"If this works," mumbled Stohler.

"You've already got *somebody else* in jail?" Helen asked.

Shelly shook his head.

"But you said—"

"Locked up, I said. Not in jail." He gave Homer a little nod, and Homer pushed a button on a videocassette player, which made the picture on the monitor in the next room skip, just as it had when Helen was watching. And again the scene shifted to an image of the lovely Snow White cleaning the dwarves' home.

Stohler leaned even closer to the glass. "Now—"

"Take it," said Foley. "Pick it up."

They watched Jenkins closely, as his hand traced the inside curve of the fire ax, sliding down toward the head, half of it painted red, the other half gleaming steel. His hand rested there, patting it.

"Go ahead," murmured Foley urgently. "We know you want it. Just grab the sucker . . ."

But Jenkins's hand moved off the ax to settle on the curve of Gunnarson's hip.

"We lost him," muttered Stohler.

"Maybe not," Foley insisted.

"He's fondling her, for Chrissake, paying no attention at all to the chimp sitting right there. If he was gonna freak at the sound of that song, the two of them woulda been mincemeat already." Stohler spat. "Somebody might as well get those two and bring 'em in."

Helen heard this recitation and stared at Stohler, and then at Homer, who arose to go out. As he passed Helen, he shrugged and said, "Just to keep them from talking to their friends about our little experiment here."

She looked at Foley, who was still staring intently through the glass.

"They're off the hook?"

"You saw them—they didn't pick it up, did they? No—just left it there, like a centerpiece."

She hesitated. "Why would the killer pick up the ax?"

"To keep *him* from getting it."

"Him?" She followed his gaze and then turned, aghast, to Shelly. "You think—Joseph killed Henry?"

Shelly shrugged. "When he's mad, he's a real animal."

26

HELEN KAUFMAN COULDN'T BELIEVE HER EARS. "JOSEPH? THE kindest, gentlest creature ever? You think he picked up Henry's double-headed ax, and—" She made a gesture of bringing it down. "Whack!?"

Shelly ticked off on his fingers the strikes against the chimp. "He was in the room already. That counts as *opportunity*. There was Harrison's souvenir ax in there with them. That counts as *means*. With a human being, we'd have to think about *motive*, too. I'm not sure we do in this case, but we have it anyway."

Helen turned from him to Ralph. "Do you believe this? What sort of motive could Joseph have harbored?"

Ralph patted her hand. "You'd better hear them out first, Helen."

"Don't judge him too harshly for it," said Shelly. "He was probably brainwashed at the time."

"You mean . . . conditioned to kill Henry Harrison?"

"People knew they were working together again—if they ever worked together before. Somebody might've known Harrison was using a certain tape with the chimp. If they trained him to go nuts when he heard a song from that tape—"

"Whack!" said Helen.

"Possibly."

Stohler looked at Shelly with a smile of amusement, trying to gauge the likelihood that the whole thing would bust in his face, like a Bronx cheer—which in this part of Jersey was known as a raspberry.

"But who would've done such a thing?" Helen wondered.

"Actually, everybody," Shelly said. "Most of you had pretty good reasons to have been willing to do such a thing. A better question is who *could* have."

"All right," Helen said testily. "Who?"

"At the moment there seems to be only one answer," Shelly replied. "But we're checking for any others." He gestured around the room. "We've collected all the people with any sort of motive for wanting Harrison dead."

"Like me?" asked Helen.

"He fired you this week, didn't he? Separating you from your one true love?"

Helen glanced at Ralph. "So why didn't you test him, too? My one true love could've done it, for the same reason."

"But he wouldn't know how," Shelly said. "Ralph's not a trained psychologist, or a psychologist in training. He's never even been a patient, experiencing the sort of treatments used around here to change people's behavior. If it works on you and me, it ought to work on a chimp."

"Maybe," said Helen. "There's some conflicting evidence in the literature. Depends on the chimp."

"It worked pretty well on Joseph," said Shelly. "He went after Harrison with an ax, all right. And he nearly went after Adrienne today. Something stopped him, right at the last minute, that didn't stop him with Harrison."

"That's easy," said Helen.

"Sure." Shelly nodded. "Joseph and Adrienne cared for one another. Whereas Harrison hated him."

"That's a bit strong," demurred Helen. She looked at Ralph. *"Hated* him?"

"That's the only word I'd use for it," insisted Lowenkopf. "Harrison never trained Joseph. Ray Singh did that—according to the Reverend he discussed his doubts with. And Dr. Mullens here, who hasn't confirmed it, exactly, but hasn't denied it either." Shelly waited a beat, and shrugged. "She's got her own ambitions at this clinic, I guess."

Helen turned to Marsha, who said, "I'm not about to pull out the rug from under Henry's reputation—the reputation on which this clinic was built. But I have at times wondered how Henry could have worked so closely with that chimpanzee, when he simply couldn't abide the stench of an animal research lab. He refused to go into one, preferring to wait in the hallway whenever we needed an animal."

"And his training procedure—the one he reported in that first book of his—just doesn't work. Neela Zapotnik was trying to repeat it."

"Replicate it," said Mullens.

"And she couldn't get her pigeons to react the way Harrison said his pigeons had reacted—because they never did in the first place. Isn't that right, Neela?"

The girl sat up, sliding off her mother's lap. "I wrote him about it. Asking where I was going wrong. Asking for help with my research design."

"That's when he invited her to lunch in his gazebo," Shelly said, "where he drove her off the grounds by torturing her—as only a shrink could do."

Stella Zapotnik took her daughter's hand, and would have pulled her back into her lap, but Neela resisted, keeping herself upright. "I never meant to challenge his work," she told Mullens apologetically.

"Of course not!" said Shelly. "You never suspected it was all a big lie—a fake to promote his theories! But I think you may have escaped, by sheer luck, a worse fate he had planned for you."

"A worse one?" Neela paled, and Stella shivered.

"You worked down at the pigeon coop every morning, didn't you? Cleaning the place out, taking notes about your experiment, feeding the birds?"

Neela nodded. Her lips were white.

"And you got in the habit, every morning, of whistling while you worked."

"It was a tune that stuck in my head," Neela explained. "I used to hear it all the time, coming through the wall from next door. Where Adrienne always played it on her phonograph!" Neela turned to her neighbor for confirmation, and Adrienne nodded at her, sickly.

"It wasn't your fault," said Homer.

"No, it wasn't," agreed Shelly. "Harrison heard it one day, and it gave him an idea. He realized how he could get rid of you, Neela, and at the same time play a terrible joke on Joseph, whom he hated. For making his career a lie."

"It wasn't Joseph's fault—" began Neela, in outrage.

"Harrison didn't see it that way," Shelly said. "He decided to prove he really could train Joseph—but not as Ray Singh had done. Harrison was going to use his own methods, this time, just as he claimed to have done in his book. He couldn't train Joseph to be a loving friend that way, of course, since Harrison had no love of his own to give. So he trained him to do what Harrison's kind of training *could* teach him to do.

"He trained him to kill on a stimulus.

"And what stimulus did he use? Why, the one he knew Neela Zapotnik would utter, because she did already, every morning. He trained Joseph to go berserk when he heard 'Whistle While You Work.' There's a tape of it in Harrison's office, which he must have used with electric shocks, or whatever aversion therapy he was most enamored of. Showing him tapes of mutilations—you all know it better than I do. He had Joseph practicing on a pigeon that day in his office, when he was killed.

"Remember the wrench in the coop? Joseph must have heard Ralph whistling while he worked on the dock. The tune got to him, and he picked up the biggest wrench around and went after those pigeons. Just as he had done in Harrison's office.

"That's why the tape was there, and the ax, and a very frightened bird. Harrison was training Joseph to swing at it. Remember how awful he looked when we came in?

Joseph *hated* doing it. He's a decent chimp, with a bigger heart than Harrison ever had—being programmed to do these awful things to other living creatures."

Helen put up her hand, trying to follow. "Are you saying . . . Henry himself trained Joseph to commit acts of violence?"

"He's the only suspect left, isn't he? We've just run all of you—the people with motives, who might know how to program a chimp—through our fire-ax test in the room next door, on the other side of the glass. You all thought the monkey in there was Joseph, didn't you?"

"I thought he seemed different today," said Helen.

Shelly frowned. "If you realized he's *not* Joseph, you might not have passed, after all."

Helen snorted. "Even if I'd known it wasn't Joseph—and I can't honestly say that explanation occurred to me—I still didn't train him to kill Henry Harrison."

"I know," said Shelly gravely. "If you did, you couldn't have risked leaving the ax right there on the table, within his reach, when the trigger song came on the TV monitor. You'd have known it would've driven Joseph berserk, just as you programmed it to. You wouldn't've risked your life on the bet that the chimp in the collar *wasn't* Joseph. So you would've had to grab the ax anyway, just to be safe—and we would've grabbed you.

"But nobody here reached for it—except Jenkins, who stroked it a few times but left it on the table. Which leaves Henry Harrison the only suspect who hasn't passed our test."

Marsha Mullens spoke up. "Not really. We haven't tested every psychologist in the world. Who knows how many of them had motives to have wanted Henry dead?"

"And I don't understand," said Neela. "Dr. Harrison never used Joseph against me."

"He didn't have to," said Shelly. "He was planning to use Joseph against you, because your research was embarrassing him—even threatening his reputation. But he knew there were risks involved with Joseph. He might have killed you. That could've proved a problem, when chasing you off was all he really needed. And then the perfect opportunity came up for him to do just that. He invited you to lunch. Helen had to leave for a supervision group—which he knew about, of course. He had all the schedules. He waited for his chance and went after you, himself, in person. So he never had to use Joseph, after all.

"But he was *enjoying* his progress with Joseph so much, he didn't want to stop. And the chimp was getting sadder and sadder every day. That's what Ray Singh noticed. I heard him say he was worried about Joseph. He must've figured out what was going on and confronted Harrison about it—maybe even threatening to expose their dirty deal. So Harrison had to get rid of him, too. That's why he slipped the brake on the truck in the driveway. He was there, right when he needed to be. I saw him, and I think Ray Singh did, too.

"And Joseph saw him do it, too."

"Just a second," said Marsha Mullens, biting her lower lip. She felt a need to say something in Henry's defense. "Are you trying to suggest that Henry trained Joseph and then triggered a violent episode against him . . . himself? He played the whistling song and then Joseph chopped him up?"

"That seems to be the drift of it," Helen Kaufman agreed, wrinkling her brow as she pictured the disaster behind Harrison's office door.

"But that couldn't be true," Mullens said. "Didn't I hear somebody say the tape was wound to the beginning of the reel? On the machine in Henry's office?"

"I noticed that myself," mumbled Homer.

Mullens looked surprised to find support from so unlikely a quarter. "So Henry *couldn't* have played it, then, to trigger Joseph's response."

"That's true," Shelly said slowly.

Mullens felt encouraged. "And Howard Davenport distinctly told the police he didn't hear any whistling coming from Henry's inner office—which he did on other occasions, the walls being so thin. Isn't that right?"

This she addressed to Stohler and Foley, who ex-

changed a glance, their first good one since Lowenkopf
began. They hadn't thought of the objections raised by
Marsha Mullens, of course, but believed themselves to be
intuitively aware of the weaknesses in Lowenkopf's
theory. Either way, they appreciated her question as a
new opportunity to watch him squirm.

For her part, Mullens felt she was on a roll—and this
gave her courage to ask the Big One.

"I can't imagine it," she cried, shaking her head as if
with regret. "I'm trying to picture how it might have
taken place in Henry's office. But I can't make all the
pieces fit. Do you really expect anyone to believe that
Henry R. Harrison, a genius in psychology, conditioned
a chimp to commit violence at the sound of a certain
song, and then played that song for him? With an ax lying
right at hand? What could have induced him to act so
negligently?"

"Nothing," said Helen.

Shelly twisted his lips. "I don't believe he did."

Marsha wanted to jump on that, but Helen got her
point in before Mullens could speak.

"But then—your whole theory falls apart. If Harrison
never triggered the response, what difference does it
make if he wired one into Joseph?"

"The difference is Joseph himself," said Shelly. "The
chimp knew what was being done to him. He had an
experience with Ray Singh that made a nice contrast to
Harrison's kinky 'treatments.' He saw what Harrison did
to Singh, and knew what he wanted him to do to the
pigeon in his office. And Joseph simply refused to be a
part of it anymore. Without Harrison—or anyone else—
playing the trigger song, Joseph picked up the ax and
went after Henry for himself. Call it an act of defiance, or
personal revulsion—whatever you like. Joseph wasn't
going to dance to Harrison's music—he just wasn't going
to do it anymore. So he put an end to it. The way
Harrison had trained him to do."

"To someone else," said Homer.

"Only it happened, in the end, to himself," Shelly
concluded with a shrug. He realized he had no proof of

these allegations, but he wasn't trying to prosecute anyone either.

Mullens and Kaufman exchanged a glance, but neither of them could find an objection. Their silence made Foley and Stohler particularly uneasy. They stood up and Stohler cleared his voice, as if to suggest the time had come for them to get to the bottom of the mystery at last.

"So Harrison was chopped up by a monkey, trained to kill at the sound of a whistle?" he asked.

"More or less," said Shelly, shaking his head at his partner when Homer was about to explain to Detective Stohler how he had mangled the details.

"And who trained this monkey to kill like that?"

"Harrison did," said Shelly.

"Are you trying to make us believe," Foley asked, eying all of the shrinks in the room, "that Dr. Henry Harrison murdered himself by proxy?"

"You could say that," said Shelly, and since none of the others contradicted this assessment, Foley jotted it into his pad, from where it was copied into their report. Stohler never did get the details right, but he never worried about it, either. The case was closed; their captain was pleased; and there was too much going down in Jersey that September for them to lose any sleep over a man who had murdered himself.

27

THEY RELEASED HOWARD DAVENPORT THE NEXT MORNING, with no further explanation than "You can go." He was met at the Sussex County precinct house by Roberta, with a summer-weight cotton suit, a neatly pressed white shirt, and a tie that picked up the tan of the suit and threw in some orange and a couple of browns for contrast. Howard sneered at the fresh clothes and continued to wear his green army trousers and white T-shirt, even though he had slept in them for three days. And when the desk sergeant on duty gave him his valuables and sent him home for a shower and some sleep in his very own bed, Howard said nothing, but clenched his jaw and resolved on another route.

Roberta opened the passenger door of her Volvo for him and he climbed in without a word. But when she buckled herself in behind the steering wheel, adjusted the seat, and opened and then closed her window; when she put the transmission in gear, turned the key—and then put the transmission back into *park* and tried the key again—he said, "Where are you driving?"

She twisted her mouth around, knowing what his question was intended to mean. "Home, of course."

He shook his head. "Take me back."

She set her foot down on the accelerator, revving the

engine for a moment, to give herself time to think.
Howard was prepared to fight, to hold his ground against
her. He knew she was in the driver's seat at the moment,
with her knuckles growing white from their grip on the
wheel, but that didn't really matter, in the end. If he had
to, he could let her drive him all the way home, and then
make his way to the clinic again. There was a bus at the
George Washington Bridge, he felt sure, that would travel
out to Sussex County. All he had to figure out was how to
make it to the bridge—

"All right," she said. "I will."

"Pardon?"

"You want to go back to that horrible place, I'll take
you back there." She threw the car into gear again, and
this time it started rolling forward.

Howard studied her smiling face. "What've you got up
your sleeve, there, Berta?"

She shook her head. "You want the loony bin, I'll give
it to you."

He sat back, stared at his reflection in the passenger-
door window, and rubbed his stubbly chin. What was she
up to now? After all the trouble and expense she'd gone
through, sending a private investigator after him, for
God's sake—what made her think she could just give up
on him now? Did she have something of her own going,
without him? Something on the side, maybe? She
couldn't have—not Roberta—but as she reached for the
dial and clicked on the radio, listening as the morning DJ
woke up New Jersey, Howard couldn't help wondering . . .

And, once started, there was no stopping him. He
viewed everything he saw suspiciously, as if the world
had taken advantage of his stay in the lock-up to trans-
form itself into a saner place than it had been when he
went in. Even the clinic, when he arrived before lunch,
seemed incredibly different to him; and it wasn't just the
absence of Henry Harrison, either, though that change
was immediately apparent. As they bounced up the
driveway, Roberta clinging to the steering wheel for dear
life, Howard craned his neck to see the crest of the

hill, and for a moment could've sworn he'd seen that hawk-nosed bastard, Harrison, still haunting his marble gazebo—but the sun chased a gray cloud from behind the white pillars, the shadows cleared, and Howard saw two women at the table in the center of the gazebo, chatting amiably as they dawdled over the remains of juice and coffee, sweetrolls and jam.

The two women were Marsha Mullens and Helen Kaufman, who were enjoying the fine morning and the prospect of taking control of the whole clinic together. Mullens had worked her way through most of Harrison's papers and discovered the significant factor in the popularity of their graduate internship program was Helen Kaufman herself. Henry had done some fancy footwork with the members of the board, but Helen seemed to have her advocates there, too. Marsha thought that Helen would make a far better friend and ally than a former employee whose tenure at the Care Clinic had been ended unfairly by Henry Harrison when she tried to protect an intern under her charge. With Helen and Ralph behind her, the members of the board would appoint Marsha permanent director. With Helen as her clinical director, and herself overseeing research, they could turn the place into a clinic that really did care.

"The only thing," said Marsha, smearing the last curl of jam from the bottom of the jar on her last crust of butter croissant, "is the sneaking around. I can't have my clinical director go to bed in her room and wake up in a cabin every morning."

"Then I won't do it," said Helen. "I'm not going to give up Ralph, job or no job."

"There's no reason to *give him up,*" said Marsha, scowling at her. "But you don't have to keep him at arm's length, either. Claim him publicly—before somebody else does."

"You mean *marry* him?"

"It's been done," said Marsha. "Even by Transcendentalists! I don't care if you see a preacher or a judge. Just acknowledge him as your own, to have and to hold . . ."

Helen gazed down from the height of the gazebo and

thought she saw Ralph by the cabin—in his faded overalls, with no shirt underneath, up to his knees in the lake. She sighed. "We'll have to think it over."

Mullens looked out, too, but said nothing, thinking her own thoughts.

Helen glanced at her watch, and leaped to her feet. "Do you know the time?"

"Almost noon?"

"I'm nearly late for a patient. First visit. Can't keep 'em waiting for that one."

"Who is it?"

"Adrienne Paglia. I thought, after all we've done *to* her, we might as well do something *for* her."

"If her father finds out you're listening to her, he might pull her out of here."

"That's a risk I'm willing to take. And, more importantly, so is Adrienne."

Adrienne Paglia herself at that moment was in the pigeon coop, helping Neela rebuild the wooden supports on which the birds built their nests.

"You're going to work with them again? Now that you know that Harrison's book was a fiction?"

"Sure," said Neela. "Now I know what was wrong with my research design. I know what doesn't work. And I also know what does." She held out her hand for another nail, which was put into it by Joseph. The chimp squatted on the floor by a tool box, holding Neela's hammer when she set it down, handing it back to her when she needed it.

"Don't you think he's enough of a project for you?"

"Joseph? He's not a project—he's a friend. Helen promised to help me heal him, and that's a labor of love. These pigeons are work, Adrienne."

Adrienne looked over at Joseph, who was still unable to meet her eyes. She sighed, watching him—the most victimized of all of them. If he was not ready to forgive himself, she at least could forgive him.

Adrienne stepped out onto the porch and leaned on the rail, watching the guests on the lake. There was a trail that ran around the lake, between the pigeon coop and the swimming area, and she thought she saw a lean blond man in a neat linen suit trekking his way around it.

"Isn't that the cop?" asked Neela, coming out of the coop. "The one who does crossword puzzles?"

Adrienne looked over and saw Homer Greeley half-stepping, half-sliding over the hill, kicking up dirt with his neat oxfords as he made a beeline for the pigeon coop.

"He does crossword puzzles, too?" asked Adrienne.

Neela nodded. "Anagrams."

Homer started calling before he reached them. "Adrienne? Stella said I'd find you here. You're going to be late for your session with Dr. Kaufman."

"Is that what you came to tell me?"

"Your mother asked me to tell you that. I'd rather tell you my own stuff later." He looked at Neela and walked up the steps to Adrienne. "When we're alone."

Adrienne looked at Neela with brilliant eyes. "I guess I'll have to wait, then."

She turned away from both of them, leaning against the rail, feeling happy. She felt like shouting her news to the people around the lake—like that woman at the end of the pier, staring into the water.

Roberta Davenport had come to the end of her line—either Howard wanted to be with her, in their life in the city, or else he wanted to stay here, in a fantasy land in New Jersey. She imagined she knew why he might want to stay, where people did not really have to take care of themselves, and could spend all their time on their problems. It was pretty, too, the hill and the lake with the clouds overhead, the little signs telling you the Latin names of all the different pine trees—and the loons at the end of the lake. She watched the squat, ducklike diving birds with their short necks and sharp beaks, as they sat back on their asses and cawed their laughlike cries. For a moment she thought they were laughing at her, and then realized they were laughing at nothing at all. Oh, yes, she could understand why Howard would like it here, where you could stroll by the lake and hear the cackling in your belly cried aloud by those birds; and then retreat to the security of the concrete Research Building, where modern science kept it all under control.

She heard a clomping on the planks of the pier behind her and turned to see Howard standing there—sheepishly, for Howard, which meant defiantly, but with no real conviction to his anger. When she saw the suitcase at his feet, Roberta's heart lit up like a cash register during a Mother's Day sale. He had put it down behind his feet, to minimize its presence, but she saw it there between his shins, and knew what it meant, and left it to him to explain how it had happened to get there.

"It's all different," he said, scowling. "I don't know what I'm supposed to do, now. By the time they get it all sorted out, without Harrison in charge . . . I might as well pass the time at home with you."

She said nothing, seeing how that might be nice.

He picked up his suitcase and waited for her.

But Howard Davenport wasn't the only guest who had decided to move on from the clinic.

Shelly Lowenkopf went to find Ralph Kotlowicz, to ask a few questions about building-wide air-conditioning systems. He found him at the Research Building, watching an evacuation of monitors and other equipment owned by the Church of the Unflagging Eye. The Reverend Illuminati had commanded his Initiates to haul every one of their things out of there, after a two-hour meeting with Marsha Mullens that left them parting company. The clinic under her leadership would take responsibility for all the treatment delivered there, which meant, she explained, that the Reverend's group leaders would have to describe just what they'd been doing with the Initiates—Eleazer couldn't stand for that! This was still a private country, wasn't it? With freedom of religion for all? Then he didn't see why, if one faith practiced observances which included hooking people up to television sets, they should be persecuted . . . yes, persecuted for their beliefs. Dr. Mullens had said they were free to practice whatever the law allowed, but if their members chose to brainwash themselves, they could do it someplace else.

Ralph sat on the hood of his delivery truck, watching two Initiates load a video monitor into the back, under Roger's close supervision. Roger the Group Leader didn't actually touch the sets himself, but he had clear ideas of just how each of the two men struggling under their weight might handle them in better accord with the laws of nature.

"Gravity pulls things down, remember. We don't want to work against it. Just lift your end a little higher there—a little more effort there, Spock—"

Ralph grinned, slapping out the drum solo in *"Wipeout"* as he observed the Church precepts in action. Inside the cab, Eduardo watched, gripping the big steering wheel, glancing nervously from his boss to the sweltering laborers.

Shelly stuck his foot up on the bumper, remembered Ray Singh and took it down again.

Ralph patted the fender. "It won't bite."

"I know it," said Shelly. "I don't usually put my feet up on murder weapons, is all."

"It wasn't the truck's fault, you know. Just like it wasn't the chimp's."

Shelly nodded agreement. "It was Harrison's. That doesn't mean I like what happened to him."

"You know what Emerson says in *Fate?* 'A man's fortunes are the fruit of his character.' Harrison slipped on a banana peel he left for somebody else."

The horn of the delivery truck beeped, and Shelly and Ralph turned to the cab, where through the windshield Eduardo touched his elbow and shook his head.

"I'd pay some attention to your boy, there," murmured Shelly to Ralph.

"Eduardo? Just careless. And I do not believe it was his carelessness that killed Ray Singh."

"Harrison did that, too," said Shelly. "I practically saw him do it. But Eduardo may be dragging himself around for a different reason."

Roger and his minions passed with another couple of monitors, and Eduardo made a worried face.

"He's not afraid I'll put him to work here?"

Shelly shook his head. "It's group identity. Sympathetic vibrations."

"You think he joined up with these TV junkies?"

"I saw him at one of their ceremonies. And those aluminum-foil finger caps we found in the cab . . ."

"His?"

"That's my bet."

Ralph studied his assistant again, and sighed, acknowledging the truth in Shelly's surmise. "I suppose I didn't want to see it," he said. Then he slapped the dog-eared volume of Emerson in his back pocket and took it out. "Maybe there's something here that'll interest him."

"Maybe," said Shelly, offering his hand. Ralph shook it, and the link between fortune and character was written plain on the face of the man.

Shelly thought of it again that night, sitting up against the headboard next to Mordred's bare feet, as she lay flat on her stomach, chin in her hands, watching Jay Leno's monologue on the little portable at the far end of the bed. Leno was doing one of his routines about signposts that said more than their authors intended—he held up a picture of one from Heaven, Nevada, where somebody had scrawled a minus sign on the altitude number so that it read: *Population 12,000. Altitude -2200 feet.* "Sounds more like the other place than Heaven to me," quipped Leno, lifting his eyebrows, and Mordred joined the studio audience in chuckling at his deadpan.

Shelly felt like a cigar—there was no denying it. He had stuck a few in his underwear drawer before he left for the clinic and thought of them now, lying there, waiting for him to unwrap them. There was an ashtray on his dresser with a book of matches in it that could be moved to his bedside table in no time at all. Mordred was watching the set with interest; he could have a cigar cut and lit before she noticed him stirring. Except he was wrong about that—she did notice, before he made a move. Something about his silence must have alerted her, because she rolled over, tilting back her head, and asked, "Are you all right?"

He almost said, "Fine," to send her back to her program, and reached for his cigar behind her back. But he didn't feel like lying to her, about this or anything else. How much did he need it, anyway?

"I was thinking about a cigar," he said.

She frowned, and crawled to the top of the bed, snuggling into him. "Do you want me to take your mind off it?"

"That would be fun," he said, "but I'll just want one even more when we're done."

"We'll just have to go all night," she said.

He stroked her crimson-black hair. "I'd like to do that anytime, anyway," he said. "But that's not the way I want to quit smoking."

"What does it matter how?" she asked, raising her head.

"It does to me," he said softly, shrugging if he knew why. He lowered her head to his shoulder again. "A man told me something about character today, and it started me thinking about it. And this."

"You've got plenty of character," she said.

"I *am* a character," he told her. "But what about courage? In here." He poked himself in the chest.

"You were a cop for how many years, Shell? And didn't they give you a medal or something?"

"I'm talking about something quieter. Standing up for what you believe in, no matter what other people try to drum into your brain."

"Nobody can make *you* believe anything," she said. "Take it from me, I've tried."

He smiled and gave her a kiss on the cheek. Then he sighed, heavily enough to solicit a face deeply creased with sympathy. "Tough case, huh?"

"I met a chimpanzee who proved himself a better human being than the person who owned him."

"A nice monkey?"

"Uh-huh—and one with real character. Who stood up

to all sorts of brainwashing, and held on to what he felt was important. After hours of clinical intimidation, when push came to shove, he refused to lower the boom."

"I'm not following."

"He wouldn't do what they programmed him to."

The volume on the television set suddenly became louder, and their attention was drawn for a moment to the screen, where Leno's sponsor tried to sell them a meatier brand of cat food by sticking a fork into it.

Mordred smiled at Shelly. "Nobody'd make *him* smoke cigars. Is that it?"

Shelly hadn't realized the connection. But now he said, "Something like that. It seems to me if Joseph can make himself a better human being than these people tried to make him, I ought to be able to manage that much, at least."

"I'm right behind you," Mordred promised.

He reached over to his dresser and opened the underwear drawer, pulling out the three cigars still inside. He held them together in his fist, crinkling their wrappers together, and then broke each one in half and dropped it ceremoniously into the wastebasket by his night table.

"One . . . two . . . three . . ." he said, wiping his hands on each other. For a moment he looked down his nose at the halved cigars in his wastebasket. Then he glanced over at Mordred with a hint of doubt in his eyes.

She took him in her arms and kissed him. "I like the new Shelly Lowenkopf. A free man at last!"

She kissed him again before he could object, and he forgot the reason he wanted to. He felt no further desire for cigars that night, or any other.

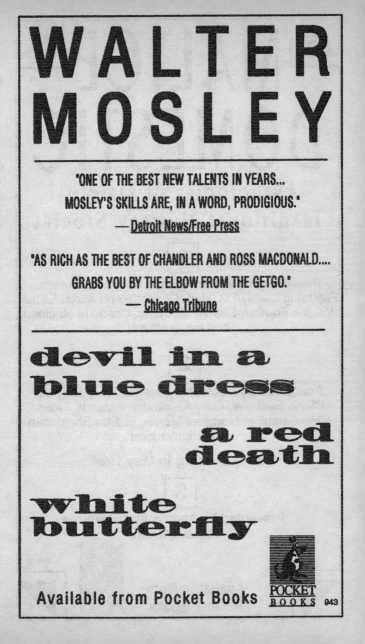